Also by Jackie Ashenden

ALASKA HOMECOMING
Come Home to Deep River
Deep River Promise
That Deep River Feeling

SMALL TOWN DREAMS
Find Your Way Home

All Roads Lead to You

JACKIE ASHENDEN

sourcebooks
casablanca

Copyright © 2022 by Jackie Ashenden
Cover and internal design © 2022 by Sourcebooks
Cover design by Eileen Carey/No Fuss Design
Cover images © Seth Mourra/Stocksy, DEEPOL by
Plainpicture/Corey Hendrickson, Mark Kelly/Alaska Stock

Sourcebooks and the colophon are registered trademarks of Sourcebooks.

All rights reserved. No part of this book may be reproduced in
any form or by any electronic or mechanical means including
information storage and retrieval systems—except in the case of
brief quotations embodied in critical articles or reviews—without
permission in writing from its publisher, Sourcebooks.

The characters and events portrayed in this book are fictitious
or are used fictitiously. Any similarity to real persons, living or
dead, is purely coincidental and not intended by the author.

All brand names and product names used in this book are trademarks,
registered trademarks, or trade names of their respective holders.
Sourcebooks is not associated with any product or vendor in this book.

Published by Sourcebooks Casablanca, an imprint of Sourcebooks
P.O. Box 4410, Naperville, Illinois 60567-4410
(630) 961-3900
sourcebooks.com

Printed and bound in Canada.
MBP 10 9 8 7 6 5 4 3 2 1

To my two best men, Dad and Tim.
Never forgotten.

Chapter 1

OH, THANK HEAVENS. THERE WAS ONE LEFT.

Bethany Grant slid back the glass door of the food cabinet and reached for the delicacy sitting in splendid isolation on the top shelf just as a large and definitely male hand reached for it at the same time.

Beth, who'd never been faster than when it came to getting food she loved, quickly whipped the sausage roll off the shelf before her rival could get a good grip on it and slid it triumphantly into the paper bag she was holding in readiness.

Getting the last of Bill Preston's sausage rolls in Brightwater Valley's General Store was a feat equivalent to being the last gladiator standing in the Colosseum, and she was going to enjoy the hell out of it.

Ready to be magnanimous in victory and maybe offer him half, or at the very least be sympathetic, Beth glanced at her opponent, her gaze settling on a broad, muscular chest covered in a black cotton T-shirt with a familiar logo.

Her stomach dipped.

Really? Did it have to be?

She glanced farther up.

Her stomach dipped more.

Eyes the color of espresso coffee, check. Black hair worn just a little too long, check. High forehead, sharp cheekbones, and straight nose, check. Beautifully sculpted mouth, the kind that made you think of kissing, also check.

Brooding as hell and radiating I-have-a-secret-dark-past-that-I-don't-like-to-talk-about vibes, double check.

It was Finn Kelly, all right.

Dammit.

The man was so reserved he made a stone seem garrulous and outgoing, and he had resisted all her efforts to make friends with him since she'd gotten here.

Quite frankly she was getting a little tired of it.

Beth had come to Brightwater Valley in New Zealand's South Island six weeks ago, along with Izzy Montgomery and Indigo Jameson, and in that time she'd successfully befriended just about everyone in the tiny town.

Everyone except Finn.

He was the younger brother of Chase Kelly, whom Izzy had fallen for and was now living with, and part owner of Pure Adventure NZ, an outdoor adventure company based in Brightwater. The business was also owned by Chase and a third, their friend Levi King, and basically offered any outdoor experience you'd care to name. Hiking, hunting, kayaking, fishing, heli-skiing, horse riding…or all of the above.

Over the past few weeks, Beth had come to know the other two guys well. Chase was officious and bossy—he was ex-SAS and that kind of went with the territory—yet he was also a caring, kindhearted man, with a delightful, funny teenage daughter called Gus, and Beth liked them both very much.

Levi, by contrast, was pure playboy. Ridiculously good-looking, charming, and just a touch wicked, Beth would have considered him a nice distraction—if she'd been in New Zealand for men.

But she wasn't in New Zealand for men.

She was in New Zealand ostensibly to find new markets for the jewelry she designed and made herself. But she also had a deeper, more private goal that she'd told no one else about.

She was here for escape and to find the happiness she'd lost back in her hometown of Deep River, Alaska.

Brightwater Valley was similar to Deep River, yet different enough that arriving here had felt like a balm to an aching wound.

It had the same snow-capped mountains, dark green bush-clad hills, and a large body of water in the shape of a lake instead of a river. But what Brightwater Valley had that Deep River didn't were total strangers.

People who didn't look at her with that awful

combination of sympathy and uncertainty, as if they didn't know what to do or what to say. As if she was some fragile thing made of glass that might break at any moment.

She'd gotten tired of that. Tired of the weight of their concern for her. What she wanted was people who didn't know her or the past she was trying to leave behind.

Here was her new beginning, where she could be whoever she wanted to be, and what she wanted to be was strong, fearless, and definitely *not* fragile. And happy. Just…happy.

Even if Finn Kelly was the one dark cloud on her blindingly bright horizon.

He was guarded, bordering on unfriendly, and had barely said more than a couple of words to her the whole time she, Izzy, and Indigo had been here.

Beth was starting to find that something of a personal challenge.

There had been some resistance from the locals of Brightwater to her attempts at friendship— they were a crusty lot, full of mutterings about a "bunch of Americans" coming in and "changing things." But Beth had been relentlessly friendly and cheerful, and soon their chilly antipodean reserve had thawed.

Except for Finn's. The chill around him remained and she was desperately curious to know why.

Beth gave him her extra-friendly, extra-wide

smile. "Hey, Finn. Sorry, did you want the last sausage roll?"

He did not smile back, his almost-black eyes impenetrable as usual, his reserve fathoms deep. "No thanks." His voice held a kind of darkness and grit that set something very female inside her vibrating.

It was annoying. In fact, her physical reaction to him as a whole was annoying. She didn't want to find him as ridiculously attractive as she did because that was a complication she so didn't need right now.

Friends. That's all she wanted. Just friends.

She and Indigo and Izzy were on the point of opening Brightwater Dreams, the little gallery they'd spent the past month setting up, selling local arts and crafts as well as locally produced artisan delicacies. It was a commercial enterprise that was supposed to help revitalize Brightwater—the town was tiny and on the verge of becoming a ghost town—by bringing in new blood in the shape of the three Deep River ladies and potentially more tourist dollars.

Brightwater Valley had sister-city links to Deep River going back to the forties, when American GIs from Deep River had been stationed here during the Second World War, so when Brightwater had called for help to save their dying town, Deep River had answered.

The three of them loved it here. But while Izzy had found love and a new future with Chase Kelly, Beth had more important things to do.

Things such as making sure she had enough stock of her jewelry. She was also trying to secure the last thing Izzy had wanted in the store before it opened—paintings by a well-known New Zealand artist that would hopefully draw in more people.

Except the well-known New Zealand artist was a recluse who lived in Brightwater and had so far refused to speak to Beth.

Okay, maybe Finn Kelly wasn't the only holdout in her friendship drive.

Evan McCahon was too.

"Are you sure?" Beth lifted the paper bag containing the sausage roll and waved it at Finn. "I can split it with you."

Bill baked many delicacies that he kept in a cabinet on the counter, and his sausage rolls, meat pies, and scones were the best Beth had ever tasted. Particularly the sausage rolls, which were rolls of delicious flaky puff pastry stuffed with ground beef, onions, and herbs.

She loved them, but sadly so did everyone else in Brightwater Valley, which usually meant they sold out by midday.

Finn stared at her a moment, his handsome face completely unreadable, while Beth fervently wished she didn't feel quite such a strong urge to stare at the fit of his black Pure Adventure NZ T-shirt, the cotton lovingly outlining the broad width of his shoulders and chest.

He was a tall guy, much taller than she was, six two, six three at least, and muscled like a gymnast or a swimmer, with wide shoulders and lean waist.

Hot. Exceedingly hot.

Beth, much to her annoyance, felt herself blushing under the weight of that dark stare.

"It's fine." Finn shoved his hands into his pockets. "You can have it."

"Oh, I don't have to." Beth waved the paper bag at him again, determined now that he should accept at least something from her. "I can get one tomorrow."

"No thanks." He turned away.

Rude.

Beth watched him stride out of Bill's store with the kind of purposeful grace that made the very female, quivery thing inside her quiver again. She ignored it.

Really, this was starting to feel personal now. Finn was nice to everyone but her, and even though she'd been telling herself for the past couple of weeks that she didn't care, she kind of did.

Had she done something to him he hadn't liked? Said something offensive? Because if so, she wanted to know so she could fix it and maybe not do it again.

Bill, a short, round man in his early seventies with a few wisps of white hair still clinging to his head, a craggy face, and bright blue eyes, gave her a knowing look from behind the counter.

"It's me, isn't it, Bill?" Beth put the sausage roll down on the counter. "I mean, is there anyone else he's like that with?"

"Who? Finn?" Bill peered inside the paper bag, then rang the pastry up on his till. "Nah, it's just you."

"Why? What did I ever do to him?" Clearly it had been something.

"Well, you're bright, you're pretty, and you're American." Bill held out his hand for the money, which Beth dutifully gave him. "But mainly you're too cheerful and Finn Kelly's not in the market for cheer."

Beth sighed. She was pleased to be called bright and pretty, but there was nothing she could do about that or about the fact that she was American. And as for cheer, if only they knew. Lucky for her they didn't.

"Thanks, Bill. But who isn't in the market for cheer? The man could obviously use some."

The old man counted the change and dumped it into her palm. "He lost his wife five years ago, so I'd say that has something to do with it."

Beth's heart gave a sudden, sharp kick.

"Oh," she said, a little shocked. "I didn't know that."

"Why would you? It's not a secret, but obviously no one talks about it on a daily basis."

So that was the dark past thing she'd sensed about him. Or at least, it must be. He was a widower.

Her heart gave another little kick, then clenched hard. She'd always been sensitive to other people's emotions—probably too sensitive—and had a strong sense of empathy.

Maybe that's why she'd been drawn to him. Why she'd wanted to be his friend. She'd sensed his grief and wanted to make it better.

"That's awful," she said quietly.

"Lovely woman, Sheri," Bill went on, since there was nothing he loved more than imparting information. "Family lived up the valley. She and Finn grew up together. He was devastated when she passed." He gave Beth a serious look. "Cancer."

Well, that was terrible. No wonder he was so silent and grave all the time.

"I should have let him have that sausage roll," Beth said, feeling guilty. "Poor man."

Bill shook his head. "Oh, no, he wouldn't have accepted it, anyway. Hates sympathy. And he doesn't like to talk about it either, so I wouldn't go around mentioning it to him if I were you."

She could relate. She hated sympathy too.

"No, of course I won't," she murmured. "But…is there anything I can do?"

"It's been a few years now, so probably not. I'd

just take this friendship thing slow. He's a very reserved, private bloke, is Finn Kelly."

Oh, she knew that already. He was so reserved it was amazing he spoke to anyone at all, let alone her. But this, at least, was some context.

Still didn't explain why he was nice to everyone except her though.

What does it matter? Do you really care that much?

Maybe she shouldn't. And maybe if she hadn't known about his wife, she wouldn't. But now that she knew...

She wanted to help him, make him feel better. Bring a smile to his fascinating, handsome face, make that hard mouth soften and curl. Relieve the darkness in his eyes.

Which was stupid because she knew that sometimes all the smiles and optimism and positive thinking in the world couldn't help some problems. But at least it couldn't make it worse, right?

She knew the darkness. She'd been there herself.

"Okay," she said. "Good to know. Thanks, Bill."

She picked up her sausage roll and stepped outside into the brilliant sunshine of a late summer day.

Brightwater Valley was tiny, the town consisting of one street and three buildings. The first was a long, low stone building that housed Bill's General Store and Brightwater Dreams, the new gallery. The second was a two-storied, ramshackle old wooden building that was the Rose hotel/pub/restaurant.

The third was also wooden and two-storied but a lot newer and housed Pure Adventure NZ, Chase, Finn, and Levi's outdoor adventure company.

Opposite the town's buildings was the lake and a small gravel parking lot where some cars were already parked, a few tourists picnicking on the grassy lake shore.

The lake was a deep turquoise blue; the mountains ringing the entire valley were white-capped and sharp, while the foothills were covered in dark green native bush.

The colors in this place constantly astounded Beth, as did the wildness of the landscape. She loved it. Her sketchbook had never been so full of inspiration for new designs.

Except right now she wasn't looking at the scenery. Her gaze was firmly on the Pure Adventure NZ building. Considering.

Finn Kelly was a man in need of a friend—she could sense that loud and clear. But it was also clear that she had to go about this carefully.

He had suffered a significant loss, so she couldn't just blunder about trying to get a smile out of him or pushing for something he wasn't ready to give. She had to go carefully and, as Bill had said, take it slowly.

Perhaps needing his help would be a good way in, such as making contact with the elusive Evan McCahon for example.

Apparently, the painter liked no one else in town but Finn, which meant if she wanted to convince him to show his paintings in the gallery, she was going to need someone to introduce her.

Evan didn't have a landline, and since there was no cell phone service in Brightwater Valley, she couldn't text him or call him on a cell. He didn't have a computer either, so she couldn't email him. In fact, the only way to get in touch with him was to visit him in person, and since he hadn't answered the door the one time she'd made the trek to his house up the valley, she hadn't managed to do that either.

All of which boiled down to a perfect excuse to talk to Finn Kelly.

The door to Pure Adventure NZ opened and Finn stepped out, heading toward the mud-splashed truck that was parked out front.

"Right," Beth murmured under her breath. "Finn Kelly, I'm sorry, but be prepared to be aggressively friended."

———

"Hey," a sweet, lightly accented female voice called. "Hey, wait up, Finn."

Dammit. It was Bethany Grant. What the hell did she want with him?

Finn debated ignoring her, but in the time it

took to decide his options, she was already walking down the street from Bill's toward him, the sun making the cloud of white-blond hair that had been tied in a loose ponytail at the nape of her neck look like a collection of thistledown.

She was of average height, though that was short to him, and had the lushest curves, especially in the jeans that molded nicely to her hips and thighs, and the green T-shirt—the exact color of her eyes—that did the most wonderful things to her chest.

Which he should not be looking at. In fact, he shouldn't be looking at her, period.

It had been five years since Sheri, his wife, had died, and in that time, he'd never once been with another woman. Initially grief had put his libido on ice for a couple of years, and after that, he'd deliberately chosen to keep it in the deep freeze. His brother and Levi would be appalled if they knew he hadn't had sex for five years—longer, considering Sheri had been ill for a while before she'd died.

But he hadn't missed it. Nothing had been the same after Sheri had gone, and he hadn't met anyone else since who even made him consider thawing a bit.

And then Bethany Grant had turned up. Bethany, with her delectable figure and the brightest, sunniest smile he'd ever seen. Bethany, with the small dusting of freckles over her nose and green eyes that stunned him every time he looked at them.

Bethany, who'd appeared like a sunbeam in the middle of the darkest pit of hell and who had not only turned his frozen libido molten in seconds flat, but who had also blown his previously rock-solid denial that he didn't miss sex to smithereens.

And he was pissed about it. Majorly pissed.

It wasn't fair to blame her. It wasn't her fault that she was pretty and sweet and sunny, and that he was attracted to her. Just as it wasn't her fault that he was a moody bastard who had lost his wife five years ago and didn't want to be attracted to anyone else.

But he didn't care what was fair or otherwise.

He'd been done with fairness when Sheri had first gotten her diagnosis.

It was too late to pretend he hadn't heard Beth calling his name, so now if he ignored her, he was only going to seem rude. And while he was fine with being rude in private, there were enough tourists around that he didn't want to do it in public since it wouldn't exactly be good advertising for the company.

Muttering a curse under his breath, Finn paused opening the door to his truck and turned in Beth's direction. Her sweet, heart-shaped face was pretty in a freshly scrubbed, girl-next-door fashion, with a turned-up nose and a generous, full mouth, currently curved in one of her infectious smiles.

In one hand she carried the paper bag that

presumably held the last of Bill's sausage rolls, the sight of which made him annoyed all over again.

He'd been looking forward to that all day and she'd bloody well taken the last one and he was pissed about that too.

"Can I help you?" he asked coolly as she approached, her sandals crunching over the gravel.

She came to a stop by the truck, close enough for him to see that exposure to the harsh southern-hemisphere sun had made the faint little dusting of freckles across the pale skin of her nose darker and that she had a touch of sunburn to her cheeks and forehead.

She always wore a lot of jewelry too, a quantity of silver bracelets chiming on her wrist, plus the necklace she always wore—a small silver pendant in the familiar, curled spiral of a koru, a fern frond, hanging from a delicate silver chain that nestled just in the hollow of her throat.

It was pretty, just like her, as were the small silver hoops in her ears, the surface of the silver etched with intricate, swirling designs.

Had she made those? She was a jewelry designer, or at least he'd heard she was. Not that he'd been paying attention. At all.

"Funny you should ask," she said. "Because yes. Yes, you can."

Great. This was the last thing he needed. He had to get up to Clint's—the horse farm he'd been helping Clint manage and was in the process of buying off of him. There were a few things he needed to finalize, and he didn't particularly want to get sidetracked into helping Beth out with whatever it was she wanted.

He didn't particularly want to get sidetracked by Beth at all, but while he didn't care about a bit of absent rudeness, he couldn't quite bring himself to be an active dick with her, especially when she'd been nothing but nice to him.

And *most* especially when the problem wasn't her.

He dragged his gaze from the necklace and the hollow of her throat to meet her clear green eyes. "Make it quick. I have to get up to Clint's."

"Oh?" Beth looked momentarily concerned. "Is he okay?"

"Yeah, he's fine. Just some horse stuff I have to do."

"That's good." Her smile crept back, like the sun slowly dawning over the sky at the end of night. "You know, I think that's the longest sentence you've ever spoken to me."

Wonderful. Like he needed a reminder of how he'd been avoiding her ever since the day she'd arrived.

Deciding to ignore it, he said, "What kind of help do you need?"

"I hope I haven't offended you or anything."

"What?"

"Oh, it's just that you...well, seem kind of annoyed with me."

She didn't sound the least bit accusing, only curious, which was somehow worse because he'd thought she wouldn't notice his reserve around her.

Seriously? You really think she wouldn't?

Okay, maybe not, but he'd hoped.

"I'm not annoyed," he said shortly, wishing she'd leave it at that because this was not the conversation he wanted to be having in the middle of town, with a whole lot of tourists around, not to mention a few locals.

Bill had come to stand in the doorway of the general store, watching them, and Finn could also see Cait O'Halloran, who owned the Rose along with her father, Jim, standing on the veranda of the Rose next door, also watching.

Even Mystery, the mystery dog, the town stray, was sitting at the bottom of the Rose's steps and staring at them.

They all liked Bethany because everyone liked Bethany. Hell, he'd probably like Bethany too if he weren't attracted to her.

But he was attracted to her.

Which apparently means acting like a sulky teenage boy.

Finn didn't like that thought, mainly because he had a suspicion it was true. In which case it was time to draw this little scene to a close.

"Can we talk about this another time?" He turned back to the truck and pulled open the door. "Like I said, I have to get up to Clint's."

"Oh sure." Beth's smile became even sunnier. "I'll come with you, if you like. We can chat on the way there."

Finn opened his mouth to tell her that she would not be coming with him anywhere, when she lifted the paper bag containing the sausage roll. "Here's a bribe," she said. "It's yours if you can bear my company for ten whole minutes."

Her green eyes danced, the color accentuated by the slight bit of pink sunburn, which made him even grumpier because she was just so pretty. And he didn't want to spend ten minutes alone with her in his truck, or indeed anywhere, but he couldn't think of how to refuse her, not without seeming like a total tool. Not a great look considering all the interested bystanders.

Also he kind of wanted the sausage roll.

"Fine," he said with what he suspected was shockingly bad grace. "But you'll have to wait around until I'm finished if you want a ride back into town."

"Oh, I don't mind. I love horses."

He suspected that she did not, in fact, love horses, since she'd never once to his knowledge shown any interest in going to Clint's before. But all he said was "Hop in, then."

Bethany's grin widened. "Yay. The sausage roll shall be yours."

She stepped toward him, and he wondered what she was doing, then she stopped and blinked. "Oops. Keep forgetting. Passenger's seat is on the other side, isn't it?" She gave a soft laugh. "I'll remember one of these days." Then before he could say anything, she'd gone off around the other side of his truck.

Of course the passenger door was on the opposite side to what she was used to.

He didn't know why he found that endearing, but he did.

Irritated with himself, he tried to ignore the sensation and pulled open the door and climbed inside.

Bethany had already seated herself and was putting her seat belt on, the paper bag containing the sausage roll on the console between the seats.

She pushed it toward him as he got in. "Let it never be said that a Grant doesn't pay their debts."

Finn grunted and started the truck, the realization slowly creeping up on him that he'd made a mistake. That he should never have agreed to have her in such close quarters. Because she was sitting close to him now and the delicate scent of something sweet was filling his cab. Like peaches or apricots, which were fruits he particularly liked.

You bloody idiot. Settle down.

Finn gripped the steering wheel and pulled the truck onto the road that wound around the lake. Clint's farm wasn't far, ten minutes down the road and then another five up a long, winding gravel drive that led up into the hills, rolling green fields on either side.

Not long. He could handle fifteen minutes of Bethany sitting in his truck, filling up the space with her warm, bright presence.

He wasn't a teenager. He could deal.

For a minute, as they drove, there was blessed silence.

Then he felt Bethany's attention turn unerringly on him, making every single muscle he had tighten up in response.

"So," she said brightly. "What were we talking about again? Oh yes. Why don't you like me, Finn Kelly?"

Chapter 2

FINN'S ATTENTION WAS STOICALLY FORWARD out the front windshield, which Beth supposed was a good thing since he should have his attention on the road ahead. Except she kind of wished he'd look at her.

His big, muscular body was radiating I-am-not-in-any-way-comfortable-with-this vibes and his handsome face was set in hard lines, his strong jaw sharp enough to cut glass.

She shouldn't have been so blunt with her question, but it had just popped out. And why not? She *did* want to know why he didn't like her, because it was clear that he didn't. And while she didn't mind that—he was allowed not to like her—she wanted to know for sure. Just so everyone knew where they stood and there were no misunderstandings.

Still, tension filled the cab, and she felt the urge to put her hand on his shoulder to soothe him, reassure him somehow, but she had the sense that he wouldn't welcome it, so she kept her hands to herself.

Perhaps you shouldn't have this conversation now?

Maybe not. It was obvious he hadn't been happy with it as they'd stood beside the truck, his dark eyes wary and guarded, his expression taut.

What was it about her that made him so tense? Did it have something to do with his wife? And if so, what was it? Because if she was hurting him in some way, she'd really like to know so she could stop.

Her instinct was to come right out and ask, but since Bill had told her that Finn didn't like talking about it, she didn't want to bring it up and perhaps hurt him even more.

She bit her lip, watching him instead.

When she'd first met him, she'd thought him a very still man, especially in contrast to the much more intense kinetic energy of his brother. Like a lake on a calm day, the surface smooth, hiding deep, dark depths.

But she realized now she'd been wrong. Because while he might be perfectly still, he radiated tension, almost vibrating with it like a telephone wire in a high wind.

"Sorry," she said into the silence. "I suppose that was kind of blunt."

"Yes." Finn's voice was curt.

Beth waited, but he didn't say anything more, his gaze firmly on the road.

Great, this was going well. Getting conversation out of Finn Kelly was like getting blood out of a stone.

Maybe you could have started with something less contentious straight out of the gate?

She let out a small sigh. Okay, yes, she should have. After all, hadn't she told herself that she had to handle this carefully? Bill had mentioned she should take it slow with Finn, so perhaps she should start doing that.

Beth automatically reached for her silver koru pendant, holding it, feeling the silver warm against her palm. It fitted perfectly there, as she'd designed it to, the reassuring warmth of the metal easing her own tension and the little sliver of doubt that had begun to crack the shell of her positivity.

She couldn't afford doubts. Couldn't afford second-guessing. That way lay a path she didn't want to go down, not again. She had to keep looking forward to the future, be confident in the new path she'd chosen for herself.

Being here, in Brightwater Valley. Where no one knew her and she could be whoever she wanted to be.

Bright. Happy. Fearless. Strong.

She took a breath. "Okay. So if you don't want to answer that question, how about this one instead? I'd like to get Evan's paintings for the gallery. They could really draw in the crowds and since he's a local—"

"He won't agree," Finn interrupted. "He hates showing his paintings. He also hates people."

For some reason that amused her and she smiled. "Hates people? No wonder you're friends then."

Finn glanced at her, his gaze a flash of intense darkness in the bright sun coming through the front window of the truck.

For some inexplicable reason, it made her breath catch.

"My advice?" he went on, ignoring her comment. "Don't even ask. You're not the first person who's tried to get to his paintings and you probably won't be the last, and you'll only end up disappointed."

Beth's amusement faltered. There was something fierce about Finn she hadn't noticed before, a kind of intensity that she found both compelling and disturbing at the same time.

He had the darkest eyes, almost black, which was strange when his brother's eyes were so light. Yet it was a fascinating darkness. She'd always been drawn to the bright and shiny, like a magpie, but there was something deep and dark in Finn Kelly that she couldn't deny was…magnetic.

"Wow." She tried not to sound as breathless as she felt. "I got a whole three sentences this time. I must be doing something right."

Finn's expression smoothed and he glanced back at the road ahead. "Don't say I didn't warn you."

"Okay, message received." She waited a moment.

"Actually, though, that's the help I was talking about. You're his friend, right? Perhaps you could—"

"No."

"Seriously? Just flat-out no?"

He didn't reply, slowing the truck down and then pulling off into a small, narrow gravel driveway. A rickety wooden farm gate stood across it, and without a word, Finn got out, strode to the gate, and unlatched it.

Beth watched him from the front seat of the truck, thinking.

He really was being quite rude, and if Bill hadn't let slip that piece of Finn's past the way he'd done, then she might have been annoyed. But he had let it slip, and it was awful, and so she didn't feel annoyed. She felt...sorry for him.

Five years, Bill had said, which meant there had been some water under the bridge. But grief didn't have a time limit, she knew that all too well, and sometimes the years were eons, and sometimes they were the blink of an eye.

So no, she couldn't be angry.

She'd be understanding and empathetic and careful instead.

Finn got the gate open and headed back to the truck, climbing back in and driving it through, onto the driveway. Then he got back out again to close the gate behind him, and all without a word.

Beth decided not to push it, so she sat there

silently as Finn drove the truck up the winding gravel drive to Clint's horse farm, looking out the window and admiring the view instead.

It really was in a pretty location, set on the green hillside, with lots of farmland around and some bush—black and silver beech mostly, which was common in South Island forests—creeping up the hills behind the house. The views over the lake and the mountains beyond were spectacular, reminding her a bit of Deep River.

Not that she was homesick. How could she be homesick for a place she couldn't wait to leave?

Finn pulled the truck up into the big gravel turn-around next to a cluster of farm buildings that also included the stables, then turned the engine off.

"Evan is difficult," he said unexpectedly.

Beth stared at him, surprised that, first, he'd actually spoken, and second, that it was something useful.

"Like you, you mean?" she said, teasing.

His expression was opaque. "I suppose I deserve that."

Beth was about to tease him again by telling him he absolutely deserved it when old Clint came out of the stables and headed for the truck, a big German shepherd trotting at his heels.

Finn gave her one last enigmatic look before he turned away, getting out and going over to greet both the old man and the dog.

Beth stayed where she was, uncertain about what to do now she was here. She'd said hello a couple of times to Clint, but she didn't know him, and despite what she'd told Finn, she didn't know much about horses either. Her affinity was with sparkly things rather than livestock.

She watched Finn and Clint chat for a moment before both of them headed toward the stables. Then she frowned as Finn abruptly stopped and turned around, striding back to the truck.

He pulled open her door. "Come on," he said shortly. "Come and see the horses."

Surprise rippled through her. "Me? But I'm only here to—"

"I'm going to be a while and I'm sure you don't want to sit by yourself in the truck for the next hour." His eyes gleamed in a way that made something fizz and spark inside her. "Anyway, didn't you say you love horses?"

Heat climbed in her cheeks, both because of the way he looked at her and by the total lie she'd given him about the damn horses. "Oh, I don't mind sitting—"

"Beth." His voice was softer this time and very low. "Come on."

The way he said her name, the deep timbre of the word, set off a small electric charge inside her.

She didn't know what was happening. Attraction was something she hadn't looked for and didn't want, still less having that attraction for a man as complicated as Finn Kelly.

Simple, that's what she wanted. That's why she'd come here. Simple and easy was the path to happiness, not complicated and dark and difficult.

Not a man still grieving.

She needed lightness and charm, which meant if she was that hard up for some uncomplicated, sexy fun, she should be looking at Levi. He was a man who was certainly up for that kind of thing, not Heathcliff over there.

Ignoring the fizz and pulse inside her, Beth put on her usual cheerful mask and grinned. "Well, okay. But only if you help me with Evan."

"You just don't give up, do you?"

"Nope. Alternatively..." She drew out the moment for effect. "I'd settle for proof that Finn Kelly knows how to smile."

A muscle twitched at the corner of his mouth. "I know how to smile. I just don't smile at you."

It was nearly a win. Nearly.

"Ouch," she said with feeling. "You really know how to win a girl over."

Something in his face eased slightly. "Come and see the horses or don't, it's up to you."

Beth debated teasing him some more, but since that only seemed to make the fizz and crackle she felt around him worse, she settled for sliding out of the truck instead.

Clint's dog came over to give her a sniff, then wagged his tail, and she grinned. "And who is this lovely boy?"

"That's Karl," Finn said.

"Hey, Karl." Beth dropped her hand to give the dog a scratch behind the ears. Karl wagged his tail ecstatically. "I guess at least someone likes me." She glanced at Finn, who'd already begun walking over to the stable block, so she followed after him, Karl trotting along behind her.

"Any reason why you want me to see these horses?" she asked. "Especially when you don't seem to find my company particularly enticing."

Finn kept his gaze on the stables ahead of them. "You said you love horses."

She rolled her eyes. "We both know that was a total lie. I just wanted to talk to you about Evan." At least, that was the ostensible reason.

"You can talk to me about Evan in the stables." He glanced at her. "Why did you want to stay in the truck?"

Beth opened her mouth to reply, then shut it, her face feeling warm. She couldn't tell him the real reason, that she was finding him far too attractive for her own good and that she was rather overwhelmed. No, most definitely not.

"Perhaps I like the truck." She kicked at a stone. "Anyway, I'm a jewelry designer, not a horse person."

Finn said nothing to that as they approached the

stables, a long, low wooden building with a corrugated steel roof. There were a number of stalls, each with an open front and a wooden gate, and as the two of them came closer, one black horse put its head over the gate, nickering at Finn.

Clint, a tall man in his late sixties whose weather-beaten, craggy face looked like it had spent decades being pounded by the elements, was already at the stall, and he put a hand on the animal's long nose, smiling. "Seems like Jeff knows you're here."

"Jeff?" Beth murmured. "The horse's name is Jeff?"

Clint, who'd obviously overheard, gave Beth a narrow glance. "Nothing wrong with that name." He stepped away from the stall. "Horse just looked like a Jeff to me."

"Of course." Beth smiled at him. "I didn't mean anything by it. Just that a black horse is usually 'Night' or 'Shadow' or something more…poetic, I guess."

Finn reached out and stroked Jeff's silky black nose, slipping his other hand into the pocket of his jeans as he did so. The horse nickered again, pushing against Finn's hand. "Take no notice of her," he murmured softly. "Jeff's a good name for a horse, a fine name. And you're a very fine horse, aren't you, Jeff?"

Beth went very still. There was a coaxing note

in his deep voice that she'd never heard before, and it grabbed on to something inside her and held on tight.

Finn's attention was on the horse, the usually impenetrable expression on his handsome face relaxing into something much warmer, almost affectionate.

For some reason it felt like she'd made a profound discovery and she couldn't look away.

Jeff leaned farther out of his stall, nosing down to where Finn's other hand was still in his pocket. "Oh, you know what I've got for you, don't you?" The lines of his face had softened completely now, and then much to Beth's shock, his hard mouth curved in a warm smile. "Demanding animal. I guess you can have this now." He pulled a small apple from his pocket and gave it to Jeff, who crunched on it contentedly as Finn stroked his neck.

"You spoil that beast," Clint grunted, though he didn't look too unhappy about it.

Not that Beth was paying any attention to Clint. A bit hard to do so when Finn Kelly, whom she swore wouldn't know a smile if it bit him on the butt, was now smiling as the animal's soft mouth quested on his palm for more apple.

And what a smile…

Finn was a handsome man, she'd always known that, but his smile, lighting his face and the darkness in his eyes, took him from handsome to devastating in seconds flat.

Now the only thing she could think of was what she could do to make him smile again. And at her.

Careful. You don't want to be getting too involved, remember? You're here for easy, for simple. Friends and a good time. That's it.

Oh, she remembered. But it was fine. All she was thinking about was making a hot dude smile so she could enjoy the view, nothing more. Certainly nothing to do with the accelerated beat of her heart or the sudden heat that washed over her skin. Or the insane urge to follow the line of that smile with her fingertips, see if his mouth was as hard as it looked or whether it would feel soft.

And she was right in the middle of that thought when Finn looked over at her, that mesmerizing smile still in place, an echo of the heat she felt inside her gleaming in his dark eyes. "Don't tell me," he murmured in the same low, coaxing voice he'd used on Jeff. "You want an apple too?"

———

What the hell are you doing?

It was a good question and one Finn didn't have an answer to.

Intellectually, he knew that staring at pretty Bethany Grant and asking her if she wanted an apple was a bad idea, since obviously she wasn't a horse and saying it in that low voice amounted to flirting.

But he couldn't help himself.

Her eyes had gone wide and she was staring at him like he'd just dropped in from the moon, and he found that he liked it.

Her wide smiles, boundless optimism, and relentless friendliness had always felt a bit forced to him. Life could be shit and people could be terrible, and surely no one could be that happy or that friendly *all* the damn time.

He'd always suspected it was a mask, and sure enough, that friendly smile of hers had fallen away, leaving a look of shock on her face, and yeah, he *really* liked it. Because he suspected it was a real, honest-to-God response this time.

A response to him.

That pleased him unreasonably.

Then her pale skin went pink, and his pleasure deepened into satisfaction.

"Um, no thank you," she said a bit breathlessly, and then, going even pinker, she added, "You know...uh...I think I might go back and um...sit in the truck after all."

She didn't wait for him to respond, turning and heading straight back to the vehicle sitting in Clint's gravel driveway.

Finn watched her walk away, pleased with

himself that he'd managed to unsettle her so completely. She was always doing that to him, so turnabout was fair play.

"You frightened her off." Karl had come up to sit next to Clint, and Clint gave him an absent scratch. "Did you mean to?"

"No." Finn turned back to the horse, who was still nosing at him for more treats, and tried to ignore the pulsing electricity that had settled in his gut. "Up to her if she didn't want to stay."

Clint, who like so many Southern men was bluff, burly, and never said anything unless it was in sentences of five words or less, snorted. "Don't give me that bullshit. You got the hots for her."

Finn bit down on the automatic denial, knowing it would come out sounding far too much like a protest to be believable. "She's pretty," he said instead. "But not for me."

"Sure." The expression on Clint's craggy face was skeptical. "That's why you offered her an apple like you were telling her to take her clothes off."

Finn shot him a look that Clint met with the kind of patience older people reserve for the very young being very stupid, and much to his irritation, Finn found himself justifying. "I only wanted to see if she had another expression that wasn't that fake smile she keeps giving to everyone."

"Huh," Clint grunted. "She the first since Sheri?"

Instantly, the entirety of Finn's being tensed at

the mention of his wife's name. Five years and he still couldn't relax when he heard it. The raw pain had eased, just like everyone said it would, but the hole in his soul was still there, and that would never go away.

It was a hole he'd never managed to fill with anything else, though working with his brother guiding people on hikes in the bush and showing them the beauty of the natural world went some ways to doing it.

The horses helped too. And he had Clint to thank for that.

So try not to be a dick to him just because he mentioned Sheri's name.

Especially when he was no stranger to grief himself. Clint had lost his wife, Marie, ten years earlier; that was how Finn had gotten to know him. He'd shown up at the Rose one day not long after Sheri's death and told Finn he needed help with the horses.

Dealing with anything that wasn't grief had felt too hard and he'd wanted to refuse, but Clint hadn't taken no for an answer. And it turned out the old man had known what was going on. Finn, at first, had found distraction in caring for the animals, then a measure of healing.

Horses didn't talk. They didn't want to know what had happened and how you were coping and how they couldn't imagine what you were going through. They didn't look upset or drown you in clouds of their own grief. All they needed was food and water and a pat on the nose.

There was a simplicity to it that he'd needed at the time, and sometimes he still did.

He'd also found that simplicity out in the bush. In nature there were no people either. Only the sun and the rain and the trees. The mountains and the sky. You could be alone there in a way you couldn't be even in your own house. A solitude that emphasized the smallness of your own being, at the same time making you aware that you were an intrinsic part of the world and the landscape, just as a tree or a rock. An eternal part of it.

He found that immensely comforting.

What he did not find comforting was Clint's question, so he ignored it, looking down at Jeff still nuzzling his hand. He gave the animal another stroke before stepping away.

"Look," he said. "Would you mind if I took Beth back down to town? The documents are going to take an hour or so to go through, and I don't want her to have to wait."

Clint hadn't moved. "You didn't answer me."

"Yeah, and I'm not going to."

"Don't be an asshole," Clint growled. "Your dick didn't die when your wife did, and neither did you. You're allowed to find other women attractive."

Tension crawled through him. He really didn't

want to discuss this. He knew damn well his dick hadn't died, and sure, he'd felt a couple of sparks of attraction when he'd been out with Levi or Chase in Queenstown's bars, the tourist town a couple of hours away and over the ranges from Brightwater.

But this thing with Beth felt…more intense. And he wasn't sure why. He only knew that he didn't want it.

He'd felt that for one person and one person only and she was gone. He wasn't ready to feel it again and he didn't know if he'd ever be ready.

What he did know was that he didn't want to feel it for some woman who was basically a self-help manual in human form.

"Fine," he said shortly. "She's attractive. But I'm not going there, okay?"

"Sure. But taking your own frustrations out on her and everyone around you is getting old, Finn."

Finn tried not to wince at that, because as usual Clint managed to home in on the bare truth. A truth he'd already acknowledged to himself, to be fair, but had tried telling himself wasn't that bad.

Except he knew it was that bad.

He'd become the same kind of bad-tempered, moody bastard he despised. His father, in other words.

Now that was a lowering thought.

"You know why I'm selling up here, right?" Clint went on, his brown eyes uncompromising.

Of course Finn knew why Clint was selling

up. They'd talked about it many times. Clint was moving to Christchurch, the closest big city to Brightwater, because he wanted a change of scene.

"Didn't you want to go and live by the sea?" Finn asked.

"Yeah, I do. But that's not the main reason. I want to be with Lizzie."

Lizzie was a woman Clint had met a year or so ago on a trip to the city and had gotten on with like a house on fire.

Finn had assumed that moving closer to Lizzie had factored into his decision to move, but not that it was the driving force behind it.

"Right," he said. "Well, that's good—"

"I'm lonely here," Clint interrupted bluntly. "And I'm tired of being on my own. I don't want to spend my last few years in an empty house. So Lizzie and I are going to get a house together. May even get married next summer."

Finn wasn't sure what to say. There was an uncomfortable tightness in his chest, a heavy kind of ache, and he didn't want to probe too deeply into what that ache might be. He didn't want it to be there at all.

"Are you giving me advice, Clint?" he asked. "Some kind of lesson?"

"Damn straight I am," Clint said without hesitation. "You're a man of strong feelings, Finn Kelly, and those feelings have to come out somehow.

At the moment they're coming out as anger, but that's not helpful to anyone, let alone to that young woman sitting in your truck." He glowered. "All I'm saying is be a man and handle yourself. I won't ever forget my Marie, she'll always be part of me, but I've decided I've got to live my life. And you need to live yours."

Finn got what Clint was trying to say. He really did. But he'd already made the decision to live his life. And here he was, living it. Sure, he was being a grumpy bastard and he really did have to handle that, but he wasn't going to be upping sticks and taking off to the city to live with some woman.

He was fine with everything the way it was. Helping Chase and Levi run Pure Adventure NZ. Spending time in the great outdoors. Managing the stables. Yeah, all of that was good and he wasn't about to change any of it.

One day he'd probably decide to head into town, find himself someone to spend the night with. Hell, maybe he'd even go for two nights. But it wouldn't be anything deep or meaningful, and it wouldn't be anything lasting.

Short, sweet, and easy. That's all he'd ever be in the market for.

"Yeah, well, I'll take that under advisement," he said, turning back to his truck. "But I do hear you about taking my deal out on other people. I'll handle it."

"Sure you will." Clint's tone dripped skepticism. "Just make sure you don't hurt anyone who doesn't deserve it."

And it was clear who Clint was referring to.

Finn looked at the older man, held his gaze. "I won't," he said, and meant it. "That's the last thing in the world I want."

Clint grunted. "Fine. You sorted out a temporary arrangement with Miller and his boys?"

Toby Miller had a farm not far from Clint's and a couple of sons who helped him out with it. Toby had a bit of experience with horses, so Finn had asked him if he and his boys would give him a hand, since Finn wasn't going to be able to manage the stables on his own, not when he had his commitments with Pure Adventure NZ too. At least until he'd found a permanent stable manager.

"Yeah, Toby's fine with it."

"Good. Oh, before you go, there was one other thing I wanted to ask you while I remember."

"What?"

"I can't take Karl with me to Christchurch. There's no room at Lizzie's and he'll hate the city. You know of anyone who can take him?"

Finn looked down at the dog sitting at Clint's feet.

The dog looked back, ears pricked, as if waiting for something.

He didn't need another animal, not when he was already buying himself a lot of horses. Then again, why not take the dog? He'd gotten used to living by himself, but maybe it would be nice to have the company. And Karl was affectionate and obedient, a great dog.

"I can," Finn said, deciding. "He can live with me."

"Good." Clint gave Karl another scratch. "See you back here in fifteen then."

Finn nodded, then strode back to his truck.

Beth was sitting in the passenger seat, a familiar paper bag in her hands, and she started guiltily as he pulled open the door.

The front of her T-shirt was dusted with golden flakes of pastry, as were her jeans, and she was in the process of wiping away yet more from around her mouth.

"Bloody hell." Finn was suddenly extremely irritated. "You damn well ate that sausage roll, didn't you?"

Beth put a hand over her mouth. "Oops. I did. Sorry, my bad."

She did not look sorry in the least.

"That was *my* sausage roll."

She shrugged. "Well, you didn't have an apple for me, did you?"

And a pulse of heat hit him straight in the gut.

This was revenge, wasn't it? Because he'd unsettled her. He'd made her stare, wiped that smile off her face, made her blush, and now she was pissed about it. It was obvious.

"You should have waited." A rough thread wound through his voice. "I would have found one for you."

She blinked. Then another pink flush swept over her face and she looked away, brushing the crumbs from her T-shirt with slightly more vigor than necessary, bracelets chiming. "I didn't want an apple. I wanted a sausage roll."

He shouldn't be saying these things to her, shouldn't be unsettling her, yet he was—that was clear.

It was this tension between them, this electricity.

Which means you'd better pull back and not make quite such a dick of yourself; otherwise, yeah, someone's going to get hurt.

Finn gritted his teeth and put a leash on his temper as well as the libido that wasn't showing any signs of slipping back to the coma it had been in for the past five years.

Then he got into the truck, shut the door. "Now you owe me," he said in more normal tones.

She glanced at him. "Owe you?"

"Yeah." He started the engine, then turned his head, meeting her gaze. "You owe me a sausage roll."

A little flake of pastry rested on her cheek, and it was all he could do to restrain himself from reaching out and brushing it away.

A crease appeared between her blond brows,

and she studied him for a long moment, as if she found him puzzling. Then it disappeared.

"Okay, fair," she said.

"But I'll take a beer instead," he amended, knowing this was a bad idea but saying it all the same. Because he'd been a dick and he wanted to make it up to her, and he'd promised Clint he'd handle himself. "By way of an apology."

"Your way of apologizing is to let me buy you a beer?"

"Fine. I'll buy the beer and we can talk about how to get Evan to give up at least one of his paintings."

Beth's usually radiant smile was a little uncertain at first, but it slowly crept over her face like a summer sunrise, warm and sweet and full of promise.

"Seriously? That would be wonderful. But please, you're right, I do owe you, so I will definitely be buying the beer."

And he had to look away. Had to almost physically force himself not to keep staring at that beautiful, beautiful smile.

Because that one wasn't fake, and it touched him. He hated that it touched him.

"Good," he said with no emphasis whatsoever. "That's settled then."

And he didn't say another word as he drove them both back down into town.

Chapter 3

A COUPLE OF DAYS LATER, BETH STOOD AT THE big wooden counter in Brightwater Dreams with Indigo and Izzy. The gallery was a beautiful space with a high ceiling and exposed beams, a gleaming polished wooden floor, brick walls, and purpose-built wooden shelves full of stock. Light poured through the big windows that looked out toward the lake, giving the place a light, airy feel.

The three of them were exclaiming over the perfect, deep-blue sapphire that graced Izzy's finger. Chase had given it to her the night before and asked her to marry him and of course the answer was yes.

She was incandescently happy and Beth was ecstatic for her. And it only made her more sure that coming here had been the right move. Because if Izzy could find happiness here, then surely she could too.

Izzy wasn't from Deep River, like Beth and Indigo were. Izzy was from Texas, though Beth and Indigo had met her before, since she was Zeke Montgomery's sister and had visited Deep River more than once. But they hadn't expected her to join them on their New Zealand trip as a last-minute replacement for another Deep River woman who'd had to pull out for family reasons.

Izzy had been fleeing a broken engagement and a career in ruins, and so had joined their expedition as the default admin person. She wasn't creative in the same way Beth and Indigo were, but Izzy knew business inside and out and had been a godsend when it had come to setting up the gallery and figuring out logistics.

She was also kindhearted, generous, and cool under pressure, and Beth liked her very much.

"It's gorgeous." Beth stared down at the glittering blue stone with a professional eye. "Beautifully made too. Chase really knocked it out of the park."

"He so did." Indigo, standing at the counter next to Beth, leaned in to take a closer look, her brown hair falling over one shoulder as she did so.

Indigo was another Deep River native, though she and Beth had only known each other casually. She'd been brought up in an isolated homestead by her maternal grandmother. What happened to Indigo's parents, Beth had never asked and Indigo had never said, but her grandmother had been an agoraphobic hermit, homeschooling her and never letting her out of her sight. Indigo had never been anywhere, never done anything, and when her grandmother had died unexpectedly, she of course decided to come all the way out to New Zealand.

As a rebellion against her upbringing went,

it was marked and Beth was very curious why Indigo had wanted to come out here, since Indigo seemed to find people, and indeed life in general, quite suspicious.

But whenever she'd asked, Indigo had clammed up, and since Beth had her own secrets, she'd decided to leave it alone. Whatever Indigo's reasons, coming to the other side of the world to a new country took guts, and it was clear that she had plenty of that.

Izzy gave them both a radiant smile, pleased with their admiration of her fiancée. "I know, right? Isn't he amazing? So we're going to have a little town get-together tonight at the Rose. A celebration for Chase and me. You two will be there, won't you?"

"Hell yes," Beth said without hesitation, because she liked a party. Or at least, she'd make herself like a party. "Absolutely."

Indigo wrinkled her nose. "I love you, Izzy, you know that. But I really hate parties."

Izzy leaned her hip against the counter. "Don't think of it as a party. It's more of an informal get-together. A…meeting of friends."

It was not unusual for Indigo to balk at anything that required social interaction. Then again, even when she'd been doubtful about something, she normally sucked it up and came along anyway. All she needed was a bit of reassurance.

"Don't forget, you know everyone." Beth gave

her a pat on the shoulder. "It's not going to be a room full of strangers or anything."

Indigo sighed. "I know. It's just…"

"Hmmm." Izzy's gaze turned shrewd. "This doesn't have anything to do with a certain person, does it?"

Predictably, whenever the subject of Levi King came up, Indigo went beet red, and sure enough, she was blushing now.

"What person?" There was a hint of sharpness in her tone. "I don't know what you're talking about."

Except she did know what Izzy was talking about. They all did.

Levi, playboy extraordinaire, had apparently decided that Indigo was his latest challenge, flirting outrageously with her, making her blush, teasing her, and generally being a pain in the ass.

He wasn't cruel or mean, only his normal charming self, but Indigo had decided she didn't like him and, rather to Beth's surprise given her friend's shyness, had let him know that at every opportunity.

Which, naturally enough, only provoked him even more.

Watching the two of them needle each other had become one of Beth's favorite forms of entertainment.

"You have to go," Beth said. "You know how much I enjoy watching you and Levi sniping at each other."

Indigo sniffed. "I do not snipe."

"Sure you do. You snipe. Levi flirts."

"She's not wrong," Izzy said.

"What do you expect?" Indigo looked cross. "He's a dick. I keep telling him to leave me alone and he won't."

"Well, he might if you weren't always in his vicinity at every opportunity," Beth pointed out, since it was true. For all the protests Indigo made, she always seemed to be around wherever Levi was, mostly in the background, glaring at him.

Beth and Izzy found it terribly amusing, since it was clear to both of them that Indigo had a massive crush on him. It just wasn't clear to Indigo. She was such a little innocent. It was adorable.

"I don't want to talk about Levi." Indigo's blue eyes fixed on Beth. "How's it going with Finn?"

Dammit.

Beth hadn't been specific with the other two about why she'd left Deep River—that was her secret and her secret alone. So they didn't know the Beth Grant she'd once been.

All they knew was the Beth she'd let them see, the Beth she was now: friendly, outgoing, positive, and full of boundless optimism. And also, according to them, the Beth who was currently fixated on Finn Kelly.

Which was a complete and total lie.

She wasn't fixated on him. Sure, their interaction

a couple of days ago up at Clint's had been…a bit fraught. And maybe she'd let herself get ruffled by the way he'd looked at her, teasing her about that stupid apple. But then *he'd* been stupid and her reaction to him even stupider.

She didn't regret eating the sausage roll, though, and certainly not after it had ended with him inviting her for a beer. And it wasn't because she wanted to spend some more time with him, absolutely not. She just wanted to get his help with Evan and some paintings. That was it.

Anyway, he'd largely been absent since then, so she hadn't been able to take him up on the offer. Chase had told her he'd been out taking some tourists on a two-day hike, not that she'd been looking for him or anything.

Or thinking about the way he looked at you in the truck and made you feel hot. That's got nothing to do with anything either.

No, it really didn't. And he hadn't looked at her any way in the truck. He'd been annoyed she'd eaten his sausage roll, that's all.

Sure, keep telling yourself you don't feel a thing for him, that you're not attracted to him in any way.

Beth's cheeks felt slightly hot, and much to her annoyance, Izzy and Indigo were both looking at her with interest.

Double dammit.

She attempted to feign innocence. "Finn who?"

Indigo snorted while Izzy shook her head, smiling. "Okay, but the really important question is have you managed to talk to Evan about his paintings yet? We're opening next week and I was hoping to have something before then."

Beth had hoped to have something before then too.

"I'm working on it," she said. "He won't see me, but he knows Finn quite well and Finn promised to help me with him."

One of Izzy's dark brows shot up. "Oh, so *Finn* is going to help you? How...convenient."

Beth opened her mouth to tell Izzy it wasn't like that when the door to the gallery opened and a tall, lanky girl with dark hair came clattering in.

"Hey, Gus," Beth greeted her with some relief.

Augusta Kelly, otherwise known as Gus, Chase's twelve-year-old daughter, gave Beth a giant grin. "Hi, Beth. Hi, Indigo."

Indigo's sharp face, usually guarded, relaxed with genuine warmth since it was impossible not to smile when Gus was around.

"Hey, Izzy," Gus went on. "Dad wants to talk to you about tonight. Can you go see him at HQ?"

"Oh sure." Izzy stepped away from the counter, glancing at Beth and Indigo. "See you tonight, yes?"

"With bells on," Beth said.

As Izzy disappeared through the door, Gus following behind her, Indigo sighed again, just a touch dramatically.

"Yes," Beth said before her friend could say a word. "We have to go."

"Oh, I know, don't worry. I'll be there." Indigo pulled a face. "It only feels a bit much, especially with all this house stuff to worry about."

The "house stuff" was some ongoing drama with a house that Chase had initially organized for the Deep River contingent to move into. It had been meant to happen a few weeks after they arrived, but first Izzy had moved in with Chase, and then the house itself was found to have an unsafe foundation. It had been vacant awhile and the elements hadn't been kind, and while it seemed to be a good place to live in at first, Clive Grange, who used to own a construction company before he'd moved to Brightwater and bought the vineyard, had pronounced it unsound, the foundations needing to be reblocked.

All of which meant that Beth and Indigo were still living in the Rose.

The Rose wasn't bad. While it was a bit shabby and ramshackle, it was also quite comfortable.

However, it was still a hotel. And Beth and Indigo were getting a little tired of living out of suitcases.

Not that they had much choice about the matter. Accommodation was at a premium in Brightwater Valley since the place was tiny and there weren't any other vacant houses around.

Chase was trying to get in touch with the owner

of the house they were going to move into, to get the okay to do some renovations, but the man lived overseas and was proving difficult to contact.

"Yeah," Beth said, agreeing. "I know. I'll talk to Chase again tonight if you like, see if he's managed to make any progress." She searched around for a silver lining because there was always a silver lining if you looked hard enough. "On the bright side, we don't have to cook. And Cait's food is delicious."

But Indigo must have not been in the mood to be jollied, because she sighed again. "I like cooking. I miss cooking."

Beth gave her shoulder another reassuring pat. "Don't worry, we'll figure it out. How's that dyeing coming along?"

It was the right question to ask, since Indigo immediately cheered up, going into an in-depth explanation about how Cait had allowed her to use the kitchen in the Rose, and it was great because the stove was big enough for her to have four dye pots going at once.

Indigo lost her pinched look and more or less sparkled when she was talking about the things she loved, and it made Beth happy to see it. She'd been worrying about her friend and hoping that coming to New Zealand had been the right decision for her. In the past month, she'd become very invested in both Izzy and Indigo, but now that Izzy had Chase and was building a life with him, it seemed as if Indigo was the one she really needed to worry about.

"You should wear something pretty tonight," she said to Indigo as the two of them left the gallery and made their way back to the Rose to grab some lunch. "Like a dress or a skirt."

Indigo, who lived in jeans and ratty T-shirts and the odd brightly colored shawl she'd knitted, scowled. "What? Why?"

"Well, for a start, it's an engagement party, so it might be nice to make an effort," Beth said. "Plus wearing something pretty puts you in a good mood."

Indigo scowled harder. "It doesn't put me in a good mood."

"Oh come on. You're telling me that wearing a pretty sweater knitted from nice yarn doesn't make you happy?"

"That's a low blow," Indigo muttered. "Anyway, I know where you're going with this and there's no way I'm dressing to please some dumb man."

Beth put on an innocent face. "Did I say anything about dressing to please some dumb man? Besides, that's no way to talk about my boyfriend, Levi."

Indigo stopped short and glowered. "He is *not* your boyfriend."

Interesting response. Clearly she'd hit a nerve.

Feeling bad now, because as much fun as some

gentle teasing of Indigo was, it became less fun when it hurt her feelings.

"Sorry, hon," she said apologetically. "You know I don't think of him that way."

"Well, I don't either."

But Beth suddenly wasn't listening, her attention caught by the arrival of a familiar, mud-splashed truck pulling up outside HQ.

A tall male figure got out, along with some others who were looking as mud-splashed as the truck. Obviously some tourists returning from one of the longer hikes Pure Adventure NZ took people on.

They all gathered beside the truck as the tall man went to haul rucksacks out of the truck's bed.

Finn, clearly coming back from his hike.

One woman was talking to him, looking at him raptly, as if he were imparting the wisdom of the ages. And no wonder.

Even though he was as mud-splashed as the rest of them, the midday sun glossed his black hair and turned his olive skin a deep golden brown, while the black Pure Adventure NZ T-shirt he wore, damp with sweat as he hauled out the rucksacks, clung to his muscled chest.

Finn Kelly was gorgeous and any woman with eyes could see that.

Beth mouth's went dry and her cheeks heated, and even though she desperately wanted to, she couldn't look away.

This was stupid. What was she doing staring at him like that? She hadn't seen him in a couple of days, it was true, but it wasn't as if she'd missed his glowering, broody presence, not one iota.

Why would she? When they weren't even friends?

Mystery, the stray dog that everyone in the town had tried at some point to adopt but no one had successfully managed to, had trotted from around the back of HQ and was now nosing around the tourists. They all exclaimed over him, giving him lots of attention, but once he realized there were no treats on offer, he sneezed in disgust and trotted off again.

Finn pulled out the last rucksack and dumped it beside the truck with the others, nodding as the woman kept talking to him.

Then he abruptly glanced toward where Beth and Indigo stood.

And even though he was some distance away and Beth couldn't make out his face, she felt the impact of his gaze like a weight driving all the air from her lungs.

Oh hell. That wasn't good. That wasn't good at all.

Indigo noted the direction of Beth's stare and shaded her eyes, surveying the little group gathered near the truck.

"Is that Finn?" she asked.

Beth tore her gaze away and reached for Indigo's arm. "Yep," she said, turning around and starting back toward the Rose, urging Indigo along with her. "I just remembered I promised to buy him a beer in return for help with Evan."

"Hey," Indigo protested. "What's the hurry?"

"Oh, I have to…uh…get something really quick."

"What?"

But Beth's heart was beating way too hard and a prickling heat was sweeping over her skin. She knew what that meant—oh she did. She'd felt it with Troy in the first few months of their relationship.

He'd been her high school boyfriend, a calm, steadying kind of guy, and their relationship had felt like a safe haven after her somewhat emotionally chaotic upbringing.

At least until she'd gotten pregnant, lost the baby, and fallen into a pit of depression.

Until he'd decided that wasn't something he'd signed on for and left.

But no, she wasn't going to think about him or the baby she'd lost or the depression.

Fun, that's what she wanted. Fun and happy. Because she'd never had that, not even with Troy. Steady and safe had been great back then, but she was different now. She was brave and fearless now, and safe and steady seemed a little boring to her.

Not that dark and brooding and intense was any

better. Or this prickling, feverish heat that seemed to build inside her every time Finn Kelly looked at her.

You probably should stay away from him in that case.

Yes, she should. But that wasn't an option, not in a town as small as Brightwater Valley. And she couldn't anyway, not after she'd promised Izzy she'd get at least one of Evan's paintings for the gallery, not after she'd promised Finn a beer.

No, she was going to have to figure out how to live with him, and that would probably involve completely ignoring the attraction flaring between them.

At least until it had died down, which it would, of course, since that's what had happened with Troy. It would definitely happen with Finn too, no question.

All she had to do was wait it out.

In the meantime, she'd buy him a beer and ask him about Evan. Tonight even. Treat him like the friend she wanted him to be and not like the lover her body wished he were.

"Oh," Indigo said. "I'm sure there's no connection between Finn and you suddenly needing to…uh… get something."

"No, of course there isn't," Beth said as she dragged Indigo up the front steps and into the Rose. "I don't know what you're talking about."

Finn sat at his chosen table in the corner of the crowded pub in the Rose, glowering at the four people standing at the bar.

Correction. He was glowering at *one* person.

And it wasn't Chase, Levi, or Izzy.

It was the woman standing next to Levi and talking animatedly to the other three. She wore a simple, white cotton sundress that left her shoulders bare, and her pale, cotton candy hair had been piled on the top of her head in a messy bun. Tendrils fell down around her face, ears, and the back of her neck, making it look like someone had buried their fingers in all that softness and pulled at it just a little.

You'd like to pull at it just a little.

Finn growled under his breath and forced himself to look away. No, he would not like to do that. She was out of bounds, no matter how pretty and desirable she looked in her white dress, all pale skin, soft and sexy with a hint of innocence.

Radiant, that's what she was.

Shining like the moon in the darkness.

Christ, she's turning you into a poet.

His jaw tightened. He'd thought that hike he'd taken would have helped him get a handle on things, since it was a bloody hard one and for experienced hikers only. Yet it hadn't. He was still just as obsessed as he had been before he'd left.

He glowered at the wall next to him instead, pretending to examine all the things hanging on it—the pub's walls were covered in photos, newspaper articles, old miners headlamps, fishing nets, and apparently anything else that had been lying around and could be attached to a wall—going over what on earth it was about her he couldn't get out of his head.

Was it her smile? Or was it more about how fake it sometimes seemed to him? As if she was forcing it? Which then led him on a path to wonder why and what had happened to her that she felt she had to be so goddamn happy all the time. Also, why did she bother? Who was she performing for?

He didn't want to wonder those things. He didn't want to think about her at all.

Some sixth sense made him turn just in time to see Beth approaching his table.

"Here," she said, smiling that pretty yet fake smile as she put a beer bottle down in front of him. "I owe you, remember?"

The pub was crowded with the inhabitants of Brightwater and humming with the sound of conversation and laughter, all of them here to congratulate Chase and Izzy on their engagement. Yet somehow, even though it was packed, it was as if he and Beth were enclosed in their own private little bubble.

Another thing he didn't like, not one bit.

Without waiting for an invitation, Beth sat down in the seat opposite him, and he found himself noticing how she'd caught a touch of sun on her shoulders and chest, the skin there a light, pretty gold, highlighting the paleness of the rest of her.

"I thought you might want something to toast the happy couple with," she said brightly when he didn't speak. "It's your favorite, Jim said."

Ah yes, the happy couple. He was thrilled for his brother, he really was. Izzy was a wonderful woman and she was great with Gus too, and he shouldn't be sitting over here in the corner being a grumpy ass.

But he couldn't stop thinking about Beth and now she was smiling at him, and that smile… It was so bright. Yet it still looked fake, as if she was using it to cover something else.

Perhaps she's nervous around you.

He suspected that was true, though he also suspected her nervousness wasn't because she was afraid of him. In fact, he suspected she was more afraid of this tension between them than anything else.

In which case you should be putting her at ease.

Yeah, he probably should. He'd promised Clint he'd handle himself.

He glanced down at the beer, then back at her. "Thank you."

Beth put her elbows on the table and leaned on them, her bracelets making that soft, melodic sound as they fell down her arm. "You mentioned helping me with Evan…"

Behind her, Finn could see Chase and Levi still standing at the bar, while Izzy chatted to Teddy Grange, who along with her husband, Clive, owned the Brightwater Valley vineyard. Izzy wasn't looking in his direction, but Chase and Levi were, and they had distinctly speculative expressions on their faces.

Finn didn't like that either.

The last thing he needed was for them to start thinking he and Beth were a thing. Chase hadn't mentioned it to him and Levi hadn't either, but the tension between him and Beth was palpable. Levi and Chase would have to be blind not to pick up on it, and certainly it was obvious that they had. And they were wondering.

Which made sitting here with Beth a bad idea.

Chase would start making assumptions and Levi would start making pointed comments, and his own temper would take a dive since he wasn't in the mood. Better to stop any rumors in their tracks now, before people got the wrong idea and his crappy mood turned what was supposed to be a happy occasion sour.

Finn shoved back his chair and got abruptly to his feet.

Beth stared at him in surprise, her smile faltering. "What's wrong?"

"We'll do this later," he said shortly.

"But what about your beer?"

He paused for a moment, then grabbed the beer, put back his head, and drank the entire thing in seconds flat—because he was thirsty, and she'd bought it for him, and he didn't want her trying to buy him another.

Putting the bottle back down on the table, he gave her a nod, turned on his heel, and pushed his way out of the bar.

"Hey wait!" Beth called. "What about Evan?"

But he didn't pause, going straight through the door and out into the warm summer night.

It wasn't dark yet—it didn't get dark till after nine—and a dusky twilight lay over the town.

He paused on the veranda, staring out across the lake and the mountains beyond, the snow-capped peaks tinged gold and pink in the light of the setting sun. From out in the bush somewhere, he could hear the distinctive call of a ruru, a native owl also called a "morepork." Early for a ruru, but the sound set off some memories…

He used to love this time of night in summer, sitting with Sheri on the deck of their house. Relaxing with a beer after a hard day's work and talking about nothing. Talking about everything. Their future, their dreams, their plans, children…

Muttering a curse under his breath, Finn shoved a hand through his hair and tried to pull himself together.

He didn't want to be thinking about this, not about Sheri. She'd been gone for years. Not that she was ever very far away from his thoughts; it was more that he'd stopped thinking about her every day.

Initially she'd been the first thing he'd thought about every morning when he woke up.

Then she'd become the second.

Now, he sometimes went a whole day without thinking of her, which was progress of a sort, but not the kind of progress he wanted. Not thinking about Sheri, forgetting her, wasn't something he was willing to do.

She'd meant too much to him and she deserved to be remembered.

Finn stood on the veranda knowing he should go back inside and celebrate with his brother, since he really was happy for Chase. If anyone deserved a chance at happiness, it was him. It had been Chase who'd brought Finn up after their mother had died and their father had drowned his grief at the pub.

Chase who'd dedicated himself to the Brightwater community and worked hard for it.

Chase who'd tried to make his own marriage work and, when it hadn't, had done all he could for his daughter.

And now that Chase had found happiness with Izzy, Finn couldn't be more pleased for him. But he didn't feel like being in the pub with everyone around, toasting the happy couple and smiling and laughing.

He wanted to be alone, where there was silence and no one bothering or watching him, no one being concerned for him. And best of all, no Bethany Grant distracting him with her fake smile and her big green eyes, her pretty cotton-candy hair and her pale-moonlight skin.

Finn went down the steps and was just stepping onto the gravel when a highly irritated feminine voice came from behind him.

"Seriously? You drink your beer then up and leave? Without a word?"

Of course it was Bethany. And of course he couldn't have a few moments to himself tonight. She was doing what she always did, which was get in his face when he least wanted her to.

Which meant he should be angry that she'd followed him and definitely not feeling as if he'd been shocked, every muscle in his body going tight with anticipation.

He stopped in his tracks, trying to relax, get himself under control, because his physical reaction every time she got near was ludicrous and he was tired of it.

So? Do something about it then. You're thirty-two. You can't stay celibate forever.

Yeah, and that's not what he wanted to be thinking about right now, not at all.

"Finn," Beth said. "Come on. You can't just leave me sitting there."

He gave himself a moment, then he turned to face her.

She was standing on the wide veranda, the setting sun painting her in tones of rose and gold and orange and red. She had her hands on her hips, and for a change she wasn't smiling. Which sadly didn't make her any less attractive.

You are so screwed.

"What?" He ignored both the thought and the inevitable pulse of heat that went through him every time she was near. "I said thanks for the beer."

"Yeah, then you walked out. We were going to talk about Evan."

"Can we talk about that another night?" He tried to keep his voice level. "I've got a couple of other things to do."

She frowned. "I…guess we can."

"Good." He turned around and started heading toward the Pure Adventure NZ HQ, since that was the closest building he could legitimately disappear into. "We can chat in a couple of days," he added casually over his shoulder.

Beth didn't respond, and he resisted the urge to look back.

Hopefully she'd have gotten the hint and would go back to the party.

The door that led to the top floor of HQ, which

was a self-contained apartment/office area, was around the side of the building, so Finn walked toward it with no clue what he was going to do when he got there. He only wanted to put some distance between him and Beth.

Then he heard a footstep on the gravel behind him.

"No, actually," Beth said, "I don't want to chat in a couple of days."

Shit.

Tension gripped him, his muscles tightening.

He didn't want to turn around and look at her, so he reached for the door handle instead. The door wasn't locked—they only locked it during the day, when there were tourists around, since no one who actually lived in Brightwater would steal anything from it. Not that there was anything in there to steal anyway.

"Yeah, well, I don't want to chat now." He tried to keep the growl out of the words as he pulled the door open, but he didn't think he'd been successful.

"Why not?" Beth's voice was husky and very close behind him now. "It won't take that long. You either help me or you don't."

Well, if that's all she wanted, then that was easy enough to give her. Anything to get her away from him.

"Fine, I'll help you." He stepped through the

doorway. "I'll talk to him tomorrow." Then he began to pull the door closed behind him.

Only to encounter some resistance.

Oh, for God's sake.

Left with no choice, he swung around.

Beth stood in the doorway, holding on to the door and preventing it from closing. She was still bathed in sunset colors, and what was even worse was being able to see the shadow of her body through that little white dress and it was a glorious sight. Lots of delicious, rounded curves that he knew would feel warm and soft beneath his hand.

God, it had been so long since he'd touched a woman. So long since a woman had touched him...

How long are you going to remain on that particular cross?

Finn shoved the thought away. Whatever, he was tired of keeping his temper in check and he was tired of her following him, especially when he'd made it very clear he wanted to be alone.

He scowled. "What part of 'I'll talk to him tomorrow' don't you understand?"

Surprise flashed across her face, as if she hadn't been expecting him to be quite so grumpy. Well, too bad. She was the one who'd pushed herself on him, not the other way around, which meant she could suck up his reaction.

"I do understand." She eyed him. "But you got up and left without a word and I—"

"Because I wanted to be alone. I did not want to have someone following me around demanding I explain myself to them."

"I'm not—"

"Is that all?"

She blinked. "Well, I...I mean...are you okay?"

"Why wouldn't I be?"

"You...well, you walked off."

"I'm tired. And as you can see, I'm okay." He turned back to the stairs, since he wasn't going to have a bloody argument with her at the front door, and continued up them.

With any luck, she'd take his foul temper into account and leave.

The stairs opened directly onto a small living area that housed a couch, multiple bookshelves full of books and other knickknacks, a coffee table, and a wood burner. This was for the use of Pure Adventure NZ staff and it served as a break room/planning area and, before Izzy came on the scene, a place for Gus to hang out after school since if Chase was working, he couldn't take her home immediately.

There was also a kitchen off the living area and a bathroom down a short hallway, along with a small single bedroom.

Finn stalked into the middle of the living area, then came to a stop, his back to the stairs. He could smell a faint, sweet scent. Peaches or apricots...

Apparently she hadn't gotten the hint and left.

Ahead of him were windows that looked into the green fields and the beech forest that covered the hills of the valley, currently bathed in the glow of the summer sunset.

But he wasn't taking in the view. Every sense he had was concentrated behind him, on the woman who'd followed him up the stairs.

Sure enough, Beth said quietly, "I'm sorry. I'm not trying to be a pain. I just... Have I done something to make you angry? Because if I have, I'd really like to know what it is so I can stop doing it."

Finn shut his eyes.

He couldn't let her blame herself—he couldn't. He'd promised Clint he'd handle himself and that he wouldn't let anyone get hurt. Yet here he was, snapping at her when she hadn't even done anything wrong.

It wasn't fair of him to take his issues out on her. Especially when his issue was his stupid dick.

You need to tell her, be honest with her.

Finn took a breath and opened his eyes, stared sightlessly at the window and the view beyond.

"You haven't done anything," he said into the silence. "The problem is me."

"Okay." She sounded puzzled. "So...what is it? Is there anything I can do?"

Finn turned around.

She stood at the top of the stairs, her arms folded

across her breasts, a crease between her brows, staring at him as if he was a mystery she wanted to get to the bottom of.

"No," he said flatly. "There's nothing you can do."

"Are you sure?"

"Yes."

"Because you know if I'm doing something that you—"

"Beth."

She blinked at the sound of her name. "What?"

"The problem isn't what you're doing. The problem is you."

Shock rippled over her face. "Me? But I thought you said—"

"That it was me? Yeah, it is. The problem is me wanting you."

Chapter 4

BETH STARED IN SHOCK AT FINN'S TALL, BROAD figure.

He…wanted her?

Oh, come on. Don't act so surprised. You knew this attraction was mutual.

Okay, so she did.

She remembered how he'd looked at her that day in his truck on the way to Clint's, that gleam in his eyes. She wasn't experienced when it came to men—Troy was the only man she'd been out with—but she certainly knew what attraction was. And some part of her had known it was mutual.

That's why you followed him out of the Rose—don't lie.

She wished she could say she'd followed him because she was tired of him being rude to her and she was determined to find out why, but that wasn't the whole truth.

She'd followed him because some part of her hadn't been able to leave him alone.

Now he stood in the middle of the little living area, the windows at his back, tall, dark, and brooding in his black T-shirt and jeans. The light was behind him, throwing his face into shadow, but his eyes gleamed.

He was staring so fiercely at her, she felt as if she might go up in flames.

She swallowed, her mouth dry, her face hot.

The silence between them gathered weight, pulling tight, and she tried desperately to think of something to say, because she had to say something.

"Okay," she forced out at last.

Finn pushed his hands into his pockets. "You should leave."

She should. She should get back down those stairs and get back to the Rose. Get back to her friends since she wasn't here for this.

She was here for fun and easy and simple, not difficult and hard and complicated.

Yet she didn't move.

What are you doing? He told you to leave, so leave.

But something wouldn't let her.

He wanted her. That's what he'd said—that's what the problem was. He wanted her and obviously it wasn't a good thing.

"Why…" she began, then cleared her throat and started again. "Why is that a problem?"

He muttered a curse under his breath. "Seriously? Why do you think? Nothing's going to happen between us, Beth."

Her stomach lurched and it wasn't with relief.

"That still doesn't tell me why you're being such a grumpy ass to me."

He was silent a moment, then he let out a breath and glanced away. "Because I've been trying to fight it and it's not working and I haven't been handling that well." His jaw tightened and he glanced back. "I'm sorry. I'll pull it together, okay? Give me tonight to handle it, and tomorrow I swear I'll start being less of a dick to you."

Yet something was shifting around inside her, a kind of electricity, hot and crackling, along with a burst of what could only be satisfaction. Which didn't make any sense because she couldn't be happy that he wanted her, surely. Especially when they weren't going to be doing anything about it.

Why not?

The thought echoed in her head.

She'd wanted easy and fun, and Finn was not either of those things. Yet…resisting their attraction was only making things difficult between them. He was unhappy about it and it was definitely getting in the way of them being friends.

So maybe it was the resisting that was hard. And the easy thing would be to…do something about it. They could have sex, get this out of the way, and then go on with the business of being friends.

It was only sex. And sex was pleasant and made you feel good, but it wasn't anything major if you didn't want it to be.

Also, she couldn't forget that she was here to create a bright, new, happy life for herself, to be different from the Beth she'd been in Deep River.

She'd been unhappy back there. She'd been sad and gray and scared. Clinging to the life she'd thought she'd wanted: a husband and a baby and stability. Certainty.

A life that didn't have an emotionally fragile mother in it and a constantly seething father. With arguments and shouting and all kinds of other negativity.

No, she hadn't wanted that and she'd thought she'd found an escape from it with Troy. Then she'd lost the baby, and soon after that, she'd lost Troy too.

Her dream had been wrong, that was the issue. She'd wanted the wrong things and that's why it hadn't worked out.

She wasn't going to make that mistake again.

So why not have sex with Finn? It could be easy if she wanted it to be easy, and definitely it would be fun.

And while he wasn't like Troy in the slightest, she wanted him.

And he wanted her.

Beth swallowed. "Or…there is another option."

Finn was already still. Now he became a statue. Something in his face shifted and hardened, the dark gleam in his eyes becoming pronounced. "I hope you're not going to suggest what I think you're going to suggest."

She took a little breath. "And what do you think I'm going to suggest?"

"Beth..."

"What? You didn't explain why it's a problem, Finn." She paused. "You also didn't explain why nothing could happen between us."

His stare intensified, focusing on her very intently. "Why? Because I'm not having casual sex with someone who's going to be sticking around for the next couple of months, okay? If things go bad between us—"

"But why would they go bad?" Her heart was thumping hard against her ribs. Because now that she'd let in the possibility of sex with Finn Kelly, she couldn't think of anything else. "I'm not talking about an affair, Finn. We could...give in to this attraction once, deal with it so to speak. We could get it out of the way and then...hey, maybe we could even try and be actual friends. Because you know I want you too."

Finn said nothing, his gaze dark and full of shadows.

The electricity inside her seemed to have escaped, pooling in the space between them, charging the air with static, making her breathing get faster, shorter.

She hadn't been with anyone since Troy had

left. She hadn't even been on a date. Sex hadn't been something she'd missed, and even with Troy it had been kind of…samey. Which at the time had been reassuring.

Yet looking at Finn and thinking about his hands on her skin, his mouth on hers…she didn't want reassuring and samey. She wanted excitement.

He hadn't moved and he hadn't said a word, so Beth decided to take matters into her own hands.

She took a step toward him. He remained where he was, watching her. So she took another step, then another. Then another, which took her right to him, his tall, muscular figure barely inches away.

He was very warm and he smelled spicy, like the bush with a hint of something masculine and musky. It was delicious.

His eyes were so dark, a deep, velvety espresso color she couldn't stop looking into. And he had the thickest, softest looking lashes. She was jealous of those lashes.

Her heartbeat was deafening and she was breathing far too fast for comfort, and she wished she had more experience. Because she had no idea how to do this. And he wasn't moving or saying anything.

"Finn?" Her voice had gone so husky. "Are you—"

He reached out and gripped her jaw gently, and before she could finish her sentence, he'd bent his head and covered her mouth with his.

For a second neither of them moved.

Beth trembled, every thought in her head gone, every sense she had zeroing in on his mouth and his hand gripping her jaw, on his fingertips against her skin and the press of his lips, soft yet firm. And hot—so, so hot...

She could feel that heat moving through her, dragging behind it a heady, dizzy feeling, as if all her blood had turned to champagne and was fizzing inside her veins. And there was a steady, deep pulse between her thighs, beating in time with her heart.

She hadn't been expecting this kiss, but now that his mouth was on hers, she wanted more. So much more.

Beth lifted her hands and slid her fingers into the thick, black silk of his hair, leaning into his heat and opening her mouth beneath his, encouraging him to take more.

Yet he didn't move. And gradually she became aware of his tension, every muscle in his body rigid, a subtle vibration running through him, as if he was holding himself tightly in check.

Her chest constricted.

He'd kissed her, but...did he not want this? Or perhaps the kiss wasn't as good for him as it was for her. Perhaps now they'd taken that first step, he'd changed his mind.

She took her hands from his hair and tried to

draw away, wanting to ask him if there was anything wrong, but as she did so, the hand on her jaw tightened, his hold firming.

And suddenly he pushed his tongue into her mouth, taking control in a way that turned her knees to water. She put her hands on his chest to steady herself, and then, as though whatever check on himself he'd released, he was kissing her deeply, hungrily, as if he'd been waiting for this kiss his entire life.

She was caught against the hot, iron wall of his chest, crushed against it, her mouth invaded, and for a second she couldn't think and couldn't breathe.

Then the same hunger that was driving him rushed up inside her, a raw flood of need she couldn't control.

She slid her hands around his neck, coming up on her toes and kissing back, meeting him kiss for kiss, glorying in the heady flavor of his mouth, dark chocolate and whisky and some other sweet, delicious thing she couldn't name.

It made her dizzy and feverish, made her desperate to get closer to him, because just being pressed against him wasn't enough.

He kissed her harder, exploring her as if he couldn't get enough of her. Bending her backward, taking things even deeper, even hotter.

She trembled, holding on to him urgently, and then with a suddenness that stole what little breath she had left, he picked her up in his arms, took two strides to the couch against the wall, then put her onto it before following her down, pinning her there with his body.

Beth gasped as he settled on her; the hard, muscular length of him pressing against her was the most perfect feeling. Automatically, she spread her thighs on either side of his hips to welcome him, and he settled more firmly, the brush of his erection against the most sensitive part of her making her moan.

"Finn," she gasped against his mouth, wriggling against his body, not to get away but to get closer. "Oh…please."

He didn't reply, only kissed her as if somehow this kiss was the only thing that stood between him and certain death.

She felt his hands tug on her dress and heard the sound of fabric ripping, but she didn't care what he was tearing. She wanted there to be nothing between them. She wanted to feel his bare skin on hers, and his lips and his hands. She wanted him as close to her as she could get.

His mouth moved from hers, trailing over her jaw and down her throat in a series of hot kisses and nips that set every nerve ending she had alight.

Dimly in the back of her mind, a warning echoed about how wrong this could go, but she didn't want to listen to it so she didn't.

This felt too good and it had been too long since she'd felt something this real. Something that wasn't the forced brightness and optimism she had to work at every day. Something that was pure physical sensation, pure pleasure, her mind for once silenced beneath the crush of desire.

He nudged aside the strap of her dress, and since she wasn't wearing a bra, his hands soon found her bare skin, stroking her breasts. Then his mouth closed around one nipple and she groaned as sensation arced the length of her body, a lightning strike of feeling that made her arch and writhe beneath him.

She wanted to touch him too though, so she pulled at his T-shirt, finding the hem and slipping her fingers beneath it, sliding over the smooth skin she found there. He was so hot, like touching the iron wall of a stove, making her realize how cold she'd been and how much she wanted to get closer to his heat.

He muttered a curse as she touched him, and then his hands were on her thighs, caressing her before sliding between to the hot, wet center of her.

She groaned as he stroked her through the fabric of her panties, small electric shocks of pleasure that made her quake.

"Beth." Her name was a raw whisper against her breast. "Beth…honey…I want you."

She knew what he was asking and she couldn't think of anything she wanted more.

"Yes," she panted. "Yes, Finn. Please…*please*."

Every one of Finn's thought processes had vanished. Every single one.

He was buried by need, choked by desire. Only a ghost of his conscious mind was left, enough to make sure she was with him in this, and then, hearing the heat in the word *please*, even that vanished too.

Then there was nothing but soft, slick skin, warm curves, and silken hair. Her breathing, fast and desperate, and the husky murmur of her voice as she pleaded with him. The scent of apricots and a delicate musk that made his mouth water.

He wanted to take his time, but there was no time to be had.

It had been too long—so very, *very* long—and now that she was here, beneath him, he thought he might die if he didn't get inside her.

He pulled open his jeans, his hands shaking, and then tugged aside her underwear. He touched her, feeling silky wetness and heat, and she gasped yet again, lifting her hips against his fingertips, clearly desperate for more.

He wished he could spend his time touching her, tasting her, exploring her the way she deserved to be, but he couldn't wait. He just couldn't wait.

Positioning himself, he thrust hard inside her, and it was all he could do to pause as the tight heat of her body welcomed him. To look down into her flushed face and make sure she was okay.

But she made it so easy, as if she knew exactly how difficult it was for him, reaching up to pull his mouth down on hers, her thighs closing around his waist, her hips lifting to take him deeper.

Christ. She felt so good. He wasn't going to last.

He began to move, trying to take things slow, to pace himself, but it was impossible with the way she shifted beneath him, matching him stroke for stroke. Her mouth was heaven beneath his, her taste so sweet, her kisses hot and silken and tasting of everything he'd ever wanted.

He could feel the sunshine in her. It was there, a ball of white heat that she kept locked away. Perhaps it wasn't so feigned after all, all her brightness. Perhaps he'd been wrong and it had been there all this time, warmth and summer sunlight shining down on him.

He reached for it, moving deeper, thrusting harder, letting the heat of her spread all over him, spread through him, lighting up the dark places inside him.

God, it felt like he'd been in those dark places too long, lingering in the shadows like a ghost.

But he wasn't there anymore. He was here, inside her, and it was the most glorious thing he'd ever experienced.

"Oh…Finn…" she groaned, her body trembling and he knew she was on the brink. So he slid his hand between them and touched her, giving her the extra friction, and he felt her convulse around him, her cry of release in his ears.

And then he was moving even faster, even harder, every check he had on himself gone. Everything vanishing the way it had when she'd come close and he'd realized he wasn't going to refuse her, that resisting her had become impossible and the only way forward was this.

Was her beneath him, writhing in ecstasy, and him surrounded in her heat and sweetness, following on behind her.

His movements became jerky and out of rhythm, and then he stiffened as the pleasure came rushing up his spine, exploding in his head, annihilating him. And he lost himself for whole minutes afterward, lost in the glory of a sensation he hadn't felt for years, not with another person.

Then when he came back to himself, he realized he'd collapsed on top of her and that he was likely crushing her with his weight.

He muttered a curse and tried to move, only for her arms to close around his neck.

"Wait," she whispered, the sound husky and shaken. "Just...wait for a moment. Please."

Automatically he relaxed, still in the warm grip of pleasure. "Okay. But I don't want to crush you."

"You're not. Believe me, you're not."

He shifted anyway, so she was more comfortable,

then he looked down into her flushed face. "Are you okay?"

Her green eyes were startling against the deep pink of her skin. She looked so thoroughly and utterly sexy he felt himself begin to harden again. "Yes," she breathed, her kiss-reddened mouth curving. "Yes, I'm okay. I'm very, *very* okay."

Awareness was coming back to him, of what had just happened: this was the first time he'd slept with a woman since Sheri died.

For an instant he waited for the cold shock to hit and for the guilt to come along with it and the flood of memories that would no doubt swamp him like the tide.

But…nothing happened.

And he realized, with a different sort of shock, that he hadn't felt any of those things while he'd been in the grip of passion either.

He hadn't thought of Sheri once the whole time.

Another sensation shifted behind his breastbone and he braced himself, because surely here came the guilt now.

But again, nothing happened.

He just felt…good.

Which was not what he was expecting.

He'd never wanted to forget her. He'd always wanted to keep a place for her in his heart because she deserved no less. And he'd expected making love to another woman would be fraught with memories too painful to bear. Memories of Sheri and what it felt like to take her in his arms, to kiss her, to do all the things to her that he'd loved doing that he'd never do again.

But there had only been Beth in his arms just now and no memories at all to haunt him. And there was a certain bittersweet pain in that, yet also relief.

Beth didn't deserve for him to be thinking of his dead wife while he was with her, and Sheri didn't deserve it either.

Neither do you.

Yeah, well, that was up for debate.

Still, as he looked down into Beth's eyes, he could only see her, not Sheri's light-brown eyes gazing back. Only see a very well-pleasured woman looking rather dazed and not a little awed.

A long-forgotten and very male part of him stretched out in satisfaction.

He'd done that to her. That was all him.

Automatically he smoothed back small tendrils of hair that had stuck to her cheek and forehead before shifting again to pull up the strap of her dress and adjust the fabric, easing everything back in place.

"You sure you're okay?" He reached to tuck another rogue strand of hair behind her ear. It was very soft.

"Yes, I'm fine." She was studying him with that same slightly awed look.

"Nothing sore?"

"No, not at all."

He reached to secure her strap more firmly on her shoulder and this time her hand came out, gripping his.

"Finn," she said softly, "I'm fine. You don't have to fuss."

Another realization filtered through him, of what he was doing and why. He was a caregiver, like his brother, and he always had been. It came naturally to him, which was why he'd found looking after the horses after Sheri's death so therapeutic. He'd needed something to care for and animals, rather than people, were all he could handle.

Now here he was caring for Beth.

Are you sure that's a good idea?

A stupid thought. As if caring for a woman after sex meant anything, which of course it didn't. He was just being gentlemanly and he wasn't going to apologize for it.

"I'm not fussing. I'm taking care of you."

She flushed deeper. "You don't have to do that."

"Too bad. I'm doing it." He frowned at the tear in one of the straps of her dress. It was a very narrow piece of fabric and it had torn straight through. "Sorry about that," he murmured. "I'll buy you a new one. In the meantime I'll find you a safety pin."

But gently Beth pushed his hand away. "I don't need a new one and I don't want a safety pin. I'm okay." She reached for him, sliding her fingers into his hair again, her body shifting languorously underneath his. "Let's stay here awhile."

He got even harder at the husky note in her voice and the scent of musk and sex and sweet apricots surrounding him. The thought of pushing her back on the couch and exploring her properly was very appealing, and for a second he couldn't think of anything he wanted to do more.

But something was making him uneasy and it took him a second or two to put his finger on it.

Shit. Had he used a condom?

Obviously you didn't. You don't have any, not when you haven't had sex for five years.

A cold feeling twisted in his gut. "Beth," he said hoarsely, "I didn't use protection."

Her eyes went very wide for a moment, and she paled, shock rippling over her face. And then came unmistakable relief. "Oh, it's okay. I'm on the pill." The delightful pink flush returned to her cheeks. "Period issues, you know."

He didn't know, obviously, yet he'd never been so thankful for "period issues" in his entire life. "Okay, that's good. That's…very good."

Beth wriggled beneath him in a way that made him catch his breath. "So?" She lifted her head and brushed those soft lips of hers down the side of his neck. "Can we stay here for a little bit?"

Heat gathered inside him yet again, eating away

at his resolve. And why not? Why shouldn't he stay here with her? It had been a long time, after all, and this was a gift.

No memories, no guilt. Just pleasure.

Pleasure and sweetness and sunshine.

"Okay," he murmured, his own voice gone husky. "But just once more. Before people notice we're not there and wonder where we've gone to."

"Sure. With any luck they won't notice for a while." She slid her hands up his back, her fingers hot on his skin. "Kiss me, Finn."

So he did and left the world behind him for a time.

Chapter 5

A WEEK LATER, THE BRIGHTWATER DREAMS
gallery held what Izzy termed a "soft launch,"
opening its doors to the inhabitants of Brightwater
so they could get a first look at the place before its
official opening the next day.

Chase and his team had organized a town barbecue on the lakefront to celebrate, but a fair few
of the townspeople were in the gallery, poking
curiously around at the various items on display.

Beth stood with Izzy behind the big wooden
counter in the middle of the gallery, watching
people look around the big, airy space. All the
products looked so good displayed on the rustic
wooden shelves that lined the exposed stone walls.
There were lots of different products too, all produced by the inhabitants of the valley. Artisan
preserves and cheeses from Teddy and Clive's
vineyard, handmade wooden furniture and other
items from Jim in the bar, who turned out to be a
dab hand with a chisel. A rainbow of brightly dyed
skeins of yarn hanging from wooden pegs courtesy
of Indigo, plus knitting needles and crochet hooks,
and other hand-knitted items that Shirley, who

helped Bill out in the general store, had made. A big glass case contained some of the jewelry Beth had brought with her from Deep River, as well as some that she'd made here in Brightwater, plus other items that she'd sourced from nearby Queenstown.

She was nervous, though, and trying not to show it. She'd sold her jewelry to cruise ship tourists at the farmer's market in Deep River, so it wasn't as if she'd never sold jewelry before. But this felt different somehow and she wasn't sure why. She had a variety of different pieces on display, necklaces and bracelets and earrings, plus a couple of pendants. Silver mainly, with etched designs and some with semi-precious stones. She'd found a lot of inspiration in the New Zealand bush, with curled fern fronds and delicate rata flowers and kowhai.

She hoped people would like them. She hoped the gallery would be a success because one thing she was very certain of: she did not want to go home.

She and Izzy and Indigo were supposed to be here for three months initially, and one month and a bit had already gone. They had another nearly two months to make sure the business worked out, and she was crossing everything she had that it would.

At the counter beside her, Izzy was busy pouring celebratory champagne into glasses Cait had supplied from the Rose, and handing them out to people. Indigo was over by the yarn, talking to

Shirley and another couple of ladies from farther up the valley.

There were quite a few people standing around sipping champagne and talking, and they appeared to be enjoying themselves, which was a good sign. Several townspeople—Bill especially—had been against the gallery opening, or rather "a bunch of Americans coming in and taking over," so it was nice to see the people who'd grumped about it chatting and obviously having a good time.

Beth took a surreptitious look around the gallery, purely to see who was here and not at all to check whether a certain tall, dark, and handsome someone had come into the gallery yet.

She hadn't seen him so far this evening, so maybe he hadn't. Not that she cared whether he was here or not. It didn't matter to her.

In fact, she'd been very, very clear how little Finn Kelly mattered because she hadn't thought of him once the whole week since they'd had sex.

She definitely hadn't gone over every minute of their encounter, thinking about it in the moments before she went to sleep, and it wasn't still in her head the instant she woke up either.

About the hungry way he'd kissed her or the desperation in his touch. How he'd been so at the mercy of their shared chemistry that he'd lost control, putting her down on the couch and being inside her in seconds flat.

She didn't think about her own pleasure either, of how good he'd felt, how the heat of him and the fire she'd seen in his dark eyes had set her alight.

And she definitely *wasn't* still burning a week later, no, not at all.

Once, they'd agreed. And okay, maybe it had turned into twice and possibly a third might have snuck in there, but then they'd finally managed to tear themselves away from each other, going back to the bar (separately) and continuing on with the evening as if nothing had happened.

That's how they would go on, they'd both agreed on that too. Neither of them would mention it again.

Finn had been as good as his word, though, about being friendlier to her. The couple of times she'd run into him, he'd actually smiled and said hello. And if there was still a crackle of electricity between them, both pretended it wasn't there.

No one else had picked up on anything either, which was good.

Yep, it was all great.

The only dark cloud on the horizon was the apparent difficulty Finn was having getting to talk to Evan about his paintings. Certainly there were none of them in the gallery, and though Izzy had assured Beth it wasn't a problem and they didn't need them, Beth was still a little disappointed.

They'd pull in bigger crowds, she was sure, if

the world famous Evan McCahon had a painting or two hanging in the gallery. Plus, Finn had said he would help and he hadn't told her that Evan had refused.

A tall, male figure caught her attention, but it was only Levi, heading in Indigo's direction.

Momentarily diverted, Beth watched her friend suddenly scowl as Levi held out a glass of champagne each to her and Shirley.

Sneaky to get one for Shirley too, so it didn't look like he was only getting one for Indigo. And of course the added pressure of Shirley looking pleased and taking the glass ensured Indigo had to take hers as well.

Beth leaned her elbows on the counter, waiting for the fireworks. But then Levi inclined his head, turned around, and walked away. Indigo at first looked surprised, then she scowled even more furiously, watching Levi the whole way to the door.

"One," Beth murmured under her breath. "Two and…three."

Exactly on the count of three, Indigo put her champagne down on a nearby shelf and headed straight for the door that Levi had just walked through.

Beth grinned. She wasn't sure what Levi had done now, but she'd love to be a fly on the wall when Indigo caught up with him.

Suddenly there was movement by the door.

A tall, thin man in his early sixties, dressed in muddy jeans, a black-and-red-checked sweater-thing that everyone here called a "swanny," and black rain boots (aka gumboots), came in with something large wrapped in a sheet under one arm. He had closely cropped salt-and-pepper hair, a face that was all sharp edges and hard angles, and eyes almost as dark as the man following him.

Beth's heart gave the strangest leap.

Finn's gaze connected with hers as if she was the only thing worth looking at in the entire place, and that raw, crackling electricity that seemed to spark whenever they were in the same room arced between them once again.

She ignored it the way she ignored her frantic heartbeat because the man in the swanny was Evan McCahon. And it was clear he'd brought one of his paintings with him.

Beth straightened as Evan came straight up to the counter where she and Izzy stood.

"I hear you wanted one of these to hang up," he said shortly, banging the sheet-covered painting down on the counter.

Beth gave him her widest, most welcoming smile. "We did."

"Well, you can have this one," Evan said.

"That's so amazing of—"

"Don't thank me," Evan interrupted. "Kelly was the one who did the convincing." He jerked his head at Finn, who'd come to stand beside him. "He's going to give me a bottle of his best Macallan."

Beth didn't know what a bottle of best Macallan was—some kind of alcohol likely—but she was very pleased that Finn had offered it.

"We're very grateful," Izzy said smoothly, pushing a glass of champagne in Evan's direction. "I'm sure you have some ideas about where to hang it too."

The painter narrowed his gaze first at Beth and then Izzy. "I didn't want you ladies here, as you probably know. But Finn thinks this gallery nonsense will be good for the town, get some more money flowing to the people that live here." His white brows came down, his dark gaze glittering. "I don't like tourists."

"There's not much to be said for people in general," Beth said, wanting him to know that she got where he was coming from. "Let alone tourists."

His gaze darted to her and stayed there for a second, disturbingly penetrating. "No," he muttered after what felt like a long time. "There isn't." He grabbed a glass of the champagne. "I'll see where to put the painting. Don't disturb me."

"Wow," Beth murmured as Evan stalked off to examine the bare stone walls. "How did you manage that?"

Finn leaned against the counter. "Evan likes whisky."

"That's it?" Izzy looked at him in some disbelief. "You promised him a bottle and he said yes?"

Finn lifted a shoulder. "It's good whisky."

She knew she was staring, but Beth couldn't help herself. This was as close as she'd been to him since those hours upstairs in HQ, and his presence was doing stupid things to her heartbeat.

"Thank you, Finn," she said, conscious of how husky her voice was. "Honestly, that's amazing of you."

"I did promise you I'd help."

"You certainly came through."

Something glinted in his eyes and one corner of his mouth curved slightly, making it feel as if all the air in the gallery had been suddenly sucked away.

All she could think about was how that gorgeous mouth of his had felt on hers and how hot his skin had been. How hard his long, lean body was and how good he'd felt as he'd moved…

Her thoughts scattered like a flock of birds as the knowing gleam in Finn's dark eyes met hers, and she became aware that not only was Finn looking at her, but Izzy was too. And that Finn had said something she hadn't taken in.

"I'm sorry?" Her voice also sounded suspiciously throaty, worse luck. "What did you say?"

His gaze was unreadable. "I said, apologies that I wasn't able to get anything from Evan before the gallery actually opened. He likes playing hard to get."

A blush was rising in her cheeks whether she wanted it to or not, and she hoped like hell Izzy couldn't see it. Or Finn, for that matter.

"It's okay," she said hurriedly. "Tomorrow is the big day and it's great we've got something before the doors open then."

"True," Izzy murmured. "Thanks for that, Finn. We really appreciate it."

"No worries," he said easily.

Okay, smile and then let him walk away.

Yes, she absolutely should. There wasn't any point prolonging this conversation, not with Izzy standing there looking at them both with interest. And why would she do that, anyway?

She and Finn weren't in a relationship, nor did they have any plans to begin one. All they had was a couple of hours of great sex. That's it.

And it had been *truly* great sex. An eye-opener, that was for sure. She didn't need it again though. Or at least, not with him. She could find it with some other guy, when she was ready for a relationship or maybe just for a little fun.

Finn was a friend. That was it.

In which case, a good friend would definitely offer him a glass of champagne.

Before she could think better of it, Beth grabbed one of the full glasses on the counter and pushed it in his direction. "A drink? In return for all your hard work?"

Finn glanced at the drink, then at her, his mouth curling. "You're always plying me with alcohol."

That tantalizing suggestion of a smile and the gleam in his dark eyes… The combination made her heartbeat, already quick, get even quicker.

"Always?" She grinned, her cheeks hot. "Come on, it was once. And you didn't seem to mind."

"No." There was a note in his voice that made her breath catch. "No, I did not. And it really wasn't once, either."

He wasn't talking about the alcohol now, and she could feel the knowledge of what had happened that night pulse in the space between them, alive with hunger.

He hadn't forgotten.

Look away. Izzy is right there.

Beth tore her gaze from his, reaching for a glass for herself and fussing with it to cover the moment.

Finn shifted against the counter and she thought he might leave, but he didn't. His gaze flicked around the room instead, as though he was looking for someone. "Where's Indigo?" he asked, as if that tense moment hadn't happened.

"She went outside with Levi," Izzy said levelly.

Beth resisted the urge to glance at her to see whether she'd noticed the tension between her and Finn. That would only give herself away even more.

Get it together, come on. It was one night and now it's over. He's a friend now, that's all, okay?

Yeah, definitely that was all.

"What do you want with Indigo?" Beth leaned against the counter, going for casual.

Finn folded his arms across his broad chest. "It's both of you. We need to chat about that house you two were supposed to move into. Chase mentioned he still hasn't had much luck contacting the owner."

It was true, he hadn't. And Indigo was starting to get depressed about continuing to live in the Rose, which was understandable. Beth was getting tired of it herself. It would be nice to have her own space and a bathroom with an actual bath, not just a shower. And having a proper workbench for her jewelry would be good; though Jim had let her use a portion of his workshop, she still felt as if she was imposing.

"No," she said. "He hasn't. What's that got to do with me and Indigo?"

"I might have a solution to your housing issue."

Beth stared at him in surprise. "Seriously?"

"That's great, Finn." Izzy looked pleased. "I mean, I'd offer some rooms in Chase's place if he had any."

"Yeah, he's not going to allow that," Finn said casually. "And besides, that wouldn't solve the issue."

Izzy sniffed. "Chase doesn't get to decide that all on his own. I have a say too."

Finn lifted one dark brow in a way that spoke volumes and Izzy flushed.

"He doesn't," she insisted.

Beth was too busy gazing at Finn to be amused at Izzy's discomfort. It took a lot to fluster Izzy, but Chase Kelly managed to do it on a regular basis, even now that they were engaged.

No, it was the realization of how much Finn managed to say without speaking. A raised brow. A curl of his mouth. A gleam in his dark eyes. He might be a man of few words and his expressions mostly impenetrable, but if you knew where to look, you could get hints of his mood.

Apparently, both Kelly men had what it took to fluster a woman.

"What's your solution?" Beth asked, leaning on her elbows again, staring up at him. His black T-shirt let her see the pulse at the base of his strong throat, a regular, steady beat.

She'd made his heart beat fast that night, though, hadn't she? She'd made him groan her name, made his usually guarded expression fracture into need, into hunger...

Finn's gaze settled on hers and he gave the minutest shake of his head. As if he knew exactly what she was thinking and was warning her not to go there.

Dammit.

Beth took a deep breath and tried to pull herself together.

"Clint signed the sale documents last week and he's moving out in a couple of days since he wants to get back to Christchurch ASAP. I'm not going to be living there, I have my own place, but the farmhouse is very decent and there'd be plenty of room for you and Indigo."

Beth blinked. "You mean…we could move into Clint's?"

Something shifted in Finn's expression, though she couldn't have said what it was. "Yeah. What do you think?"

———

Finn had had himself well in hand the moment he stepped into the gallery. Or at least he thought he had. So Beth's big green eyes meeting his the second he walked through the door shouldn't have been such a gut punch.

He'd managed a whole week seeing her a couple of times, giving her a smile and a nod, without feeling anything much.

Except the second her gaze met his, he realized how completely he'd been lying to himself. It felt like someone had plugged him into an electrical socket and flicked the switch.

She was looking quite frankly adorable in a bright-blue T-shirt that clung to her generous curves, the deep V of the neckline showcasing her pretty cleavage and the koru pendant nestled there. And her hair was caught up in that messy bun again, the same one he'd pulled down that night up in HQ. Tendrils of curly, white-blond hair clustered around her neck and ears, making him itch to touch them, smooth them back behind her ear.

Which was not happening. None of it was. He'd well and truly broken his drought with her last week, and he'd always be grateful to her for giving him those couple of hours of sweet oblivion. But a couple of hours was all it was.

He wasn't looking for more, no matter what his body was telling him.

He was fulfilling his promise to her by finally getting Evan to bring one of his paintings in—the old guy hadn't taken much convincing, truth be told, not when Finn had put a decent scotch on the table—and then he was going to chat to her about his idea of her and Indigo moving into Clint's farmhouse.

A friendly conversation and that's all.

So he ignored the heat gathering in his gut, ignored his persistently wandering attention that kept settling on things it shouldn't, such as her cleavage, and concentrated instead on the deep green of her eyes, which were wide with surprise.

Then she smiled, that bright one that neverthe-less looked fake to him. "That's a wonderful idea," she exclaimed as if she'd never heard of anything so amazing. "Seriously, that's great. Are you sure?"

"What's the problem?" Because despite what

she'd said, it was clear to him that she did not think it was that amazing and there was a problem. "You don't like the idea?"

Izzy frowned. "I'm pretty sure she just said she loved the idea, Finn."

"Yeah, she did. But she didn't mean it." He glanced back at Beth. "Did you?"

She hadn't. He'd heard the note of uncertainty in her voice even if Izzy hadn't. He'd seen the slightly forced nature of her smile too, though he'd always seen that. But especially now, when he knew what the real thing looked like. Beth on her back, having just been thoroughly pleasured, smiling up at him like he'd taken the moon from the sky and handed it to her...

Shit. Don't think about that.

Yeah, he really shouldn't.

Beth's bright smile wavered for a second before holding firm and becoming even brighter. "Sure I did. Indigo is getting sick of not having her own space, and while I love Cait's cooking, it would be really nice not to live out of a suitcase for a change."

Finn studied her while she stared back, and this time there was no wavering in her smile.

"Is there some workshop space?" she asked. "Or at least somewhere I could do some metalworking?"

He didn't even need to think because it was something he'd considered when Chase had mentioned that he was having difficulty finding the owner of the house the women were supposed to move into and how problematic finding alternative accommodation was.

Clint's farmhouse seemed perfect. It was unoccupied and Finn wasn't going to move into it because he already had his own house. Plus there was a huge workshop space near the stables that would be perfect for Beth and her jewelry making, not to mention Indigo and her dyeing operation.

"Yeah," he said. "There's a big shed near the stables with a big workshop bench and other stuff. Clint isn't going to take it all with him, so I said he could leave his tools here. They won't be what you want, but I'm sure you'll like the bench space."

Beth eyes glowed and this time it was totally genuine. Yes, it would seem she'd definitely like the bench space.

"When you say 'big workshop bench,'" she murmured, "exactly how big are we talking about here?" Something playful glinted in her eyes. "Not that size matters, of course."

Finn shifted against the counter again, everything male in him wanting to respond to her, flirt with her, because she was definitely flirting with him. She'd been doing so from the minute he'd walked in the door.

But while he liked it and wasn't immune to it, he couldn't in good conscience keep doing it. Not while their chemistry was still so strong.

One night, he'd told her, and she'd agreed, so there wasn't any point in continuing to belabor something that wasn't going to go anywhere.

Ignoring her comment he only said, "I'm not sure how big you need for your purposes, but it's a decent size. Plenty of places to store tools and things too."

The brightness of her smile dimmed. Obviously, she'd taken note of his refusal to flirt back and had been disappointed by it.

That couldn't be helped. He'd been very clear about what he could give her and she hadn't refused him. In fact, she'd told him she hadn't wanted anything more either, so why she was being flirtatious he didn't know.

It had to stop though.

"Think about it," he said, deciding that now was a great time to take himself out of her immediate vicinity. Especially before she said something else that might give them away. And most especially with Izzy looking interestedly on.

Stepping away from the counter, he gave them both a last smile, then turned and walked out of the gallery.

It was early evening, a late summer heat lying over the valley, the air full of the smell of dry grass and the earthier, spicier scent of the bush.

It was peaceful—or it would have been peaceful if there hadn't been a town barbecue.

Down by the lakefront, a grill had been set up, along with fold-out tables and chairs; a good number of townspeople already clustered around. Cait had brought out food for everyone—salads and rolls—while Jim dealt with handing out beers and shandies from a big cooler full of ice. Mystery was nosing around, a black streak of fur looking for a dropped sausage no doubt.

A couple of kaka, a native parrot, were perched on the roof of the Rose and eyeing the goings-on beadily. Kaka and their cousin, the kea, weren't regular visitors to the town, but Finn appreciated their presence when they did appear. Even if they turned stealing food into a high art form. One of the kaka flapped its wings, revealing the bright red feathers underneath. It made a screeching sound as if displeased at having to wait for scraps like an ordinary scavenger.

Finn grinned at them as he strolled over to where Chase stood manning the grill, cooking steaks and sausages with the same kind of intense focus he reserved for every task.

Levi was down on the lakefront with Gus and a few others, apparently teaching Chase's daughter to skim stones, while Indigo, looking irritated, watched from a short distance away.

"Planning your third Michelin star?" Finn asked casually, coming up to stand beside his brother. "I'm sure they give them out for sausages."

Chase didn't look up. "If you've got some issue with the way I cook sausages, then by all means, let's hear it."

"Does Izzy know how seriously you take sausage cooking?"

"Is there another way to take sausage cooking?" Chase glanced at him. "Careful, you might be in danger of cracking a smile."

"Nah, it's just a figment of your imagination." Finn put his hands in his pockets. "I just asked Beth if she and Indigo want to move into Clint's."

"Oh?" Chase gave the sausages a critical look. "She keen?"

"Yeah, I think so. From the sounds of it they're both sick of living at the Rose."

"Understandable. What about when you find someone to manage the stables?"

Finn had been considering this. He didn't have time to oversee the running of the stables in the long term, not when Pure Adventure NZ took up so much of his time. And he loved guiding and spending time out in the bush. He didn't want to stop doing that.

Toby and his sons were a good temporary solution, but what he really needed was a permanent stable manager, and finding someone was going to be tricky. People generally didn't want to be stuck way the hell down a long and treacherous unsealed road, in a tiny town that consisted of three buildings and no internet service. Even if accommodation in a spacious farmhouse was part of the deal.

"*If* I find someone to manage the stables," he qualified.

Chase nodded sagely while turning over a steak. "Tricky. Are we going to have to find a temporary guide to pick up the slack?"

"No. I've got Toby Miller and his sons helping out until I find someone. Plus we're heading into shoulder season."

They'd already seen a drop-off in terms of summer tourists, and now that they were heading into autumn, they would only get fewer and fewer. In winter there were still a few but not many, which made the purchase of Clint's ranch good timing. It would give him some breathing room in which to find a manager.

"Fair enough," Chase said. "Well, it would certainly solve the issue of accommodation for them if they could live at Clint's. Even if it's a temporary solution for the winter." He paused a moment, then added, without any discernible change in tone, "You've been in a good mood lately."

The comment made an odd tension crawl through him, though why Finn wasn't sure. "Have I?"

"Yeah." Chase turned over another steak. "For the last week I'm sure I even saw you smile at people."

"What?" He tried to keep his tone casual. "A man isn't allowed to smile?"

"It's noticeable." Chase's attention was still on the grill. "Because for the past few months, you've been tense as hell."

Finn didn't like the direction this particular conversation was heading in. "And you haven't been? You've stalked around snapping at—"

"Yeah, and you know why too." Chase cut him off, turning his head, his gray gaze meeting his.

Of course Finn did. Chase had been bad-tempered as hell because of what had gone on with Izzy. The two of them had resisted each other for a whole month before they'd finally gotten together.

Finn attempted to relax all his muscles and not snap at his brother, because then that would be turning this into a case of protesting too much, which Chase would definitely pick up on because he was by no means a stupid man.

You think he hasn't noticed the chemistry between you and Beth? Come on.

Finn ignored the thought, making sure his posture was loose and easy. "Are you suggesting Izzy might have something to do with it?"

Chase scowled. "Don't be a dick, Finn. You know I'm not suggesting that."

"Then spell it out for me, big bro. Because if you've got something to say, then just say it."

"Okay, fine." Chase's silver gaze narrowed. "Did something happen between you and Beth?"

Finn had to keep a tight hold on his expression to not give himself away. "What? What are you talking about?"

"You think I haven't seen the way you look at her?" His brother's gaze was far too knowing. "And the way she looks at you?"

A muscle jumped in Finn's jaw. So much for assuming he and Beth had been secretive about it.

It shouldn't matter. It shouldn't matter that his brother knew, because really, it had just been a one-off thing and it wasn't going to happen again. And anyway, being secretive about it only made it more of a big deal and it definitely wasn't a big deal. So it was the first time he'd had sex with a woman in five years. So what? Chase didn't know that and Finn wasn't in a hurry for him to find out either. Maybe, to keep it casual, he'd tell his brother. Chase could be like a dog with a bone about some things, especially when it concerned Finn's well-being.

He was such a big brother sometimes.

The only issue was it rebounding on Beth, and Finn didn't want that. Not that Chase was a gossip. He'd keep it on the down low.

"Why do you want to know?" Finn asked at last.

"Because my little brother's well-being is import-ant to me," Chase said flatly. "And you've been a bastard on wheels for so long, I've forgotten what the old Finn Kelly is actually like. That was until last week."

The old Finn Kelly. As if he'd been a different person before Sheri had died. And, well, to be fair, he had been. Grief was a journey and that journey changed you. Irrecoverably.

Finn raised a brow. "So naturally you assumed I'd gotten laid?"

"It is a great mood enhancer, you can't deny that."

He wished he could. But Chase was right. Since that encounter with Beth, which had been nothing but pure unadulterated pleasure, his mood had been...well. It had been fantastic, something he should have done years ago.

But that was before you'd met Beth.

Yeah, and he didn't want to start thinking things like that. He didn't want to start thinking that Beth made it different or special or any of that kind of crap. He'd slept with her because he wanted her, because they had a fair amount of physical chemistry, but that was it.

It had nothing to do with her smile or the sunshine he'd sensed inside her, that he'd gotten to hold for a brief little while...too brief...

Chase coughed ostentatiously. "I'm going to take that as a yes."

Finn scowled. "I didn't say anything."

"No, but the look on your face did. That's a 'I'm

just remembering the great sex I had' face if ever I saw one."

It was too late to deny it, so all Finn said was "Yeah and it's not going to happen again, so don't get too excited."

Chase studied him a moment, then looked back down at his grill. "And why not?"

"Do I really need to explain why?"

"Twice doesn't make it a relationship. Even three times doesn't."

But Finn was getting tired of this conversation. "I have my reasons and I don't need to explain myself to you. Also, just so you know, she felt the same way."

"Right."

Finn narrowed his gaze at his brother because that was the most carefully neutral sounding "right" he'd ever heard. "We discussed it. She was fine with it."

Chase didn't say anything for a long moment, the pause punctuated by the sounds of the meat sizzling on the grill. "It's been my experience that when women say they're fine with it," he said finally, "they almost never are."

That Finn had also had that experience wasn't helpful. Sheri had been a great one for acting as if everything was fine, ignoring her inexplicable tiredness and the pain she'd get in her shoulder. Working too hard, she'd said. Probably just slept weirdly, she'd said.

And she'd kept on saying those things right up until the day she'd told him that it wasn't nothing after all. That she had cancer.

But he didn't want to talk about that either, so all he said was "Yeah, well, that's why it was a one-off. No point promising something that's not going to happen."

And it wouldn't.

Of that he was utterly certain.

Chapter 6

THE NEXT THREE WEEKS WERE BUSY ONES FOR Beth. Now that the gallery was open, she, Izzy, and Indigo found their schedules filled with stock sourcing and production, record-keeping and banking issues, not to mention having gallery shifts to cover.

Because as it turned out, Brightwater Dreams was a hit with the tourists. Many came to view Evan's paintings (Finn had managed to wheedle another couple out of him) and were thrilled to find out he was a resident of the town. Then, once they finished looking at the paintings, they started looking at the gallery's other offerings, and once they started looking, they started spending.

It was very, very pleasing, and the three of them were ecstatic about how it was turning out.

Izzy had met with Cait to see if the Rose could start doing café meals and/or lunches for the tourists during busy weekends, so those who weren't doing outdoor adventure activities could poke around the gallery, then have a nice lunch afterward.

Beth was over the moon that her first lot of jewelry sold out quickly, then got slightly panicked when she realized she was going to have to make more—and keep on making more to satisfy the demand.

Which was why, despite her initial worries about living in Clint's farmhouse, mainly based around Finn owning the place and possibly being around far more than was comfortable, the shift from the Rose to Clint's was a welcome one.

She and Indigo moved in the week following the gallery opening, and it was great to finally have her own room again after over a month of living out of a suitcase at the hotel.

Clint's farmhouse was a rustic wooden building with a steeply pitched roof of red corrugated steel, a gabled front room, and a wide porch at the front of the house.

Inside it was basic but comfortable, with a front room that housed a big wood-burner, a small kitchen and bathroom at the back, and a couple of bedrooms on the other side of the hallway.

Clint had been happy to leave all his furniture behind, so they didn't have to face furnishing it, but Beth had already privately decided she was going to get a new bed when she had some money, because the one in the bedroom she'd claimed was uncomfortably hard.

Not that she was complaining. Because the best part about Clint's was the workshop space and the bench that Finn had talked about, which was indeed big, and there were plenty of places for her to put her jeweler's tools.

She hadn't been able to do any work since she'd left Deep River—or not proper work—and having the space to put everything away and store the raw materials she'd collected over the past month was fantastic.

Indigo was insanely happy there was enough room to do her dyeing too, bustling about with dye pots and drying racks and bins full of undyed yarn, then doing some more bustling in the house, making it habitable.

The only downside was the house being a good fifteen minutes' drive from the town, which would have been a problem if Clint hadn't also left them his old truck and a quad bike to use as runarounds.

Beth loved the quad bike but she didn't know how to drive it, so she stuck with the truck instead to ferry her and Indigo—who didn't drive—up and down from town. It took some getting used to driving a right-hand drive vehicle, and several times she accidentally drove on the wrong side of the road, but it didn't matter too much, not when there were so very few other cars on the road too.

She didn't see a lot of Finn. He and the other Pure Adventure NZ team offered to help her and Indigo move, but since there was really nothing to move but their suitcases, she and Indigo graciously declined.

He'd visited once, briefly, to see how she and

Indigo were doing and to tell them that if there was anything they needed to let him know, but apart from that, she didn't see him much at all.

Toby Miller and his two sons from the neighboring farm managed the day-to-day running of the stables, while Finn would visit every couple of days to keep an eye on things, Karl at his heels since apparently, Izzy had told her, Clint had given his dog to Finn. But he didn't come inside the farmhouse, not even to say hello. Not that she was there even when he did, because she was usually doing a shift at the gallery.

She only saw him on the periphery, helping tourists out by the lake or sitting with Chase and Levi in the pub. Once, she saw him take a small group out on a horse trek and found herself watching him as he rode, his lean, muscular body at ease in the saddle.

It was sexy. He was sexy.

Not that she was looking for him or anything, or even noticing him. And she definitely wasn't *still* thinking about that night on the couch in HQ. No, most definitely not.

What she was doing was concentrating on this new life she'd built for herself in Brightwater Valley, with the gallery and making her jewelry. Surrounded by nature and making friends with a whole new bunch of people who only ever knew her as the positive, sunny Beth she was here.

Not the sad, gray, scared Beth she'd been back in Deep River.

Life was good.

So good that at first she didn't realize how much more tired she was in the evenings, a lot more tired than normal, and that she was falling into bed sometimes as early as eight o'clock. And sometimes she felt a bit sick in the mornings, but surely that had to be a virus.

Then one morning in the gallery, a customer came in with an egg sandwich from Bill's general store next door, and Beth abruptly knew she was going to be sick.

She only had a moment to excuse herself before stumbling into the tiny bathroom out the back of the gallery, her stomach deciding it was done with the toast she'd had for breakfast and it needed to be empty right the hell now.

Afterward, she splashed some cold water on her face and stood in front of the little mirror above the basin, cold and shaky and distinctly fuzzy around the edges, and wondering why this bug she'd picked up wasn't getting any better.

This is very familiar.

The thought drifted idly through her brain, because yes, it was familiar. She'd felt this tired and this sick before, back when—

No. No, it couldn't be.

She shut down that thought hard, but a cold

feeling was creeping through her, winding around her like a giant snake, constricting so tight she could barely breathe.

No. *No.* She hadn't been with anyone…

Only Finn Kelly.

And suddenly her knees felt weak and she was sitting on the floor of the bathroom, the wall at her back, her breathing way too fast, her thoughts spinning around and around.

Yes, they'd had unprotected sex. But it had only been the once. Finn hadn't had any condoms on him, but had found some in HQ's little bathroom and they'd used those.

So, only one time. And anyway, she was on the pill. She'd been taking it to regulate her period and for other hormonal issues, and she was sure she'd taken it religiously.

But maybe you didn't? Maybe you missed one?

Beth tried to think. It was a month ago and she'd been busy with the gallery opening and trying to get Finn to be her friend… It was possible that she'd missed one and hadn't noticed.

Oh God.

A wild uprush of feeling swamped her, an emotion so complicated she couldn't untangle all the threads. Mainly grief and fear, but mixed in was a tiny bit of joy, like a nugget of gold at the bottom of a bitterly cold lake.

For a long moment she just sat there against the

wall, her eyes full of tears, because if this wasn't a bug, if this was indeed what she thought it was, then her life here was about to change.

She'd done this once before, a couple of years ago, with Troy, and the baby they'd conceived had been very much wanted. But the pregnancy had been difficult and then…

Beth swallowed.

You idiot. How could you not be more careful?

She put her hands over her face, pressed her palms hard against her eyes. He'd overwhelmed her, that was the problem. She'd been so obsessed with him, had wanted him so much, she hadn't been thinking straight, not at the time. And neither had he.

Then her breath caught.

This was going to affect him too.

"Hey," a deep male voice called from the gallery. "Is anyone around?"

Yet more cold washed over her as she recognized it.

Oh hell. Talk about timing. It was Finn.

She shoved herself to her feet, her heart racing, and as soon as she came upright, black spots began to swim in her vision. Her hands and feet felt cold. Everything felt cold.

She tried to ignore the feeling as she came out of the bathroom and went into the gallery. Or at least she tried to go into the gallery. But the black spots in her vision multiplied and her feet were numb, and she had to lean against the doorway for support.

Oh, please, not in front of Finn. Please don't let her faint in front of Finn.

He was leaning against the counter, looking unbelievably gorgeous in a pair of black utility pants, black Pure Adventure NZ T-shirt, and boots. It was clear from his clothing that he was either about to take a group out or had just come back in.

His eyes met hers, widened slightly, then narrowed into thin slits of obsidian.

"Beth?" His dark, husky voice was a whip crack in the silence of the gallery. "Beth, what's wrong?"

She opened her mouth to tell him nothing was wrong, absolutely nothing, she was fine, just a little upset tummy, no biggie, when the doorway she was leaning against moved and she wasn't upright anymore but falling.

Things went black for a couple of seconds, and when her brain decided to work again, she found herself lying against something very warm, very hard, and covered in black cotton.

She blinked.

Someone was holding her. Finn was holding her.

For a moment all she was conscious of was his warmth and his delicious scent—spicy and earthy and masculine—and the strength of the arm that was circling her, holding her against his chest.

Feeling was coming back to her hands and feet, making them tingle, and her heartbeat was slowing, and long seconds passed where all she wanted was to simply exist there, lying against him, feeling safe and warm.

But no matter how badly she wanted to deny it, no matter how desperately, the truth was sitting inside her and she couldn't escape it.

She wasn't sick; she was pregnant. And Finn was the father.

And she had no idea, no idea at all, what she was going to do.

━━━━━━━

Finn had a group of tourists waiting down by the lake and a trip to Glitter Falls to manage, and he'd nipped into the gallery to find Izzy to let her know that Chase had another booking mix-up, and since it was taking him a while to sort out, he might be home a bit late.

It shouldn't have taken long. Only a minute or two. But what he hadn't expected was to find the gallery empty at first, before a very pale Beth staggered out of the bathroom and promptly fainted in front of him. And it had only been lightning-fast reflexes, honed by years of guiding tourists around who did stupid things constantly, that had had him catching her before she hit the floor.

Now he was sitting on said floor, holding her against his chest, a complicated mixture of anger, frustration, worry, and unholy desire tangling in his gut. She felt small in his arms—small and warm and very vulnerable.

He did not want her to be vulnerable. He did not want to be holding her either, but it was clear she was unwell and he couldn't leave her in this state.

So much for three weeks of distance.

Finn ignored the thought, glancing down at the woman in his arms. He could only see the soft curve of one cheek, her pale, silvery lashes resting against it. Her hair was in a messy ponytail and he was conscious of the sweet scent of apricots or peaches. A familiar scent. A scent that was haunting his dreams...

The desire inside him coiled tighter, but he shoved it aside the way he'd been shoving it aside for the past three weeks. The last thing Beth needed was him getting inappropriately turned on while she was feeling crappy.

"Beth?" He shifted her so he could see her face. "What's wrong? Are you sick?"

Her eyes were firmly shut, and she didn't open them. There were big black circles beneath them, and she looked so white she was almost green. A sour smell was coming from the bathroom, a sure sign that someone had thrown up and recently.

Well, not just someone. Beth.

The worry he'd tried to tell himself he didn't feel tightened its grip. "Come on," he said, securing her more firmly against him. "Let's get you to the Rose and I'll call a doctor."

That seemed to galvanize her because she moved abruptly, pushing at him. "No, I'm fine. You can let me go."

He didn't want to. Especially since she'd fainted just before and quite clearly wasn't fine. "Beth," he began.

But she pushed at him harder. "Please, Finn."

Color was returning to her cheeks, though they weren't at their usual pretty deep rose yet, and since he knew it was for the best if he wasn't physically close to her, he loosened his hold. He did keep an arm around her as he helped her to her feet though, because she was unsteady, noting that she pulled away almost as soon as she was standing.

Used to assessing people's well-being as part of his job when he was guiding tourists, he gave her a rapid scan. Yeah, she was still pale, and she looked exhausted.

"What's going on, Beth? Tell me." It was an order, and he made no effort to soften it. If she was unwell, he wanted to know, because if so, he was here to help. He, Chase, and Levi were all up-to-date with first aid since the closest ambulance was two hours away in Queenstown, which made them also first responders in an emergency.

That's not the only reason you want to know.

Yeah, well, if so, he was *not* going to be interrogating those reasons just now.

"It's nothing," she said faintly. "A stomach bug, I think."

He wasn't sure he believed that. She'd given him the oddest look when she'd come out of the back room and leaned against the doorframe, her face chalk-white. It was almost as if she was…terrified.

People with stomach bugs usually weren't terrified.

"Beth," he began again.

"Really, I'm fine." She turned to him, the biggest, fakest smile he'd ever seen plastered on her pale face. "It's only a virus."

He had people waiting for him, and he didn't have time to stand around arguing with her about how fine or otherwise she was. But he was a caregiver first and foremost and he couldn't leave it alone.

Sheri had told him she was fine, that he didn't need to worry, and look how that had turned out. The doctors had told him there would have been nothing he could have done if he'd known about her illness earlier, but he'd never been able to shake the feeling that he could have. That perhaps if he'd noticed Sheri's symptoms earlier he could have done something that might have made a difference.

"You're not fine," he said tersely. "You just fainted and I'm guessing you threw up as well."

She waved a dismissive hand. "And I feel tons better for having done so."

He ignored that. "You look exhausted. You should be in bed, getting some rest."

"Yeah, yeah, I hear you." She turned away, moving over to the counter. "But there's only a couple of hours before Indigo takes over for the afternoon, and I'm not exactly run off my feet. I'll be fine."

This was his cue to accept what she'd said and leave, because she was an adult. She could look after herself. And besides, he had a crowd of people to take over the lake to visit the falls. He didn't have time to fuss around with her.

"Will you though?" he persisted.

Beth fiddled with one of the displays of preserves stacked neatly on the counter, then looked at him. Her green eyes were very direct and there was no sign of the fear he'd seen in them earlier. "Yes," she said with great certainty. "And if I feel sick again, I'll drive home and go straight to bed. Promise."

Doubt still nagged at him, though since he couldn't quite pinpoint why, he had no real reason to believe she didn't just have a virus. In which case he couldn't really protest about it.

He left her, in the end, with assurances she'd look after herself, but the doubt wouldn't leave him alone. It dogged him the whole day, sitting in the back of his mind as he took the tourists across the lake to the falls, making him grumpy and foul-tempered by the time he got back.

"What's up with you?" Chase, who'd come out to meet him and help with any remaining equipment, asked as the last of the tourists got off the boat and Finn finished stowing the life jackets.

Karl—whom he'd started bringing along on trips since the dog loved being out in the bush and was a hit with the tourists—had already leapt from the boat and was wagging his tail hopefully at Chase.

"Nothing," Finn said, then winced at how short the word sounded.

"Yeah, sure." The skepticism in his brother's voice was obvious. "You're supposed to smile at clients, remember?"

Finn finished with the life jackets, then stepped off the small runabout they used to ferry tourists to and from the Glitter Falls trail across the lake.

Chase was standing on the little jetty watching him, silver gaze narrowed. He dropped an absent hand onto Karl's head to give him a scratch, but the dog, clearly sensing his half-heartedness, bore it dutifully before trotting off down the jetty after spotting Mystery enjoying a few pets from the tourists and deciding he wanted in on the action.

"This isn't McDonald's," Finn said. "We don't have to smile constantly and ask people whether they'd like fries with that."

Chase's gaze narrowed still further. "You should go see Beth again. That'll put you in a better mood."

It was on the tip of his tongue to tell Chase it was Beth who was the problem, but he decided against it. Telling his brother he was concerned about the fact she was sick and that he suspected it wasn't actually a bug would only lead to more questions. Which in turn would lead to supposition and probably some advice that he hadn't asked for and didn't want.

So all he said was "No. It was a one-time thing, remember?"

The tourists were climbing back onto one of the big buses that had brought them here, some coming out of the Rose and a couple from the gallery. A kea had flown in from somewhere, obviously having decided to join the party, and was now perched on top of the bus, flapping its green-feathered wings and screeching at the tourists. Levi was pointing at it and talking to one woman, the late-afternoon sun picking out the gold strands in his tawny hair, and she was laughing.

"You should tell Levi to stop flirting with the tourists," Finn muttered, mainly to distract Chase from mentioning Beth again. "It's not professional."

Instantly his brother's head whipped around, his gaze zeroing in on Levi and the woman.

Then Indigo came out of the gallery. She took

a couple of steps toward the general store, then stopped, her attention also on Levi at the woman.

Finn didn't particularly care what was up with her and Levi, but there was probably only one way he was going to stop thinking and worrying about Beth and that was to ask Indigo if she was okay.

"You deal with Levi." Finn strode past his brother. "I've got something I need to ask Indigo."

Chase muttered something, but Finn ignored him.

Indigo was scowling in Levi's direction, her expression clearing as she noticed Finn coming toward her. "Hey, Finn," she said, a shy smile appearing.

"Hey." He stopped in front of her. "Just wanted to check in on Beth."

Indigo frowned in obvious puzzlement. "Oh? Why? Is something wrong?"

Right, so Beth hadn't told Indigo she hadn't been feeling well. Interesting. Why was that?

Briefly, Finn debated whether to tell Indigo that Beth had fainted in front of him earlier that morning, then decided against it. There must have been a reason Beth hadn't wanted her to know, in which case she wouldn't appreciate Finn running his mouth about it.

"No," he said smoothly, covering his lapse. "I only wanted to make sure everything was okay in your neck of the woods."

Indigo blinked. "You mean with the farmhouse?"

"Yeah, of course the farmhouse."

"Oh, everything's fine. We're good."

"Great. You know where Beth is?"

"She went home at lunchtime." Indigo's attention drifted back to where Levi and the woman stood, now joined by Chase, the three of them plus the other tourists, all of them staring at the kea who was doing a little dance on the roof of the bus. "Said she had a migraine."

First a stomach bug, now a migraine. What was going on?

Seemed like if he wanted to know, he was going to have to go talk to her himself.

Why? You slept with her once and she can damn well look after herself. And it's not as if you don't have a lot on your plate already.

That was true, he did. The past three weeks had been extraordinarily busy, what with managing his commitments at Pure Adventure NZ, then overseeing Toby and his boys at the stables, not to mention still trying to find a permanent stable manager. So he hadn't had a lot of time to think about anything else, which was quite frankly a blessing.

"Anything else" being Beth and the couple of hours he'd stolen with her up in HQ that was *still* haunting him even a month later.

So really, did he have to go and check on her?

He had a horse trek booked the next day, and even though it was only a day trip, he had to do some organization and an equipment check for it. Then he'd promised to have dinner with Chase, Izzy, and Gus.

Then again, the equipment he needed to check was at Clint's and if he was going up there anyway...

"Why do you need to see her?"

Still going over things in his head, it took Finn a second or two to realize that Indigo wasn't looking at Levi anymore, but at him, and her expression was far too speculative for his liking.

"Was going to ask her the same question I just asked you," he said easily. "Unless you know of anything that she needs?"

Indigo's mouth curved in what could only be termed a smirk. "I could think of a few things."

Her tone was suggestive, which made him wonder what Beth had told her and Izzy. Then again, maybe it was nothing, merely some friendly teasing between friends.

"Oh?" He raised an eyebrow, wondering idly what she'd say. "What things?"

She flushed. "Uh...don't worry, it's nothing."

"Good." He turned toward HQ where his truck was parked. "If you think of anything important, let me know."

He gave Karl, who had given up trying to get Mystery to play with him and was now fawning all

over Levi, a whistle, then strode to his vehicle. And
once the dog had leapt into the back, he started the
engine and drove up to Clint's to find out just what
the hell was going on.

Chapter 7

BETH SAT AT HER WORKBENCH AND STARED AT the small piece of silver she was currently filing. She was in the process of making a pendant, but she couldn't quite get the right shape. To make things worse, her brain was still fuzzy and her stomach was starting to roil once again.

She'd gone home when Indigo had arrived at the gallery at lunchtime, then had a shower before determinedly trying to push everything out of her head and have a nap.

But her brain wouldn't let her sleep.

You're a coward, it said. *You know what this is and you're going to have to do something about it.*

Beth put the piece of silver down on the workbench and stared at it.

It was true. No matter how much she wanted to hide, she couldn't, not from this. And there was only one way to be sure she was really pregnant and that was to take a test. But the thought of going into Bill's and asking him if he had any pregnancy tests…

Ugh. She could only imagine the gossip that would spread, since gossip was Bill's lifeblood, and the very last thing she wanted was everyone knowing. There would be questions about who the father was and that would drag Finn into it.

He's going to be dragged into it whether you like it or not.

Yes, but only if the pregnancy was a viable one. It might not be. So surely it was better to leave him out of it until everything was certain?

No, she couldn't get a test from Bill's. She'd have to get one from somewhere and the most logical place for that was Queenstown, which was the closest large town. Except Queenstown was two hours away by car, so not exactly the place for a quick trip.

You could, of course, keep on pretending everything's great, the way you always do.

Beth let out a soft breath, put her file down, and shut her eyes.

She could pretend. That had gotten her through in the past. And sometimes, if you kept pretending long and hard enough, eventually the pretense became the reality. Could she do that with this though? After what had happened the last time?

So much for your brand-new life.

Her eyes stung, a sick fear tightening its grip.

She'd lost her first baby. A little girl, born far, far too early. And afterward she'd fallen into a depression so bleak and black it felt like being trapped at the bottom of a cold, dark lake with the weight of the water pressing down on her.

Postpartum depression without a baby and it had nearly destroyed her. Troy hadn't been able to deal with it and had left, and her parents had been no help. "Just like your mother," her father had said. "Crying about it doesn't help. Pull yourself together and get on with it." Then he'd absented himself the way he always did when things were hard.

So that's what she'd done. She'd pulled herself together and gotten herself out of that pit on her own—with the help of Deep River's doctor, medication, and her newfound interest in jewelry making. And a determination within herself never to fall into that pit again.

Which was why she was here. To get as far away from it as possible.

Except now it had followed her.

Dear God, what a mess.

"Beth?" The voice was deep, male, and came from the doorway.

Sucking in a sharp breath, she turned her head.

Standing in the entrance of the corrugated iron shed that currently housed her jewelry workshop and Indigo's dyeing operation was Finn Kelly, because of course it was Finn Kelly. Who else would it be? Who else could possibly make this situation even more difficult? And naturally he hadn't taken her at her word earlier today when she'd told him she was fine. No doubt he was here to check on her, which would then mean her having to lie.

She certainly couldn't tell him the truth, not yet. Not when she could barely cope with it herself, let alone having to deal with him as well. Besides, pregnancies were precarious, as she of all people knew.

It was barely a month from conception and nothing could be counted on until at least three months after that date.

And not even then.

No. Not even then.

Her hand crept to the curl of silver at her throat, her fingers closing around the warm metal, the feel of it sitting in her palm reassuring.

"Hi," she said with a forced brightness she didn't feel. "You need anything?"

He came into the shed, giving her a brief, impersonal scan as if he were a doctor assessing her for injuries. "Not specifically. Just wanted to see how you were doing."

"I'm fine." She let go her pendant and picked up her file again. "Trying to do some work, as you can see." With any luck he'd get the hint and leave, and she wouldn't have to deal with him.

Except he didn't move away, coming closer to stand beside her workbench instead, watching her.

"You still look pale," he said after a moment. "Are you sure you should be sitting up?"

She lifted a shoulder, concentrating on the piece of silver in her hand and not on the man standing at her elbow. "I was going to have a nap, but I couldn't sleep. So this is a nice distraction." Which was absolutely true. "Hey, where's Karl?"

"He's probably saying hello to Jeff." Finn was apparently not picking up on the "please go away" note in her voice. "Have you had anything to eat this afternoon?"

"No," she said. "Why would I when I've been puking my guts up every time I put something in my mouth?"

There was a silence, and she could hear the sharp note in her voice echoing.

Crap. He was going to know something was up now. Snapping at people was unlike her.

God, she needed to get it together.

Putting down the file yet again, she glanced at him, fixing her usual bright smile to her face. It had never felt more fake.

"Look," she said, "I appreciate the concern. But I'm really fine, Finn. I mean, if you keep coming to check on me, I'm going to think you might want something else."

She'd hoped the terrible attempt at flirtation would send him packing.

She was wrong.

Finn ignored the comment and stared at her, his gaze very dark and very direct. "You're not fine.

You're far too pale, you have huge dark circles under your eyes, and you still look green."

Oh great. This was going well.

"So?" Beth smiled harder, trying for a more jokey tone. "You probably would too if you'd spent the morning hunched over the toilet."

He ignored that too. "You looked terrified down in the gallery today. Why?"

All the breath left her body in a rush and suddenly she didn't feel like joking anymore. Her lungs felt heavy, laboring to draw in air.

How had he seen that? How had he known?

Somewhat desperately she said, "I'm not—"

"Don't do that," he interrupted, his voice quiet. "Don't pretend like you always do. You were sick. You threw up and then came out of the bathroom looking frightened. Why?"

She swallowed. She couldn't tell him she was fine, not again, not when he hadn't believed her the first time around.

He will need to know eventually.

Yes, but only if that eventuality happened, which it might not. In which case, why cause him more stress that might end up being pointless anyway? She didn't want that. She didn't want anyone to have to deal with that if they didn't have to, which was why she didn't want anyone to know, not even Indigo and Izzy.

She'd gotten herself into this mess and it was her

problem to fix. No one had pulled her out of that black pit. She'd done it herself and she'd do the same now. That's what strong, positive Beth would do.

So she forced that smile back in place and opened her mouth to tell him that yes, she *had* been feeling sick, but it was getting better, when abruptly the look on his face changed, his dark gaze intensifying.

"What are you not telling me, Beth?" His gaze narrowed. "Wait..."

Oh no, he couldn't be guessing. How could he? *Why* would he?

"Finn," she said quickly. "It's nothing. It's just a virus—"

"Are you pregnant?"

The words hung in the air between them, a crushing weight.

"W-what?" Beth stammered, everything inside her going into free fall.

"I think you heard me." He took another step. "Could you be pregnant? I know you said you were on the pill, but is that a possibility?"

Her mouth was dry, her heart beating so hard it felt like it was going to come out of her chest. She wanted to keep smiling, wanted to tell him that of course she wasn't pregnant, don't be silly.

But she was tired, and she felt ill, and his eyes were glittering like sharpened pieces of obsidian, the expression on his face hard, and all she wanted to do was cry.

Everything was falling apart, and the bright dream she'd had about what her life in New Zealand would be like was in jeopardy.

And it was all her fault.

She hadn't been strong. She hadn't been looking to the future. She'd let her desire and her passion do her thinking for her, and now look what had happened.

The need to run away swamped her, and she shoved her stool back, slipping off it and making to stride past him, but his hand shot out and he grabbed her arm. His fingers were warm and strong, stopping her in her tracks.

Beth faced the doorway, breathing very fast. She didn't want to look at him, didn't want to see the expression now on his face.

Coward.

"Beth," he said quietly, "I think it's time you and I had a chat."

———

She'd gone rigid in his hold and her face was chalk-white, and if her sudden break for the exit hadn't been enough of a giveaway, the mere fact that she wouldn't look at him now told him all he needed to know.

It was a guess. He'd been thinking about her symptoms and why she'd lied to Indigo about having a migraine and why she'd looked so afraid in the gallery that morning. Plus she hadn't wanted anyone to know, it was clear, and that made no sense. Why would she not want people to know she'd picked up a virus?

There was only one explanation that would cover all of those things. And either she had the plague or she was pregnant, and he was pretty sure there was no plague in New Zealand.

Shock at the confirmation gripped him, along with a host of other more complicated emotions, but he couldn't take any of that in just yet. Because this was a crisis, and one of the first rules of managing any crisis was to deal with the immediate problem.

So first things first.

Beth was obviously in some kind of shock too and he didn't like that. He didn't like that she was so upset either, though it was understandable. Whatever, he needed to take care of her until she was in a better space.

Which is your job?

Hell yeah it was his job. If his guess had been correct, and judging from her face right now it was, then looking after her would be his responsibility for some time to come. And he wasn't going to walk away from that.

It took two to create a child, after all.

Are you ready to be a father though?

An emotion he didn't care to name twisted

inside him, but he shoved it away for the moment. He'd deal with his own issues later. Right now, he had Beth to deal with.

"We don't need to talk." Beth still wasn't looking at him. "Nothing's certain yet. I haven't had a test or anything."

But he didn't let her go. She was still too pale, and he didn't like how fast the pulse at the base of her throat was beating. If she hadn't had anything to eat all afternoon, then that wasn't going to help her feel any better.

"Yeah, we do." He let go of her arm and took her hand instead, threading his fingers through hers in a way he hoped would be reassuring. "Come on." And before she could protest again, he moved toward the workshop exit, pulling her gently along with him.

She resisted for a moment, then followed without a word.

Outside the sun was bright as he led her from the shed and across the gravel turnaround in front of the farmhouse, the silence broken only by a kereru, a wood pigeon, cooing contentedly on the roof of the porch, its iridescent feathers gleaming in the sun.

"We can chat in the workshop," she muttered behind him. "We don't need to go into the house."

Finn ignored this, going up the steps and opening the front door.

When Clint had owned the place, the

housekeeping had been rather haphazard, since he wasn't a man who particularly cared about such things. But it was obvious from the moment Finn stepped into the hallway that a new sheriff was in town. Things had changed. Radically.

For a start, the place was spotless, the wooden floors gleaming, the little hall table that had once been piled high with an assortment of items and never dusted now home to a small peace lily and all the dust gone. As were all the cobwebs.

Before, the house had smelled of mustiness and damp parka with a tinge of unwashed socks, but now all he could smell was lemon furniture polish, the faint traces of freshly baked bread, and the loamy scent of the fields outside.

It was certainly a welcome change.

Finn went into the front living area, which was also spotless, and sat Beth down on the old couch positioned in front of the big wood burner that dominated the room. Her fingers were cold in his, and since he didn't want to stand over her like a disapproving father, he crouched in front of her instead, taking both her hands in his.

Her attention was on the floor, her usual bright-ness dimmed. It made his chest feel tight, which was odd considering he'd always thought her brightness way too fake.

Then again, he hadn't that night in her arms. That night she'd been nothing but sunshine.

And look what happened.

Irritated by the thought, Finn told his brain to shut the hell up.

"Okay, so, want to tell me what's going on?" He kept his voice quiet and his tone very neutral.

She gave a short laugh but didn't look at him. "Not really."

"Beth."

"Okay, okay. Yes, I think…I think I'm pregnant." Her lashes lifted, her green gaze flickering with what he thought was defensiveness. "And before you ask, no, I haven't been with anyone else but you."

An unfamiliar sensation caught him, one that felt almost like possessiveness, which was strange when he'd never felt that way about a woman before, not even with Sheri.

"I wasn't going to ask that," he said mildly. "I know you haven't."

Beth scowled, which was an expression he hadn't seen on her face before, and it made him stare. She was even pretty when she scowled, which was quite something.

"Hey," she muttered, "I could have been with a lot of men, you don't know."

"You haven't though." He rubbed her cold fingers absently in his to warm them. "Which men would you have been with? I mean, have you been carrying on a secret affair with Bill that somehow no one knows about?"

She gave a little snort of disgust, her gaze returning to the floor once again. "I might. It would be worth it for the sausage rolls."

"Hey, I'd have an affair with him for the sausage rolls."

As he'd hoped, the tightness around her mouth eased. "Don't try to make me smile. It's not going to work."

"I wouldn't dream of it."

A breath escaped her, and there was a silence he made no attempt to fill, allowing her a couple of moments to get herself together.

At last she said, "I haven't had a test, so nothing is certain. It might not even be true." She left her hands where they were. "And if I am pregnant, I might not stay that way because it's early days."

It occurred to him, almost idly, that he could be angry about this, because if things *were* certain and she did stay pregnant, there would be a child at the end of it. And it would be *his* child.

He and Sheri had always planned on having children. A couple of years to enjoy a child-free marriage first, Sheri had said, and then they could get on with the business of trying for a baby. He'd been fine with it and hadn't minded waiting. Both of them had thought they'd have all the time in the world...

But you didn't have that time, and now the child you might potentially have isn't Sheri's.

That was true. And yeah, he could be angry

about it, about all the missed opportunities and futures he would never get to have.

But he couldn't find it in himself to be mad about it, at least not now. And he certainly couldn't be mad at Beth.

There had been two of them that night on the couch at HQ. And he was the one who'd lost control. He should have thought about condoms and he hadn't; while she might have missed a pill, it could also have failed. Either way, no amount of recriminations would help now.

Besides, apart from anything else, even if he had been angry, pacing about and shouting would only make things worse since Beth was clearly shocked and upset, not to mention ill.

He couldn't do that to her. He wouldn't.

Finn squeezed her hands, then let them go, rising to grab the thick woolen blanket that hung over one arm of the sofa, then wrapping it around her shoulders and tucking it in firmly.

"You don't have to do that," Beth protested weakly, "I'm not actually sick."

"You are," he said. "You're as white as a sheet and having nothing to eat all day is only going to make you feel worse."

She looked up at him, green eyes shadowed, the circles under her eyes pronounced and very much *not* the Beth she usually was. "Why are you being so nice about this?"

"Because getting angry and upset won't help. Plus it doesn't change the situation, so what's the point?"

"But I—"

"One step at a time," he interrupted gently. "That's the way we're going to deal with it. And right now, the first step is making sure you're warm, that you're hydrated, and have something in your stomach. Then we're going to talk about where to go from here."

"Yay," she said with some sarcasm, clearly trying to make a joke out of it. But he could see the fear in her eyes. The same fear he'd seen down in the gallery earlier that day.

Before he could think better of it, Finn reached down and cupped her cheek, her skin soft and warm against his palm. "It'll be okay," he said, rubbing a reassuring thumb across her cheekbone. "I promise. Whatever happens, we'll handle it. But first, you need something to eat."

She stared at him for a long moment, and this time he couldn't tell what she was thinking. Then she sighed. "Thanks, but I don't want anything."

"Oh, you'll want this." Finn dropped his hand, trying to ignore how the warmth of her skin lingered on his fingertips. "Now why don't you lie down and rest for a bit, while I get you a little something?"

Beth muttered under her breath, but he decided to ignore that, striding out of the living room and going down the hallway to the kitchen.

He'd do his special chicken soup for her. That was easy on sick tummies but contained plenty of liquid for hydration and some protein too. Sheri had liked it when she was in the middle of chemo.

You're going to make her Sheri's special soup?

An old pain coiled in his gut, and for a moment, he stood in the kitchen doorway, grief gripping him tight.

Sheri had loved the soup he made for her, and he'd loved making it because it helped him feel like he was doing something. As if he could make a difference somehow. It was her meal, so really, what right did Beth have to it?

Except he couldn't think like that. It would be making far too big a deal out of it if he could only make it for Sheri. It was only soup, for God's sake; he couldn't be precious about it.

Anyway, Sheri would be appalled. It wasn't *her* soup, she'd tell him. Don't be so bloody sentimental, Finn. She'd been a very down-to-earth, practical sort of woman, yet one with a big heart. She wouldn't want to deny Beth the soup.

She wouldn't want him mooning around feeling sad about it either.

Shoving thoughts of his wife away, Finn started opening and closing cupboards in the small kitchen, poking around for ingredients.

Luckily all the things he needed were there—it was a simple recipe—and soon he had a big pot of soup on the stove. While it was simmering, he went out and sorted through the equipment he needed for the trek the next day, then checked on the horses and Karl, who *was* saying hello to Jeff since the mutt liked the horse for some inexplicable reason. Then he finished up any remaining chores.

After he'd done that, he looked in on Beth and was pleased to see she'd fallen asleep on the sofa. A good thing. She'd looked exhausted, and no wonder—all of this had to have been a big worry for her.

Not long after that, the soup was done, so Finn filled a bowl for her, grabbed a spoon, and went back into the living room. There was a small, very rustic-looking wooden coffee table near the sofa that he put the bowl and spoon down on before going over to where Beth still lay asleep.

Her hair had come loose from its ponytail, lying in a pale tumble over the old, worn dark-green upholstery of the couch, and she had her hands curled beneath her chin like a child. She looked very small and vulnerable, and a protectiveness he didn't want to acknowledge gathered inside him.

He looked after people, that's what he did, and it was fine with clients—there was nothing emotional about the way he looked after them. With his brother and Levi, it was a bit different because them he did care about. But they were grown men, big enough and ugly enough to look after themselves.

Then there was Gus, and he'd lay down his life for her. But again, that was different. She was his niece, and he had no choice in the matter.

He didn't understand this protectiveness that filled him now as he looked at Beth, that also had an element of possessiveness to it that was alien to him.

He didn't like it. Possessiveness assumed that she was his or that he had a claim on her and neither of those things were true. They'd slept together once, then had decided to be friends, and they'd both been happy with that—or at least, he was happy with that.

You think you can just be friends with her now that she's expecting your child?

The feeling coiled tighter, making him aware that if he didn't like it, he liked the thought of Beth being "just a friend" even less. Though he really didn't have any idea of what else she could be, or not right now at least.

One thing was clear though: they were going to have to talk it through and figure out where they were going to go from here, and they were going to have to do this together.

Responding to an impulse so deep he didn't question it, Finn put a hand out and touched her hair. It felt silky against his fingers, just the way he remembered. Her hands had felt good in his too.

Sensing his presence, she sighed, her lashes fluttering and then lifting, the deep, shadowed green of her eyes meeting his.

"There's soup here for you, honey," he said, the endearment slipping out before he could stop it. "And then you and I need to talk."

Chapter 8

BETH FELT GROGGY AND SICK, AND SHE WANTED to tell Finn that she wasn't his honey, not in any way, yet the endearment got under her skin before she could stop it, making her feel warm inside.

He'd called her that before, when she'd been in his arms, and she'd liked it then too because it had been a long time since anyone had called her anything other than just Beth.

In fact, *he* made her feel warm inside, which she hadn't expected given the hard, intense look in his eyes when he'd asked her if she was pregnant.

She *so* hadn't wanted to tell him, yet he was far too perceptive and far more interested in her well-being that she'd ever thought he'd be, and she hadn't been able to hide it from him. All she had left was to admit it and bear the consequences.

She hadn't realized she'd been bracing herself for his anger and displeasure until it hadn't come. Because that was usually the reaction her family had to any announcement she made. Her emotionally unstable mother would always react negatively, which would then feed into her father's constant anger at his family and life in general.

He wasn't violent, never lashed out at anyone,

but the constant aura of rage was difficult to live with, making her feel as if she were living in a glass house, afraid one wrong move would bring the whole thing crashing down.

It had been a relief to move out and live with Troy, who at least wasn't angry all the time. But he had his own issues. He hadn't been able to deal with hard emotions, and when things were fraught, he'd simply leave.

She hadn't known what she'd get with Finn, but his warm, strong fingers threading through hers and his deep, calm voice telling her they needed to talk wasn't it.

He hadn't been angry, hadn't shouted, and he hadn't left either. He'd been calm and measured, dealing with it very matter-of-factly, his certainty and strength soothing her ragged nerves, so she didn't even want to protest as he'd led her inside and tucked her up on the sofa, telling her to get some rest.

She hadn't thought she would, since she hadn't been able to before, yet for some reason, now that Finn was in the house, filling it up with the strength of his steady presence, she could relax and let her exhausted brain sleep.

It's good to know you don't have to do this by yourself, right?

No, she couldn't start thinking stuff like that. She'd thought Troy would be a great support since he was as unlike her family as it was possible to get, yet when she'd needed him most, he'd left. After she'd lost the baby, he'd withdrawn, and then when she'd fallen into depression, he'd just…gone.

Most everyone did, either physically or emotionally. The only person she'd ever been able to count on was herself, and she couldn't go blindly trusting that Finn Kelly would stick around to help. Some things you *did* have to do all on your own.

Slowly, Beth sat up, drawing the blanket more firmly around her as Finn went over to the coffee table and picked up the bowl and spoon sitting on top of it.

The room was full of the delicate, savory scent of chicken soup, and her stomach cramped, deciding it was hungry and that chicken soup was the perfect meal.

"First, you need to eat." Finn came over to her holding out the bowl and spoon. "Then we'll talk about where we go from here."

Beth considered protesting, then decided she didn't have the energy, taking the bowl and spoon from him without argument. "You're just like Chase," she grumbled. "So bossy." Finn didn't say anything to that, so she added, for good measure, "Stupid Kellys." Then she eyed the soup warily, because although she did feel hungry, her stomach was still unsettled.

"It's chicken soup," Finn said, going into classic

dude pose with his thumbs hooked into his belt loops. "It's good for upset stomachs."

Beth glanced at him in surprise, since she hadn't picked Finn as a man who even knew what chicken soup was, let alone how to cook it.

Are you kidding? If any of those guys knows how to cook chicken soup, it's Finn.

"You made this?" she asked, just to be sure.

"Yeah, it's a specialty of mine." An expression she couldn't interpret flickered briefly across his face, like wind ruffling the water of a still pond. "I…used to make it for Sheri when she was sick."

Sympathy wound through her, threaded with a curiosity that pulled suddenly tight.

Sheri, his wife. The wife he didn't talk about.

"Oh." She wanted to ask all kinds of questions, but that wasn't a great idea. He probably wouldn't welcome them. And this was, after all, hardly the time to be asking questions about the wife he'd lost. "And she…uh…liked it?"

"Yeah, she did." Finn's dark gaze was on the bowl on her knees, his expression distant. "I made it for her when she was having chemo and feeling sick."

Sympathy throbbed in Beth's chest. Yes, that's right, he'd lost her to cancer, hadn't he?

Which means you can hardly spurn the soup he made for his dead wife.

Not that she was going to spurn it, but even if she'd been feeling really sick, she wouldn't.

"I'm sure it's delicious." Beth carefully dipped her spoon into the steaming liquid and brought it to her mouth, taking a sip.

Holy cow, yes, it *was* delicious.

"Oh," she breathed, suddenly ravenous. "Your wife wasn't wrong. This *is* really, really good."

Finn said nothing, but a faint, pleased smile curved his mouth as he watched her eat, his dark gaze enigmatic.

When she'd eaten half of it, he asked, "Feeling better?"

She nodded. The delicate, salty, savory taste of the soup had been divine and not too heavy, settling her uneasy stomach down nicely.

She took another couple of spoonfuls before she finally let Finn take the bowl away, returning it to the coffee table.

Then he sat down beside her on the sofa, engulfing her in his warmth and the delicious smell of sunshine, horse, and Finn's intrinsic musky, masculine scent.

It reminded her of things that she shouldn't be thinking about. Things that had gotten her into this mess to start with, and she wanted to pull away. But she also didn't want him to know he still had an effect on her, even a month after their little interlude, so she stayed put.

God, why hadn't she moved on from that already?

"Okay," he said, leaning forward, elbows on his knees, fingers loosely laced together. "So, like I said, we take this one step at a time. And the first step is getting a pregnancy test done."

We, he'd said. As if this wasn't only her responsibility. As if he was sharing in it too, which was another thing she hadn't expected.

Come on, you know he's a guy who takes his responsibilities seriously.

Okay, so that was undeniable. And maybe, now she thought about it, that was why she hadn't wanted to tell him. Because he *would* take responsibility and she wasn't sure if she wanted him stepping in and being all up in her grill.

He wasn't as openly take-charge as Chase, usually standing staunchly and quietly in the background, watching people. But it didn't mean he didn't have a strong will in him or an intent to use it when the situation called for it. And given his ordering her to eat the soup, the situation was definitely calling for it now.

But this was her responsibility too. He could walk away at any time, but she couldn't, and she really didn't want him coming in and calling all the shots.

Unless you decide not to have the baby, of course.

As if he'd read her mind, Finn said, "If you're pregnant, will you want the baby?"

There was zero judgment in his tone, yet much to Beth's horror, from out of nowhere came a rush of unexpected grief, tears filling her eyes. She looked away quickly, hoping he wouldn't notice.

Yet he must have, the asshole, because he asked softly, "What's up?"

She didn't want to talk about it, not now, yet she knew lying or even pretending that there was nothing wrong wasn't going to cut it anymore. Not with him.

He was far too perceptive. He saw through her in a way no one else did and she wasn't sure why. It was extremely annoying, not to mention painful, since it made her more aware of all the things she was trying to leave behind, the things that kept dogging her no matter how much distance she put between them and her, or how hard she tried to forget them.

Finn shifted, and before she could snatch it away, he put one of his large, warm capable hands over hers where it rested on her knee.

It'll be okay, he'd said to her just before her nap earlier, touching her cheek, his fingertips sending trails of fire over her skin. And she'd been conscious of something tight and sore inside her relaxing at the immense certainty she'd heard in his voice. As if there was no doubt in his mind that it *would* be okay. As if he'd make sure of it.

She'd needed that certainty then, and with the warmth of his hand over hers, she needed it just as badly now.

"I've been pregnant before," she forced out, since she was going to have to tell him at some stage and it might as well be now. "And it…didn't end well."

He said nothing, and for the first time it occurred to her that he wasn't a stranger to grief and loss. That if anyone knew how hard it made things, he would.

He hadn't lost a baby, but he'd lost his wife. He'd lost, period.

Beth swallowed and made herself tell him the rest. "She was born at twenty weeks and didn't make it. It was a few years ago now, so I'm mostly okay. But this is…well, it brings up some stuff."

Again, he said nothing, only kept his hand over hers in a way that made part of her ache. The same way she'd ached when he'd touched her cheek, as if some piece of her was desperate for reassurance and a warm touch, some contact that didn't involve her having to pretend everything was great all the time.

"I don't want to talk about it," she said into the silence. "And I'd rather you didn't mention it to anyone else because no one else knows. I thought that…given the circumstances, you should be aware."

After a moment, he said, "Thank you for telling me," and squeezed her hand briefly before letting it go. "You'll want to keep this baby, then?"

Her hand felt cold, and she had to restrain the

urge to reach over and grab his again, making do with folding her own together instead.

"Yes," she said, staring at the floor, the realization settling inside her like the ground settling after an earthquake. "I do."

And she did. Now the shock was wearing off and reality was asserting itself, she understood there was no question about it. She was still terrified and uncertain about what it would mean for her and her future, but she did want this baby and fiercely.

"Okay," Finn said as if it was no big deal. "We'll get a test. We should do that ASAP. It'll mean a trip to Queenstown, but that shouldn't be a problem. Levi's going tomorrow to pick up some tourists, so we can tag along."

She glanced at him. "But aren't you taking a trek?"

"Yeah, but Chase can take it. Or we can cancel it. It's not a problem."

"Or you don't have to come," she pointed out. "Believe it or not, I can buy a pregnancy test on my own."

"Sure you can." He pushed himself off the couch and went over to the coffee table to pick up the bowl and spoon. "But you're not going to."

His insistence needled at her for reasons she didn't understand and didn't have the energy to examine right now.

"Why?" she muttered grumpily. "I don't need your assistance."

Finn straightened and turned around. The expression on his strongly carved, handsome face was mild, but the glitter in his dark eyes was not.

"Here's the deal," he said. "This is not solely your responsibility. I'm a part of this too, and if you're expecting me to stand back and let you handle this on your own, you're going to be disappointed. That's not how I operate."

There it was, that will of his—tough as iron and just as certain. It made part of her want to argue, to see how far she could push him, see where his line was, while another part wanted to throw up her hands and let him take charge so she didn't have to.

Not that anyone could push Finn Kelly once he'd made up his mind about something, she suspected. Chase had even muttered on more than one occasion that the guy was mule-stubborn when he wanted to be, and Beth guessed she was looking at the mule right now.

So why bother arguing? He *was* part of this, and actually the only reason she wanted to handle it on her own was because she was afraid to trust that anyone would stay.

But Finn Kelly wasn't going to go anywhere. He owned a business with his brother and he owned this horse ranch. He had a house here, and if his wife hadn't passed away, he'd likely have had a family here too.

Plus he had the same strong sense of community responsibility that his brother did and a tendency to be an immovable object to any unstoppable force that came his way.

He wasn't emotionally fragile, like her mother, or coldly raging, like her father, and he wasn't avoidant, like Troy. He could have ignored her illness, let her pretend nothing was up, and gone about his business, yet he hadn't. He'd come after her and insisted she tell him what the problem was.

Asshole.

"Okay," she said, actually throwing up her hands. "Fine. Do that then. I don't care. I just don't want anyone else to know, okay? Not until I have to tell them."

"We," he amended irritatingly. "We have to tell them."

"You. Me. We. Whatever."

His gaze narrowed, and she was aware that whatever was going on behind those enigmatic dark eyes, it probably wasn't something she'd like.

"What are you thinking about now?" she demanded.

"If the test comes back positive," he said, "I want people to know."

Beth scowled. "There's no point, not until twelve weeks. Anything could happen before that."

"I still want people to know."

"Why?" she asked, exasperated.

"Because I'm thinking you should move in with me, that's why."

Beth's eyes went wide, and he didn't blame her. This would be a shock. But hell, it made perfect sense to him.

She wasn't having a great time of it, and she could do with someone taking care of her, most especially given what she'd told him about her earlier pregnancy.

He was glad she'd told him, even though he could tell she didn't want to.

Even though he heard the pain in her voice loud and clear.

Even though it set off a sympathetic echo inside him too, making him think about Sheri and his own grief.

It clarified a few things for him though.

He'd always thought her cheerfulness and positivity was fake, and he wondered now whether she wore it like a mask to cover up the pain of losing her baby. And surely, no matter how long it had been, there was still pain.

Time might blunt the edges, but it didn't heal it. Nothing healed it. You only learned to live with it, that's all.

He knew how it felt to pretend though, to keep on pushing through because that's all you could do. The *only* thing you could do.

His preferred method of pretending was to simply

never speak of his own grief or Sheri. That way people forgot to ask him how he was doing and gradually stopped giving him concerned, pitying looks. Being silent tended to deter questions anyway.

But his way of dealing with it was a mask, just as Beth's was.

And while he didn't absolutely need her to move in with him, he knew himself. He knew that he wouldn't be happy if she was living here on her own, even if she did have Indigo. He wanted her close so he could keep an eye on her himself.

She's yours now...

The possessive feeling wound tightly around him, though he tried to ignore it. Because he didn't want to start thinking like that. It was more him wanting her to be close so if she got into trouble, he'd be there. He'd worry about her otherwise, and he'd worry about the baby.

His baby.

He gritted his teeth as the feeling became even stronger. Sure, the baby was his, but nothing was certain. Hell, both of them knew how easy it was to lose something. Miscarriages happened all the time.

"Move in with you?" Beth yelped. "Are you insane? I mean, actually insane?"

"No." He tried to sound as reasonable as possible and not like a carbon copy of his brother giving orders. "Think about it. You wouldn't have to worry about driving Indigo up and down to town all the time, and you'd have someone to look after you when you're sick. It would make it easier when it comes to organizing doctor's visits and—"

"Finn," Beth interrupted, "we don't even know if this is going to be happening or not, so please, take it down a notch."

The way she said it, as if she were speaking to an overexcited child, irritated him, making him want to dig in. Because regardless of what he was telling himself about uncertainties and wait-and-sees, he had a gut feeling that this *was* going to be happening. They were going to have a child together, and in nine months' time, he would be holding that baby in his arms. There was certainly no other reason for him to be feeling so... Neanderthal about it.

He was going to be a father. He was going to have a child. And while it wasn't with the woman he'd thought he'd end up with, he was still going to have one. They would be a family.

The possessiveness shifted, became certain and sure, making Finn realize that he had strong feelings about what that family would look like.

His own mother had died when he was young, his father passing off his responsibilities to his two sons immediately after her death, which had made for a difficult childhood. His father had spent more time and money in the pub than he had at home, and sometimes Chase had been forced to beg Bill for food when they'd been kids because their father had forgotten to buy any.

Finn didn't want that for any kid of his. He didn't want to put a child through having to bring themselves up because their parents were gone, either physically or emotionally. Nope. No way in hell that was happening, not if he had anything to do with it.

He'd be there for them, and he wanted Beth to be there for them too.

They both would be.

So no, he would not take it down a notch.

Finn stared at her, debating whether to let her know what his line in the sand was now or to wait for a better time. He was in favor of now, but since she still looked pale and the conversation they were having was a difficult one anyway, he probably didn't need to make things worse by insisting on something she'd need time to come to terms with.

He'd pick his battles and right now wasn't the time for one.

So all he said was "Okay. We'll talk about it later. The most important thing is getting that test done, so we know what's happening."

Beth's green eyes narrowed, obviously picking up on the fact that she was being placated. "What do you mean we'll talk about it later? What if I want to talk about it now?"

Finn opened his mouth to tell her that they would not be talking about it now, not when she was still looking so pale, when he heard a car pulling into the gravel turnaround outside. Karl gave an excited-sounding yip in greeting.

Car doors slammed, then the front door opened.

"I know you didn't want a ride," Levi's voice drifted down the hallway. "So if you didn't want a ride, why did you get into my truck? Oh hey, Karl. How are you doing, boy?"

In hindsight, it was lucky Indigo appeared in the hall outside the living room doorway because it was obvious Beth wasn't going to let the whole moving-in thing slide, no matter how unwell she was feeling. And if she'd kept on at him about it, things would have no doubt degenerated into an argument.

So he let it go as Beth glanced at Indigo, who'd turned to glare at someone coming through the front door.

No, not "someone." Levi.

"I got into your truck because you'd have driven alongside me all the way up to the farmhouse," Indigo snapped. "And quite frankly, I wanted to get rid of you as quickly as possible."

"That's not true." Levi's tall figure came into view, an excited Karl nosing at his hand for a scratch. "I wouldn't have driven alongside you. I would have driven behind you, keeping a respectful distance."

Indigo looked like she was going to reply, then obviously aware of the fact that Finn and Beth were staring at her and Levi through the doorway, she shut her mouth, glancing at them and blushing.

"Oh," she muttered. "You're both here." Throwing Levi a dark look, she came into the room, her expression clearing as she approached the couch where Beth sat. "Hey, are you okay? Migraine gone?"

Beth gave her friend her usual "I'm okay" smile, the one Finn had always thought was fake as hell and still was as far as he could see. "Yeah, it's getting better."

Indigo frowned; she wasn't fooled by Beth's smile either. Then that frown deepened into yet another scowl as Levi strolled in behind her, Karl frisking happily at his heels.

"Hey, you two," Levi said casually. "Indy was telling me you're not well, Beth."

"Oh my God," Indigo muttered. "My name is *not* Indy."

"Sorry, Indigo, I mean." Levi lounged against the arm of the couch, looking very pleased with himself. "My bad."

That there was something going on between Indigo and Levi, and had been ever since Indigo, Beth, and Izzy had arrived in Brightwater Valley, was obvious. Levi could be a pest sometimes, because there was nothing he liked more than winding people up. But he always backed off when people asked him to, especially when it came to women.

But for some reason, he couldn't seem to leave

Indigo alone, and while she was, on the surface, grumpy as hell with him, she nevertheless always seemed to be around him. Finn was certain she even put herself purposefully in his way.

Finn wasn't sure what was up with the two of them and he really wasn't interested, but it was good timing Levi was here, since he and Beth were planning on hitching a ride with him tomorrow.

"You still doing a pickup tomorrow?" Finn asked him as Indigo fussed around Beth.

Levi's gaze was firmly on Indigo, as if he couldn't bear to look away from her for even a second. "Yeah, definitely."

"Good. Beth and I need a ride if that's okay."

"No problem." Levi glanced at him and grinned, though his gaze was suddenly very sharp. "Got a hot date?"

"No." Finn refused to rise to the bait. "Beth has some suppliers to meet and I need to start asking around to find a permanent manager for this place."

Not actual lies. Well, at least not on his end. He did need to find a stable manager, plus there were going to be a few issues to iron out if Beth was to move in with him.

"Uh-huh." Levi's gaze turned speculative, then he glanced at Beth, which made the back of Finn's neck prickle for no apparent reason.

Levi knew nothing about him getting together with Beth, and he certainly wouldn't be able to guess the real reason he and Beth were going to Queenstown, so why Finn felt antsy he had no idea.

"What did you do to Indigo?" Finn asked to distract him. "She looks like she wants your guts for garters."

"Nothing." Levi's expression was all innocence. "I simply had the temerity to offer her a ride up to the farmhouse." His hazel eyes flicked back once more to Indigo, who was now gazing down at Beth, looking concerned. "She kept saying no, yet she got in my truck anyway."

Indigo shot him a baleful glance. "Haven't we had this discussion?"

"It looked like it might rain." Levi grinned at her. "I didn't think you'd want to get wet."

Finn noted with interest that despite her bad temper, Indigo was blushing fiercely.

"Can you two take it outside?" Beth murmured, rubbing tiredly at her forehead. "The sexual tension in here is making my head ache."

"Sexual tension?" Indigo squawked. "What are you talking about? There's absolutely zero sexual tension. What you're feeling is probably testosterone poisoning from all the posturing from that idiot over there."

"Seriously?" Levi said rather unwisely. "Okay, first, I'm not an idiot. Second, while it's true that I do posture at times, I'm not actually doing it right now. And third, you love a bit of testosterone, don't deny it."

Since things were probably only going to go downhill from there, Finn decided to take charge, moving over to the couch and gently urging Indigo away while giving Levi a very direct "cut it out" look.

"You heard the lady," Finn said. "How about we give her some space?"

Indigo let out a breath and shot Beth another concerned look. "I'm sorry, I shouldn't have—"

"It's fine," Beth interrupted with another of those fake smiles. "I'm just tired. I'll be okay tomorrow."

"Come on." Finn herded the other two out of the living room and whistled at Karl, who followed. "Let's leave her to rest. There's chicken soup in the kitchen if you're hungry, by the way."

"Chicken soup?" Levi gave him a sharp look as they walked down the hallway. "You've been making her chicken soup?"

Levi had been in Brightwater Valley for nearly ten years. Chase had met him in the SAS, and when Chase had left the army, so had Levi. And when Chase had come home to Brightwater Valley, so had Levi. He had no family and having been kicked around in the system as a foster kid, Brightwater was the only real home he'd ever known.

Finn knew Levi thought of him and Chase as his brothers, and for all that Levi could be a pain in the ass sometimes, the feeling was mutual. Being a pain in the ass was pretty much mandatory for brothers

anyway. Besides, Levi could fly anything with a pro-
pellor, was a magician when it came to engines, the
clients loved him, and he'd lay down his life for his
friends and the community here.

He'd also known Sheri, had viewed her as a sister-
in-law, and was well aware of the significance of the
damn chicken soup. And Finn was kicking himself
for having mentioned it, because Levi, being the
annoying brother type, would now imagine there
was importance attached to it where certainly none
had been intended.

Importance attached to Beth too, which he was
not pleased about.

He shoved away his irritation and merely lifted a
shoulder. "It's just soup, Levi. No big deal."

"Seems like a big deal to me," Levi said.
"Especially the way you're fussing around her like
a mother hen. What's really going on?"

"Nothing. If we're going to talk about people
fussing around other people, I could ask you what
the hell you're doing with Indigo." He lifted a brow.
"Or is that a conversation you'd rather have in the
heli tomorrow?"

Levi grinned widely, then threw a companionable arm across Finn's shoulders. "Tell you what,
bro. Let's never speak of either of these two things
again, okay?"

Interesting. Normally Levi loved nothing better
than to wax lyrical about whichever woman of the

moment he was interested in, and it was very unlike him to not want to talk about it.

It half made Finn want to push, but since he really didn't want to talk about why he was fussing around with Beth, all he said was "Deal."

And went into the kitchen to dole out some soup.

Chapter 9

THE HELICOPTER TRIP FROM BRIGHTWATER Valley to Queenstown only took twenty minutes, and it was a pretty and very scenic trip, especially when the weather was good.

The weather was good now, yet Beth found it hard to concentrate on the scenery and not because she was feeling sick. Her nausea had settled down earlier that morning, after a piece of toast, but nothing was going to help the nervousness that gripped all her muscles tight.

Neither Indigo nor Izzy had commented when she'd told them she was heading into Queenstown for the day, Izzy merely shrugging and offering to take on her shift in the gallery.

Indigo had been more suspicious, muttering something about Beth perhaps needing to stay at home, seeing as how she wasn't well.

Beth had ignored that, meeting Finn at HQ and following him to the little Airbus helicopter that Pure Adventure NZ owned. Levi had already completed the preflight checks, so within a couple of minutes of her getting in, they were in the air and flying over the mountains that ringed the valley to Queenstown.

Finn and Levi were chatting in the cockpit while she sat behind them, happy not to take part in the conversation, her brain going around and around with what Finn had told her yesterday.

Move in with me, he'd said. As if it were no big deal. As if it were the most logical thing in the world rather than being completely insane.

They weren't together, not in any way. He wasn't her partner. Hell, he was barely even her friend, so why on earth would he want her living in his house? Surely that was taking responsibility too far?

And what if something happened during the pregnancy? Would he then want her to move out? Get rid of her like an unwanted gift?

That wasn't even considering Indigo and what she would do if Beth moved out. She didn't drive, and someone needed to ferry her up and down from the farmhouse since it didn't seem fair to leave her having to walk.

Then there was the wonderful workshop and her newly acquired workbench. Would she have to leave those behind too? Did Finn have a place she could work, or did he simply think she'd give up her job now that she was pregnant? Because that sure as hell wasn't happening.

Beth glared at the back of Finn's dark head, since he was seated in front of her.

How dare he make this difficult, and yes, he *was* making this difficult.

Or are you just feeling ill and scared and taking it all out on him?

Uncomfortable awareness shifted inside her. Perhaps she was. He'd been so good yesterday, remaining calm and certain and looking after her, while she'd been...

Well. She hadn't handled it, had she? She could blame tiredness and feeling sick, but the reality was she'd gone to pieces, and he'd picked those pieces up and put her back together again.

Which wasn't exactly in line with the strong, brave person she was supposed to be here. The person who looked forward to the future positively and who was ready for anything that came her way. Ready to create happiness for herself, leave all that depression stuff behind.

She wasn't going to be that Beth again, the one that let herself fall apart.

She couldn't be that Beth again.

The thought settled her, and by the time the helicopter went in to land at Queenstown Airport, she was feeling stronger if not any less nervous.

Queenstown was a picture-perfect little alpine town. Like Brightwater, it sat on the edge of a beautiful lake, jagged snow-topped mountains soaring around it.

It was very much a tourist town, full of cafés and bars, and shops supporting the outdoor adventures the town was famous for. Skiing and hiking were its main draws, but it was an area famous for its vine-yards and restaurants too.

There were also docks at the water's edge where boats were tied up, as well as a giant old-fashioned paddle steamer that took people across the lake and back again.

Beth loved Queenstown. It was big enough to feel like a bustling town yet small enough not to be too overwhelming like a city would be. There were quite a few little artisan stores scattered around that sold jewelry and other cool, arty things, and Beth had made friends with a number of the people who owned them in the hopes of one day being able to sell her jewelry there as well as at the gallery.

Except you're not going to be doing that anytime soon, are you?

Beth ignored the snide thought as Levi dropped her and Finn off in the town center. Levi had a place in Queenstown, up in the hills, and an old truck he used for running around town in, even though he spent most of his time in Brightwater, either sleeping at the Rose or in the little bedroom in HQ.

Beth was curious about his Queenstown house, but Levi had never offered to show her around, and she didn't like to ask. She thought Levi was actually quite private, despite his open and charming persona.

Now, though, she wasn't thinking about Levi's

house. She was thinking about how she was going to have to go into a pharmacy and buy herself a pregnancy test, and how it brought back uncomfortable memories she didn't want to deal with.

Finn, picking up on her mood, glanced at her as they stood on the sidewalk, and frowned.

"Let me buy it," he offered. "I know where the pharmacy is."

"I know where the pharmacy is too," Beth said, irritated. "Several pharmacies actually. Also it's better if I do it since you know a lot of people here and they'll probably want to say something if you suddenly start buying pregnancy tests."

Finn gave her a look, his dark eyes enigmatic, and she thought he might start insisting. But he only lifted a shoulder. "Fine. You go and buy one. I'll wait outside for you."

"Don't you have other things to do?"

"No. Nothing that's this important."

Beth felt her stupid chest get tight, though really his dogged persistence at being involved should annoy her, not make her emotional.

Stupid potential-pregnancy hormones.

Without speaking, they walked down the little pedestrian mall that led to the docks, stopping outside the big pharmacy situated there.

Beth went in, leaving him standing outside by the door.

There were very few people inside, and she

found the pregnancy tests easily enough. Taking one to the counter made her feel self-conscious, so she smiled extra brightly to make up for it.

The woman rang her up without comment—thank God for Kiwis who'd rather die than pry into your personal business—and Beth soon found herself standing outside again, a brown paper bag clutched in her hand.

Finn's expression was impenetrable. "Do you want to find some place to sit? Go to a café? We can leave doing the test until we get home again if you'd prefer."

"You keep saying *we*." Beth shifted on her feet, antsy and restless, the nerves in her gut gathering tighter. "As if we're both going to be peeing on that stick."

His mouth twitched. "I mean, I can if you want me to. If you'd like some company"

Beth bit her lip. No, he was not going to make her smile. She didn't want to be cheered up, not when her future was currently barreling along on the road to hell, sitting pretty in a handbasket.

"Thanks," she muttered, "but I'll pass. And I don't want to wait until we get home. I want to get this over with."

"There's a public bathroom not far away."

Great. She was going to do this in a public convenience? How…wonderful. Then again, wanting privacy and cleanliness seemed a bit precious when this was her fault. She had to suck it up and deal.

"Okay," she said, shoving down her distaste. "Let's get on with it."

She turned in the direction of the public bathrooms only to have Finn reach out and take her arm in a gentle grip.

"Let me call Levi," he said quietly. "We can do this at his place."

Beth shut her eyes for a second because there was nothing more she wanted than to do this at Levi's—where she could find out the truth in private, without screaming kids and tourists and a hundred other people all in her vicinity.

But that was silly. Who cared where she did it as long as she and Finn got some answers?

"I'm fine with it," she said staunchly. "Come on, let's go."

Yet Finn didn't release her. "You might be fine with it, but I'm not. I'll tell Levi you're not feeling well, okay? We'll get a cab to his place, and I know the lock code. We don't even have to involve him."

He made it sound so…easy. Reasonable even. No big deal at all. Making her wonder like she had yesterday what the point was in arguing with him. Especially when the idea of doing this at Levi's was so attractive.

She swallowed, resisting the urge to lean into the strong hand holding her arm. "Okay. Let's go, then. The sooner we get this over with, the better."

Levi's place was a ten-minute ride away, up the side of the mountains that ringed the town. It was very private, set in among tall trees and overlooking the town itself and the lake. It had a distinct log-cabin vibe to it, with a pitched roof and an impressive deck with views across the lake.

Beth also had the distinct impression that it was worth a lot of money.

"So," she said as Finn keyed in the code on the heavy wooden front door, "what's a mountain guide who lives mostly in a hotel or his office doing with a luxury Queenstown hideaway?"

"Levi's got money he stashed away years ago," Finn said as he held open the door for her. "Though to be honest with you, I've never asked him where he got it. That's his business, not mine."

"Fair enough."

She took a step inside and looked around.

A hallway ran down the middle of the house, with one side opening up into a big, open-plan living area and kitchen. It was all exposed wooden floors, white walls, and a big stone fireplace.

It looked like a five-star hotel.

Finn went past her, showing her to the sleek, white-tiled bathroom down on one end of the hallway.

Beth stepped inside and closed the door, then leaned her forehead against the cool wood of the door, her heart pounding.

Maybe she wasn't pregnant. Maybe this was just a bug, a virus that she'd soon throw off.

Yeah, and Finn Kelly is the smiliest, chattiest person you've ever met.

She gave a little groan.

Okay, here went nothing.

A few minutes later, Beth stared down at the pregnancy test sitting on the white vanity, watching as two pink lines slowly appeared.

Yep. She was pregnant, all right.

———————

Finn didn't need to see Beth's white face as she came out of the bathroom holding the small plastic test stick.

He already knew. He'd known yesterday, pretty much as soon as she'd told him, give or take half an hour.

The test was for her benefit, and it was clear she'd been hoping for another answer, even though some part of her had known for sure just the way he had.

He was going to be a dad.

Something kicked hard inside of him, something that had already been building since the day before, hardening into a sure certainty.

She would move in with him. He wanted to be near her to look after her and the baby, and hell, if she didn't want that, then he'd move into Clint's, though he thought she'd be more comfortable at his place.

So, what? You're just going to ride roughshod over her?

Sheri used to complain about how stubborn he could be at times, and yeah, he could be unyielding and a bit too rigid. But then he'd had to be, growing up with a father like his, to suffer all the criticisms his old man had dealt out and with no one but his big brother to rely on.

Sheri understood because Sheri had grown up in the valley like he had and knew him, but Beth?

Yeah, she might not.

Finn stood in the living area by the big windows that looked out across the lake and watched as Beth came into the room and walked over to him, her hand outstretched with the pregnancy test in it.

"I know," he said. "You're pregnant."

Beth shook the test at him. "You don't want to look at it?"

"I don't need to. I know already. I was certain of it yesterday."

"How nice for you." The sharpness in her voice betrayed how upsetting this news must be for her. "We must have made this trip for nothing then."

Finn took the stick from her, stuck it in his pocket, then before she could pull away, and following an instinct he couldn't resist, reached out and slowly drew her into his arms and held her.

She went rigid at first, then unexpectedly relaxed against him, her body warm and soft as she allowed herself to be held.

"You needed to take the test," he said quietly, running a hand over her silky white-blond hair, soothing her like he'd soothe one of the horses. "You needed to see the lines. It's good. Now we know, we can start making plans."

"What plans?" Her voice sounded muffled, her cheek turned against his chest. "The only plans I'm thinking of making are going back to bed and sleeping for the next nine months."

He smiled. "That's okay. I'll tuck you up and feed you sausage rolls."

Her shoulders trembled and he could feel the warmth of her breath against his T-shirt. And it came to him that he hadn't hugged a woman this way in years. Not simply held her in his arms to comfort her.

In fact, the last woman he'd hugged had been his mother-in-law at Sheri's funeral. She and his father-in-law had moved from Brightwater to Christchurch after Sheri had died and he didn't blame them. He didn't see them much anymore.

But it was good to hold Beth. Good to hold her curvy body against his, to breathe in the sweet scent of apricots and sunshine. She reminded him of summer, of blue skies and the green peace of the bush, the heat of the sun on the back of his neck and ice cream melting on his tongue…

There were no painful memories associated with holding her, in the same way that there hadn't been any making love to her either. Because she was different from Sheri, there was nothing to scrape the edges of his grief raw, nothing to cut him.

Even this was different.

He and Sheri had never had a pregnancy to deal with, not even a scare.

But Beth has, don't forget.

His heart constricted. Ah shit, that's right. There would have to be memories associated with this for her and not good ones.

Finn let her go and took her face between his palms, tilting it back so he could look into her eyes. They were darkened and he could see the fear in them.

"Are you okay?" he asked gently. "I know this can't be easy for you."

She looked up at him, and he was very conscious of her warmth and the echoes of sunshine he could see in the shadowed gleam of her eyes. And he knew that despite those shadows, there was a genuine core of lightness in Beth Grant and he was looking at it right now.

He wanted very much to hold it in his hands, wrap it around him, let it chase away the darkness he sometimes felt inside himself, the darkness that had settled there after Sheri died.

They were standing very close, the small space

between them abruptly becoming charged with a certain familiar electricity.

Finn caught his breath, his body hardening in response.

Here they were in Levi's house. Alone. No one would know if they decided to indulge themselves again. No one but them.

You're thinking of sex? Now?

Yeah, not ideal. But shit, he was a man. And considering, bar that night in HQ, he hadn't had it for five years and Beth was pregnant with his child and—

She flushed and abruptly pulled herself out of his grip, taking a couple of steps back, putting some distance between them.

"That's…probably not a good idea," she muttered, not looking at him.

He took a breath, fighting to get his physical response under control. He'd thought after a month of not being around her this desire would lessen, but apparently not. And not for her either.

Great. Just…great.

"Yeah, probably not." He shoved his hands into his pockets once again.

"And to answer your question, I'm fine." She'd turned away, moving over to the long line of windows that gave magnificent views out over the lake and the jagged teeth of the Remarkables, the mountain range on the opposite side of the lake.

Irritation wound through him.

Shit, he was tired of hearing those two words over and over from her. Especially when he knew it wasn't true. She wasn't fine and they both knew it.

Knowing that a fair bit of his irritation was also due to his ridiculous physical response to her didn't help either.

"Bullshit," he said shortly. "You're not fine."

She turned and glanced at him. "I'm absolutely—"

"Yeah, and you said that yesterday after I caught you puking your guts out in the gallery, right before nearly fainting in my arms."

Color tinged her pale cheeks.

With the morning light coming through the windows and making her white-blond hair glow and her eyes seem green as grass, she looked almost ethereally lovely.

"You're not fine, Beth," he repeated for emphasis. "So why do you keep pretending you are?"

"So I don't get stubborn assholes all up in my grill telling me what to do." She crossed her arms, sans bracelets today, her jaw getting a mulish cast to it. "Anyway, you're a fine one to talk, acting so calm and sure of yourself. You can't tell me you're any more fine with this than I am."

"Not especially, but there's nothing we can do to change it. The only thing we can do is handle the situation the best we can."

Her chin lifted. "Oh right, so I guess 'handling

it' involves telling everyone and me moving in with you, right?"

Clearly, she did not think much of this idea. At all. Which wasn't a surprise. It was plain he was going to have his work cut out for him convincing her it was a good idea, which was fine. He liked a challenge.

"Yeah, that's right." No point beating about the bush with it.

"And what about me? Do I get a say in all of this?"

"Of course you do. It'll be your decision, Beth. I'm not that much of a dick."

She eyed him balefully. "That's debatable."

Finn didn't respond. This whole situation was going to require tact and care, especially given how upset she was. Getting all hard-line about her moving in wasn't a great plan, but she had to know he was serious and he had good reasons for it too.

He let the silence hang there a moment, then asked, "Okay, so what do you want, then?"

"What do you think? For everything to carry on as normal. Me living in the farmhouse. You living in your house and taking tours and whatever touristy stuff you do."

"So what happens when you start to show? When people start asking who the father of your baby is? What are you going to do then?" He kept his voice very neutral, betraying nothing of the protective, possessive feeling getting stronger inside him, urging him to start striding around and making all kinds of pronouncements that would only enflame the situation.

She bit her lip and glanced out the windows again. "I…don't know. Maybe I'll cross that bridge when I come to it."

There was the issue right there, wasn't it? For him it was "we." For her it was "I." As if he had no responsibility, no role to play in this at all.

Part of him wanted an argument, to tell her in no uncertain terms that he would be part of this whether she liked it or not. But again, not helpful.

"Right," he said, still calm and measured. "So here's what I want. I want to be involved with your pregnancy every step of the way. I want to make sure you're okay, that you're happy and safe and well looked after."

She glanced back at him again, frowning. "You can do that while living in your own home, Finn."

"And I want that," he went on as if she hadn't spoken, "because I lost my wife. She was ill, and for a long time she pretended she was fine, that there was nothing wrong. And I believed her. And I didn't see how sick she was until it was too late."

The frown faded from Beth's face. "Oh, Finn…I…"

"She was trying to protect me," he continued, because this was how he'd tackle it. With honesty. So she'd understand why he was being such an insistent asshole. "She didn't want me to worry about her, and while I disagreed strongly with her decision, I understood it. And I'm at peace with it. But I'm not doing it again. I need to know you and the baby are well. I need to know you're protected and looked after, and I need to see that with my own eyes." He paused, holding her gaze. "So you can live with me at my house, or I'll move into the farmhouse, your choice. But I'm going to be there, Beth. Whether you like it or not."

Chapter 10

BETH WAS SORELY TEMPTED TO FIRST PUNCH stupid Finn Kelly in the nose and then to put her arms around him and give him the same hug he'd just given her.

Punch him because he was being such a stubborn ass about this pregnancy.

Hug him because he'd lost his wife and the look in his eyes as he'd told her how Sheri had wanted to protect him had torn at her heart.

That had hurt him, she could see, and no wonder. Much like his brother, he was a protector, and finding out he hadn't even known Sheri was ill must have been exquisitely painful for him.

Sympathy ached inside her, both for Sheri, who'd tried to protect him from the worst, and for him, for not being able to protect her. They must have loved each other so very much.

Unlike you and Troy.

Beth turned away to look out the windows again so Finn wouldn't see her face or read the complex mix of emotions that was no doubt plastered across it whenever she thought of Troy.

No, she'd loved Troy and he'd loved her. At least,

she'd thought he'd loved her. Turned out he'd only loved her when things were going well and when they weren't, not so much.

But Finn isn't like that. You saw the expression on his face. It hurt him badly that she didn't tell him…

Well, yes, and the thought of him being hurt was oddly upsetting to her. But she didn't know why she was thinking of Finn in conjunction with Troy. The two had nothing to do with each other. And she definitely wasn't thinking of Finn as a husband because no way.

He was a…friend. That's all.

And the father of your child.

Not to mention a stubborn ass.

"Well?" His deep voice scraped over her raw nerves.

She glanced at him.

His expression was very neutral, all traces of the grief and anger she'd seen glittering in his eyes just before gone. It was as if he'd closed a door between them, shutting his emotions firmly away.

It made her want to reach out and open it again, the way it had opened that night they'd spent together up in HQ, when she swore she'd caught a glimpse of his soul.

Don't go there, girl.

No, she really shouldn't. Not when she could still feel the heat that had ignited between them when he'd given her that hug.

Wow, had that been a mistake. His arms had felt so good around her, keeping her safe and protected as he'd held her against his iron-hard body. She'd had the sense that nothing could harm her while he was near, not with his strength and utter certainty at her back.

But that was the issue, wasn't it? It wasn't so much their physical chemistry as it was their emotional connectedness. Because whether she liked it or not, she was connected to him now. They were having a child together, and he had a lot of qualities she admired very much.

He was standing there looking at her, sexy as hell in his usual uniform of well-worn jeans and black Pure Adventure NZ T-shirt. The one that clung to his broad shoulders and muscled chest. His dark eyes didn't move from her face, and she had the sense that he would wait there forever for her response if she wanted him to.

You could be in trouble so easily…

Beth turned away again, her heart beating uncomfortably fast.

No, no. Absolutely not. She was not going to fall for Finn Kelly, no way. Except now he was telling her that he was going to be around her, keeping an eye out for her and their baby—yes, *their* baby— and she didn't know how she was going to cope with that.

Every instinct she had was telling her Finn Kelly

was a man she could rely on, and normally she had no problems with her instincts. She could trust him. It was her heart that was the issue and always had been. There was the potential for things to get messy, and that's not what she wanted. Not now that she was pregnant.

She was going to have to keep her boundaries very clear.

"What exactly is the issue, Beth?" Finn's voice was quiet in the silence when she didn't speak. "Because I can see there's an issue. I'm not going to crowd you or anything, or tell you what to do all the time, you know that, right? It's just about being around and making sure you're okay."

"I know," she murmured, staring at the view outside, struggling to make sense of her own complicated feelings.

She had to keep him at a distance somehow for the sake of her own sanity, especially if he was so insistent about staying close to her. Because yes, it wasn't him crowding her that was the issue so much as it was *her* feelings for him.

She didn't want to feel sympathy for him or curiosity about him. She didn't want to feel safe in his arms. She didn't want to want him, and she most definitely didn't want to fall for him.

But she couldn't tell him that. She needed some other kind of honesty that would keep him at arm's length.

Perhaps she should be up front about what happened after she'd lost her baby. It would mean giving him a window into the poor, sad, weak Beth she'd been back in Deep River, and that was uncomfortable. But there was nothing like mental health issues to keep people at bay.

She sighed. "The issue? You don't really want to know, Finn. But since you asked…I had some pretty awful postpartum depression. I was sick for…quite a while, and it took me a long time to pull myself out of it. But…" She took a breath and turned to face him, meeting his gaze, because she was brave now. She was brave and positive, and most of all she was *not* falling back into that pit again. "I got a good doctor and some medicine, and I got better. And I guess it's an issue because I don't know whether it'll happen again with this baby. It might. In which case you'll have a front row seat, and are you ready for that?"

His gaze didn't even flicker, as if people told him about their mental health issues every day and it was no big deal. "Of course. If I can handle cancer, I can handle postnatal depression."

"Finn, it's not—"

"Let's just see what happens when the time comes," he said calmly.

Except she knew what happened when the time came. People couldn't handle it. People only wanted to support you when you were feeling good. They didn't want to do the hard work and support you when you were struggling.

Ah, but there was no point in thinking about that. In the end, that had been for the best because it had taught her a certain amount of strength and self-reliance. It had also taught her that no one was going to rescue you.

You always had to rescue yourself.

"So…that's it? That's all you're going to say?" she asked, a little surprised by his acceptance. "Just 'let's see when the time comes'?"

"I didn't think you'd want to talk about it." He lifted one brow. "Unless you *do* want to talk about it?"

Something inside her tugged, as if she really did want to talk about it. Because she had the sense that she could tell Finn Kelly anything and he'd simply nod in that calm, accepting way he had.

Another reason why having him around all the time is a very bad idea.

True. Then again, if she refused, she suspected he'd probably put up a tent in the farmhouse's yard and camp there for the next nine months, the idiot.

"No," she said. "No, I do not want to talk about it."

"Okay. So where are we at? Am I going to move in with you, or do you want to stay at mine?"

God, he was like a dog with a bone.

Beth sighed. "I'd like to see your place before I make any firm decisions."

"Fair enough. How about I give you a tour when

we get back, then? You can take a look around, see what you think."

Gah. He was being so reasonable. She couldn't think of a good enough excuse to refuse.

"Yeah, okay." She tried to hide her reluctance because she didn't want him asking any more questions. "That sounds good. And what about telling people?"

"How do you want to play it? Shall we wait until we've got our living arrangements sorted out?"

She didn't want people to know at all, at least not until everything was certain, but people would notice if Finn was suddenly in her vicinity all the time. And she couldn't exactly hide it if they were living in the same place.

Telling Izzy and Indigo was a drama she wasn't looking forward to though. Not because she was afraid they'd be judgmental. More because of the questions that would be asked about her relationship with Finn.

"We could wait until then," she said. "Except I don't know what to tell them."

"You mean about the pregnancy?"

"No, about us. About our relationship." She met his dark gaze. "Like…what exactly *is* our relationship?"

Something hot glittered briefly in his eyes and then it was gone, that door shutting again.

"Well," he said, "we're friends, aren't we?"

Yes, she supposed that they were friends, though

that implied the kind of warm, long-standing relationship that they didn't have. They were more like...distant friends. Acquaintances even.

Acquaintances who were going to have a baby together.

Come on, you're supposed to be upbeat and positive, remember?

Yes, she was. And thinking about the direction of her relationship with Finn and worrying about having him around was counterproductive.

The bottom line was if she didn't want to fall for him, she wouldn't. Hell, having him around could be a good thing. She could get him to do the tasks she hated, like putting out the trash and putting away the dishes. And it *would* be nice when she was feeling sick to have someone to make her soup and wrap her up in a blanket.

"Yes," she said. Then more firmly, "Yes. We *are* friends."

"Then we'll tell everyone the truth. We had one night together and now you're pregnant."

"Okay, so...friends having a baby and, uh... remaining friends, I guess?"

Finn's gaze narrowed, and for the first time she got the distinct impression that this was something he *wasn't* entirely accepting about.

"That's right though, isn't it?" she said when he didn't say anything. "We're friends. Definitely *not* in a relationship."

He was silent a few moments more, then said, "We'll discuss what we tell them later, once we know what's happening with the living arrangements."

Yeah, he was *not* happy with the thought of being friends; she got that loud and clear. But seriously, what else did he want? Neither of them were up for a relationship, and there was no way she was going to marry him or anything purely for the baby's sake. That was like something out of the nineteenth century.

She contemplated pushing him on it, but then decided not to since she didn't particularly want to talk about it now either.

Finn had a few things he wanted to do in town, so he suggested she stay put at Levi's and take it easy, but she felt too restless. So she looked around the jewelry shops, chatting with the designers while he went off on whatever mysterious errands he was running.

They met up again a couple of hours later and Levi picked them up, running them back out to the airport and the helicopter, muttering something about how expensive gas was and how the heli wasn't an Uber they could order whenever they wanted a ride anywhere.

Beth was tense that Levi might start asking annoying questions about what they were doing in Queenstown together, but he didn't. He seemed a tad distracted himself.

Back in Brightwater Valley, after disembarking the helicopter, Finn walked with her back to where she'd parked Clint's old truck outside of HQ.

"We should get our living arrangements sorted out ASAP," Finn said. "So why don't you come to dinner at my place tomorrow night? I can show you around the house and you can see what you think."

Surprised, Beth stopped beside the truck and glanced up at him. "I can look around the house without you having to cook for me."

Finn's dark eyes gave nothing away. "Sure, but we're friends, right? Friends can invite each other over for a meal."

There was an odd fluttering feeling inside her, though she wasn't sure what it was.

Dinner sounded...nice.

"Just a friendly dinner, then," she said, only just stopping herself from making it a question.

He raised a brow. "What other kind of dinner would it be?"

"There is dinner, Finn. And there is *dinner*. A date kind of dinner."

His expression, as per usual, was completely enigmatic. "It's not a date kind of dinner."

The feeling inside her fluttered again and she tried to tell herself it wasn't disappointment. Of course it wasn't a date kind of dinner. Why would she think that it was? She didn't want it to be one anyway.

They weren't dating. They'd had one night of sex to deal with their chemistry, and it had been dealt with. Sure, his nearness still made her heart race, but that would fade in time.

Then he'd become just an ordinary friend.

A friend you're having a child with.

Yes. Exactly.

"No, of course it isn't a date kind of dinner." She was conscious of her flaming cheeks and how he could probably see she was blushing. "I didn't think it was."

"Okay." His tone was devoid of expression. "So tomorrow night, then?"

"Sure." Beth forced a smile. "Love to."

It was just dinner with the father of her baby.

No big deal.

Finn didn't want to talk to Chase about Beth, but the moment they touched down in Brightwater Valley after their trip to Queenstown, he knew he was going to have to.

Because he couldn't leave what she'd said to him earlier at Levi's place, about what they were going to tell people about their relationship, alone.

Friends, she'd said. Friends who were having a baby together. She'd looked at him uncertainly as she'd said it, as if she knew how ludicrous it sounded too.

Because it was ludicrous. Not so much the friends having babies together—he was sure some friends did that—but the part assuming he and Beth were friends. They weren't. Not especially.

In fact, he didn't know what they were, and he didn't like that one bit. Gray areas were tough things, and this whole situation was a gray area. They weren't in a relationship, yet they weren't strangers either. It was technically a one-night stand, yet they interacted almost on a daily basis.

Now he'd made the decision to be there during her pregnancy, what did that make them? Flatmates? Platonic partners? What? And how would it work when the baby was born?

No, he didn't like any of this, and although talking about personal shit wasn't his favorite, he could use some advice. Chase, in addition to being his brother and now a prospective uncle-to-be, was also the only one who knew he'd slept with Beth.

The only problem was that Chase's advice was invariably infuriating. In which case he'd have to suck it up. Because while his brother's advice might be infuriating, it always ended up being invaluable.

Chase was still out on the horse trek Finn was supposed to take instead of going to Queenstown, so he had to wait to see him until the afternoon. Then he finally tracked Chase down to the Rose, where his brother was having a well-earned beer and a chat with Jim, the proprietor.

"Hey," Chase said as Finn came into the pub. "You want a beer?"

"Sure." Finn came over to the bar and leaned an elbow on it. "I need to talk to you."

Chase raised an eyebrow. "You coming to me for a chat? That's a first."

Finn didn't rise to the bait. "In private."

"Sounds serious," Jim said, delivering the requested beer. Then he coughed. "I'll leave you to it."

Finn grabbed his beer, turned, and headed to one of the tables in the back corner of the bar, away from the door and from anyone that might overhear. It was the table everyone went to when they wanted a private conversation.

Chase followed, giving Finn a look as they both sat down. "It *is* serious then if you want to sit here. Everything okay?"

Finn pondered how he was going to broach the topic, then took a sip of his beer, put it down on the table with a bang, and said, "Beth's pregnant." Because really, there was no other way to say it. "No one else knows, so I'd appreciate it if you keep it between you and me for the time being."

His brother's eyes widened in surprise, then narrowed immediately into thin slits of silver. "You idiot," he said.

Despite himself, Finn was pleased Chase automatically assumed it was his fault rather than

Beth's, since that's definitely where the blame lay. And yeah, he'd accept he'd been an idiot. It was true. He had been.

"I know." He met his brother's gaze squarely. "Believe me, I'm fully aware of how much of an idiot I am."

Chase shook his head. "I'd have thought—"

"Yeah, yeah, spare me the lecture. It was just the one time without a condom, and she said she was on the pill. And," he added, "just so we're clear, I believe her."

His brother snorted. "Beth's not a liar. If she said she was, she was."

"The hows and whys aren't important right now anyway." Finn picked up his beer again and took another healthy sip. "The reason we were in Queenstown was so she could get a pregnancy test and find out for certain if she was pregnant. And she is."

Chase sipped on his beer, studying him. "So what's the plan?"

Of course Chase assumed he had one since Chase always had a plan for every eventuality and he was not tolerant of those who didn't. Plus he had strong views on taking responsibility for one's actions.

Luckily, it was something Finn agreed with him on.

"The plan is that she's either going to move in

with me or I'll move in with her for the duration of the pregnancy. She's got a lot of fatigue and the morning sickness is kicking in, and I want to be able to keep an eye on her."

"How does she feel about all of this?"

Finn thought about Beth's pale face and the dark circles beneath her eyes as she'd told him about her postnatal depression. About the glimmer of fear in the green depths of those eyes.

She'd said she wanted to handle this herself and had put a lot of effort into pushing him away, but he could tell that she needed reassurance. She also needed support, especially if she had another bout of depression.

She hadn't wanted to tell him about it, he was sure of that, and he got it. Mental health was a thorny issue for some people. But not for him. He didn't care what issues she had. She was pregnant with his baby which meant he was going to stick by her whatever happened.

"She's been knocked on her ass, quite frankly," he said, which wasn't revealing her secrets. It was merely letting Chase know that for all her attempts at putting on a brave face, she wasn't feeling great about it. "Which is why I want to be around for her."

"Yeah, solid plan." Chase eyed him. "And you? How do you feel about it? Is it something you want?"

Finn didn't flinch. "Yes, I do, though it doesn't matter what I want. She's having my baby and I'm not going to leave her in the lurch. I'm not going to be an absent father like Dad was either. I'll be here for the child and for her too."

This was clearly not a surprise for Chase, who only nodded. "Is Beth okay with you doing that?"

Finn looked down at the beer bottle in his hands, smoothing down one edge of the label that had started to peel away from the glass. "That is the issue. I don't think she's entirely pleased with the idea, no."

"Ah," Chase murmured. "So she's not going to be entirely pleased when you insist on marriage either."

Finn went very still, staring unseeing at the label.

Marriage. Shit, was that something he was actually contemplating? Chase clearly thought it was, but Chase was a traditionalist about stuff like that.

The baby needs a father. And a family. Like you had once and then lost.

It had been a long time since his mother had died. So long he barely remembered what it had been like when the Kellys had been a family all together. Back before his father had drowned his grief in a pint glass.

When Sheri had died, Finn had been very conscious of not wanting to end up like that—a grieving widower chasing forgetfulness and pain relief at the pub. And now that he was going to be a father, he was even more certain he didn't want to end up like his dad.

He couldn't bear the thought of any child of his

being alone the way he and Chase had been alone, most nights trying to cook themselves dinner because their dad was out. Having to get themselves to school because he was still sleeping off the effects of the night before.

Their father hadn't cared what they were doing, not one bit.

Yeah, he wasn't going to be that kind of father. He wouldn't. He wanted to be in his child's life every day. He wanted to be around for them after school and take them fishing, take them hiking. Take them riding. Show them the glory of nature around them and let them grow up safe in the love and support of the people who lived here.

He wanted his child to have his name.

Shit. He was getting all Neanderthal about this even more, wasn't he?

"I hadn't got that far," he said, finally lifting the beer bottle and taking another sip.

"It's crossed your mind though, right?"

"Maybe. For the kid's sake. But Beth won't like it." That would be an understatement. "In fact, I'm pretty sure she'll refuse point-blank if I offer."

"Well, if she won't marry you, there's not much you can do about it." Chase was silent for a moment. "Is that something you'd want though? To get married again?"

Finn stared at the bottle in his hands, trying to sort through the complicated tangle of emotions sitting in his gut. "I wouldn't have chosen it, no. But if Beth's pregnant..."

"You don't have to marry her," Chase said quietly. "Brightwater Valley might be a bit behind the times, but we've moved on a little since the turn of the century. I'm talking about the turn of the nineteenth century here."

His brother was right—he didn't have to marry her. Yet some part of him knew already that living together wouldn't be enough, not when he was a man who when he committed to something he committed fully.

That's how it had happened with Sheri. They'd been inseparable since they were kids, making huts in the bush and pretending they were Robinson Crusoe. Fighting dragons together, then fishing for eels in the creeks, terrifying each other with stories of the *taniwha*, the sacred Māori monster that lived in the waterways.

Then came the day of the school dance, when they were both fifteen, and she'd worn a dress for the first time since he could remember.

He'd known in that moment, with a bone-deep certainty, that he was going to marry her one day. Just like he knew now, with that same bone-deep certainty, that he'd be there for his child. And he'd be there for Beth too.

It wasn't love. How could it be when they didn't know much about each other? No, it was about the fear in her eyes and the grief when she'd told him about the loss of her first baby. About her postnatal depression.

She was a strong woman, a woman used to dealing with things on her own, he could already tell that. It made him want to know why she'd felt that way and who had left her. Who had hurt her.

It made him want to fix it because that's the kind of guy he was. He was a fixer, a protector. He took care of the people who were important to him, and whether she liked it or not, she was now important to him.

Sure, his feelings about marriage were complicated ones but the choice itself was simple. He did want to marry her, give both her and their kid some legal protection. Also she was alone here. She had no one. Sure, she had Indigo and Izzy, and they were hugely supportive. But Izzy had Chase and Gus now, and Indigo...well, she was currently being very distracted by Levi.

Beth needed someone in her corner, and shit, while he didn't love her—love was something he'd been hoping to avoid for possibly the rest of his life—he'd definitely be that someone.

"No," Finn murmured, "I know I don't have to marry her. But yes, it's something I want." He finally looked up from his bottle and met his brother's gaze. "She needs someone to support her out here."

Chase stared back. "Do you love her?"

"No. But that's not the point. She's on her own. I know she's got Izzy and Indigo, but I'm the father of her child. There's a connection there and I think she needs it."

His brother was quiet for a long time, gazing at him meditatively. "You're wrong, you know. Love *is* kind of the point."

Naturally Chase would say that. He hadn't been a great believer in love a few months ago, not after his first wife had left. However, all of that had changed after he'd met Isabella Montgomery and fallen for her like a ton of bricks.

Finn could see where his brother was coming from, but it wasn't in the cards for him. Not again.

"Not for me it isn't. Been there. Done that. Got the T-shirt."

"Keep an open mind, that's all I'm saying. Anyway, what about her? She's not in love with you, is she?"

Finn gave a short laugh. "Hell no. She's pissed at me for being so insistent. She wants to take care of all of this herself. Not because she doesn't want me involved per se, I don't think. I suppose she's used to handling things on her own and doesn't want anyone getting in the way."

"Sounds familiar." Chase looked amused.

Finn scowled. "I accept help when I need it, come on."

"Sure you do. And Elvis is alive and well and living just across the lake."

Finn debated rising to the bait, then decided not to. He had enough on his plate without arguing with his brother. "Your point being?"

"No point. It's just going to be fun watching you two butt heads."

"Thanks for the support." He kept his tone dry as dust. "Don't suppose you have any other special brotherly advice?"

"Would you take it even if I did?"

"Depends on what it is and whether I agree with it or not."

Chase grinned. "Well, okay, my advice would be to go carefully. I live with an extremely stubborn woman and having a degree in stubborn myself, we do have some battles. But compromise works, as does being up front and honest about what you want and why."

It wasn't anything Finn didn't know already, since Sheri had been pretty stubborn herself. Yet they'd figured out how to live with each other in a way that made their own brand of stubborn work well for them, so perhaps he could do the same with Beth.

Of course, that was all going to depend on whether or not she wanted to, and right now that was up for debate. Either way he was going to have to go carefully.

"Compromise sounds annoying," he observed, taking a last sip of his beer.

"Tell me about it," Chase muttered feelingly.

"She wanted to see my place before she made a decision, so I offered her dinner at mine so she could have a look around."

"Food," his brother said with the air of someone with a great deal of experience. "If you want to convince a woman of something, good food is vital. Cook her a meal she likes, offer her cheese or chocolate, or both, the works. I can pretty much guarantee you'll get a good result."

Finn thought about the chicken soup he'd made Beth and how hungrily she'd eaten it.

"Hmmm," he said. "Sounds like good advice for once."

"Hey," Chase protested, looking offended.

Finn pointed his beer bottle at him in a sudden fit of inspiration. "Sausage rolls."

Chase blinked. "Sausage rolls? Is that some kind of code for—"

"Relax, Beth likes them." His brain was already thinking of possibilities, ways he might be able to win her over. "I might have to pay a visit to Bill's tomorrow."

"Go early," Chase advised unnecessarily, since everyone who lived in Brightwater knew that if you wanted some of Bill's baking, you had to be early. "And if he tells you he doesn't have any scones left, don't listen. He always keeps a batch in the back for emergencies."

"Not sure about scones."

"If you want to propose to her, which I'm assuming you're going to do, then you'll need all the help you can get." Chase got a distant look in his eye. "Oh, and if you're very lucky, he might do some eclairs. Got one for Izzy a couple of days and she was...uh...let's just say she was very grateful."

"Noted," Finn murmured, deciding that the visit to Bill's wouldn't just include a tour of the baking cabinet; it would also involve some discussion.

Because he couldn't leave anything to chance, not with this.

Bethany Grant was going to marry him. All she had to do was say yes.

Chapter 11

BETH SPENT THE FOLLOWING MORNING IN THE gallery with Izzy and Indigo, looking over Teddy Grange's latest batch of goods. Teddy was tall, slender, and pretty, in her early sixties and with still-bright blond hair in a long braid down her back. She wore jeans, a plain white linen button-down shirt, and some expensive-looking rubber rain boots and somehow managed to look effortlessly elegant as well as practical.

She had an olive grove at the vineyard and was doing a range of flavored olive oils, as well as branching out into skincare. There were also jams, jellies, and a new product Beth was especially intrigued about: olive marmalade.

Teddy had spread some on a couple of crackers with some nice cheese to try, and Beth had wondered whether she'd feel too sick to be able to stomach it. Plus cheese could be problematic for pregnant women. However, the cheese was a smoky cheddar, so not one of the forbidden cheeses; also the olive marmalade smelled divine enough that she hadn't been able to resist.

It turned out to be delicious, salty and a little

sweet and perfect with the cheese, and she was disappointed there weren't more jars available. Izzy was a stickler for making sure there was enough stock in the gallery.

"How are you feeling today?" Izzy asked after Teddy had left. "Indigo said you weren't well yesterday."

"She really wasn't," Indigo, who was sitting on the counter knitting, confirmed.

Izzy finished with the display she was fussing with and frowned at Indigo. "Must you sit on the counter?"

"Yes." Indigo didn't look up from her knitting. "Indeed, I must."

Izzy sighed and looked back at Beth, who'd brought along a couple of pairs of earrings she'd just finished and was now adding them to the list of stock. "You're okay though?"

Beth tried to ignore the little pulse of guilt that went through her, shoving it away and giving Izzy a big smile instead. "Yeah, much better today, thanks."

"Good." Izzy came over to the counter and examined her thoroughly. "You're still looking tired though. Are you getting enough sleep?"

Beth gave a sigh. God save her from overly invested friends concerned for her well-being.

If this morning sickness kept up, she wasn't going to be able to hide being pregnant for long, not when she saw Izzy and Indigo every day. Not to mention every other person in Brightwater. And yeah, she did feel guilty about hiding it from them.

But while things were still uncertain, she didn't see another choice. Finn might have no doubt whatsoever about her pregnancy being fine, but she was still on the fence. Plus there were their living arrangements still to get sorted out.

God save her from stubborn, overly involved men too.

Then again, she couldn't deny she was looking forward to seeing Finn tonight, no matter how overly involved he was being. She was curious about his place, and being in his presence was... reassuring.

Not that she needed reassuring, of course, and not that there were any other feelings involved. And definitely nothing to do with the chemistry still sizzling between them. She wasn't getting involved with him, and this living-arrangement thing was just that: a living arrangement. She was only willing to entertain it as long as he wasn't going to be a pain in the butt to live with.

"Yes, Mom, I'm getting enough sleep," she said to Izzy, who was still staring at her with concerned, dark eyes. "Stop fussing."

Izzy pulled a face. "I'm not."

"You kind of are." Indigo turned her work around and prepared to knit back along her row. "But don't get me wrong, I approve of fussing."

"Well, I don't," Beth said firmly. "You've done your shift, Izzy, so run along, there's a good girl."

"Hey, far be it from me to be a kind, considerate friend looking out for you." Izzy reached over the counter to grab her purse. "Oh, by the way, do you want to meet at the Rose tonight for dinner? Gus did well with her latest report card and Chase wants to do a little something special for her."

"I'd love to," Indigo said before Beth could speak, "but Beth has a date."

Beth had told her friend that she wouldn't be home for dinner that night, and while she'd debated giving her a tiny white lie about who she was going out to dinner with, in the end she'd gone with honesty since everyone was going to find out about her and Finn at some point anyway.

However, she'd absolutely told Indigo it was *not* a date.

"It's not a date," she insisted, giving Indigo an annoyed look. "I told you that already. It's just a friendly dinner."

Indigo knitted on calmly. "A friendly dinner date."

"I'm sorry, did you say something? *Indy?*"

Indigo stopped knitting and scowled. "Stop that."

"Hey," Izzy said, frowning. "What's all this about a date? And with who?"

"Finn," Indigo said and smirked.

Oh boy. Indigo was on fire today.

Beth leaned her elbows on the counter. "What's

got your goat? Did Levi give you another ride home that you apparently didn't want?"

Indigo opened her mouth to reply when Izzy, clearly losing patience, said, "Can at least one of you please stop sniping at the other long enough to fill me in?"

"I'm going to Finn's for dinner tonight," Beth said before Indigo could stick her oar in yet again. "He asked me over and I said yes."

"Oh." Izzy's tone was determinedly, suspiciously neutral. "How nice."

"We're just friends," Beth felt compelled to point out. "It's a friends dinner."

Izzy held up her hands. "Hey, I didn't say anything."

"You didn't have to," Beth muttered, not in the mood to be teased. "I can hear your skepticism from here."

Indigo lowered her knitting and reached out to pat Beth's hand apologetically. "Sorry, I didn't mean to be snarky."

Beth wasn't in the mood to be placated either and gave Indigo a narrow look.

"Seriously." Indigo patted her again. "I'm grumpy today."

Her irritation eased, followed by a rush of love for her two friends. She really did appreciate them and the support they gave each other, and she hated lying to them.

"It's okay." She gave Indigo's hand a squeeze back. "I'm grumpy today too."

"Any particular reason?" Izzy asked, still looking concerned.

"Just hormone stuff." Which wasn't a lie. There *was* hormone stuff going on.

Indigo resumed knitting. "That's lame," she said. "Do you want me to cover your shift for you this afternoon?"

Beth shook her head. "It's okay. I can manage. I'm going to Finn's after I've finished anyway." She frowned as a thought struck her. "Do you need a ride up to the farmhouse?"

"No, thank you." Indigo finally put her knitting down. "I think I might walk back."

"I can take you," Izzy offered. "I've got Chase's truck so I can pick Gus up from school in a couple of hours."

Indigo paused a moment, as if thinking about it, but Beth didn't miss the way she glanced out the windows that looked over the main street outside, as if she was looking for something.

Or someone.

"Uh," she said, "thanks, Izzy, but I'll pass." In a sudden flurry of movement, she put her knitting in her project bag, slipped off the counter, slung the bag over her shoulder, and hurried to the door. "Gotta go. Bye."

Beth and Izzy watched her rush out, both of

them noting Levi standing outside HQ chatting with the Granges.

"Interesting," Izzy murmured.

"Very interesting," Beth agreed.

After Izzy finally left, Beth spent the afternoon setting up a display for some handmade quilts she'd sourced from Queenstown, looking at stock levels, and chatting with a few tourists who'd come out to Brightwater Valley to look around. Shirley, who often helped Bill out in the general store, came past and talked to her a bit about more craft things she was working on that the gallery might want to showcase, mainly some supercute soft toys and hand-knitted shawls.

Then Beth sat at the counter with her sketchbook, sketching out some new design ideas that she'd had, trying to keep her brain occupied and not worrying away at the situation she found herself in.

Which worked quite well until five o'clock came around and it was time to shut up shop and head to Finn's. He'd knocked on the farmhouse door that morning to let her know he was taking a trek out for the day but he'd be home by five and that she should come around when the gallery closed.

After she'd finished closing-up duties, she went into the little bathroom for a last-minute fuss with her appearance, berating herself even as she did so for caring. Because as Finn had already told her, it wasn't a date. Her appearance shouldn't matter one iota.

Yet still she found herself fiddling with the bits of hair that had come down from the bun she'd put it in and wondering whether the pale green sundress she was wearing, that she'd bought in Queenstown a couple of weeks back, didn't make her look a bit washed out.

In the end, sick of herself and her angsting, she left both her hair and her dress as is, left the gallery, got in Clint's truck, and drove along the gravel road that headed past town. Chase lived about ten minutes away, up a winding gravel drive, and Finn's house was just beyond that. They shared the same driveway, and as she drove past Chase's place, Gus gave her a cheerful wave from their deck.

The deep, dark green and spicy dampness of the bush closed in around her as she got farther up the driveway before it suddenly opened out into the brilliant sunshine of late afternoon as she rounded a bend.

Finn's house was built high on a flat bit of land on the side of the hill, overlooking Brightwater Lake. The house itself was wooden, with the same pitched roof as Clint's farmhouse, but unlike the farmhouse Finn's had an upper story. It was also surrounded by a wide, wooden, covered deck that had various chairs and sofas on it, plus a coffee table, as if sitting out there enjoying the sun and the view was something Finn and his guests did on a regular basis.

There was also, sitting near the edge of the flat area, overlooking the bush and the lake, an outdoor bath.

Hanging from the eaves of the awning covering the deck were wind sculptures made of metal and adorned with beads that glittered and twisted in the light breeze, while wind chimes made of bamboo made soft clacking sounds.

It was a welcoming place. Beth felt it immediately as she drove up onto the level gravel parking space beside the house and got out.

The sounds of the chimes and the whispering of the wind in the trees around the house, the warmth of the sun shining down, and the evening chorus of bellbirds, tūī, and kereru from somewhere in the bush made her feel as if there was something settling in her soul—as if something that had been tight and fearful was relaxing.

There was peace here. Maybe that was fanciful, but she felt it all the same.

As soon as she closed the door of the truck, Karl came bounding out of the house and along the path toward her, tongue hanging out.

"Hey, boy," she murmured as he approached, tail wagging frantically. "How are you enjoying living with Finn, hmm?" She gave him a scratch behind the ears, and he gave her a big doggy grin in return. "Does he tell you what to do too?"

Karl, unbothered by such disloyalty, licked her

hand, then turned away and bounded back up the stairs to the deck, where a tall figure had appeared.

Finn.

He was in his usual jeans, but instead of a T-shirt, he had on a casual, soft-looking black cotton shirt. His feet were bare, and his black hair was damp as if he'd just had a shower, and he was the sexiest thing she'd ever seen.

Her breath caught as she approached, her heart suddenly beating way too fast.

Karl nosed at his hand for pats, which Finn duly gave; then, the visitor having been properly greeted, the dog disappeared back into the house.

Finn watched her, his dark gaze giving nothing away, but there was what looked like the beginnings of a smile at one corner of his beautiful mouth, and she was blushing like an idiot.

"For the record," he said as she came up the steps to the deck, "yes, I do tell Karl what to do, and yes, he likes it."

"Of course he does. He's a dog." Beth found herself full of awkwardness, her cheeks burning even more intensely. "Uh…so…how was your trek today?"

"It was good." His gaze roamed over her as if he was hungry for the sight of her, and she felt herself get breathless.

This was stupid. It wasn't a date. They were friends having dinner together while she looked over his house, that was all. So why she should be getting wound up about his sexiness and the way he looked at her, she had no idea.

"This is great." Beth gestured at the house. "It's kind of like standing in a…a crow's nest or something."

Unexpectedly and very badly for her poor heart, Finn's mouth curved in a brief but blinding smile that momentarily stole what breath remained in her body.

"Yeah, it is, isn't it? I like being able to see the landscape, and Sheri didn't want to be buried in the bush, so we built here, where there was a view, and we didn't have to do much clearing."

"It's honestly amazing," Beth said quite truthfully, because it was amazing. Then she nodded at the wind sculptures twisting in the breeze. "Are those yours?"

"Gus." The smile lingered around his sexy mouth. "She makes them and gives them to me for my birthday and for Christmas. She made the wind chimes too."

Beth wouldn't have thought Finn was the kind of guy who'd like such whimsical things, let alone display them, and maybe he didn't. But he hung them out anyway for his niece because she gave them to him.

Are you sure he's not the perfect man?

Beth shoved that thought aside.

"They're really pretty," she said. "I love them. And I like that bath too. Do you use it?"

Finn's smile abruptly disappeared. "No," he said, his voice getting that flat, uninflected note in it again. "Not anymore."

Beth thought she knew why he didn't use it anymore, but she wasn't going to question further. Clearly it was a subject he didn't want to talk about, which likely meant it had something to do with his wife.

And sharing griefs and their pasts wasn't really what this evening was about. It was about seeing whether she could live here and having a companionable dinner, and that's all.

So she left it, and when Finn gestured to the door, she stepped inside without another word.

———

Finn showed Beth inside, determined not to watch her expressions like a hawk, looking for signs as to her opinion on the house.

He'd thought he was fine with her choosing to stay at the farmhouse and him moving in there; in fact, he thought he'd maybe even prefer it, since this was the home he'd shared with Sheri.

Yet the moment he saw her come up the steps to the deck, looking so pretty in a light green sundress, her pale hair blowing around her face in the breeze, the color of her eyes enhanced by the color of her dress, he knew he wouldn't prefer it after all. That somehow Beth belonged here.

It was a disturbing feeling and he didn't like it, because Sheri had belonged here too and surely the two women couldn't coexist in the same space, even when one of those women was a ghost.

He tried to ignore it, yet when she'd mentioned his house being like a crow's nest, he'd felt a sudden rush of pleasure. Because the observation was exactly what he'd thought when the house had finally finished being built and he and Sheri had stood on the deck looking at the view, masters of all they surveyed.

He shouldn't be pleased about that. Beth was supposed to be different so she could occupy a different space in his head from the space he'd reserved for Sheri. She wasn't supposed to be the same.

Then she had to go and mention the bath, which wasn't her fault; she didn't know that it had been Sheri who'd had it put there, but still. That had only made him even more uncomfortable.

Perhaps having her come here was a mistake. Perhaps he should move into the farmhouse instead. Then again, he'd already prepared dinner for her and had spent a good half an hour this morning convincing Bill to make her some sausage rolls for hors d'oeuvres and eclairs for dessert.

Finn took her through the short hallway to the big open-plan living area, with a galley kitchen down one end, a dining table in the middle, and a couple of sofas grouped around a big wood burner down the other.

One wall was all windows and big glass sliding doors that opened out onto the deck and gave views over the bush and the lake beyond, while the opposite wall was lined with wooden bookshelves stuffed with books and photos and other bits and pieces.

Karl was on his big cushion next to the wood burner, his tail making thumping noises as they both came in. But he didn't get up. Clearly, he thought all his doggy duties were done for the day, the lazy beast.

Beth looked around curiously, then after he'd showed her down to the kitchen end of the room gave a little exclamation of delight as she spotted—of all things—his kitchen cabinets.

"These are beautiful, Finn," she said, running her hand over the dark honey-golden wood of the cupboard doors. "Did you make them yourself?"

"Yeah." He pulled open another cupboard and got out a couple of glasses, trying not to be pleased at the admiration he heard in her voice. "Chase made some for his kitchen and I thought they'd look good here too."

"The wood is beautiful." She ran a slender finger along the countertops that he'd also made, silver bracelets chiming gently. "What is it?"

"Rimu. It's a native tree."

"Gorgeous." She glanced at him, green eyes dancing in the way that had so fascinated him when he'd first met her. "Who knew you'd be so good at woodworking?"

A shiver of heat went through him. She was so desirable, shining like the sun outside, teasing and a little flirtatious but so warm with it. A genuine warmth, not that fake bullshit she gave the others where it was all just plaster covering up the cracks.

And now you know just what cracks there are.

It was true; now that she'd told him a bit about what had happened to her, he had some insight into why she might be so determined to put on a brave face. Another man might have been put off by it, but he wasn't. No, if anything, he wanted to know even more. Such as who the father of her baby had been and where was he now and why he'd left her to twist in the wind after she'd lost their baby, since clearly that's what he'd done. Because if he hadn't left her, if he'd been any kind of man, Beth wouldn't have come halfway around the world to Brightwater Valley.

Yeah, you're screwed.

Finn shoved the thought away along with the flirtatious comeback he wanted to give her about how he was good at other things as well. Instead, he turned and went to the fridge, getting out a beer for himself and the orange juice he'd bought specially for her.

"We're jacks of all trades here," he said, putting

his beer down on the counter so he could pour the juice. "We have to be. So yeah, I can do some cabinet making if I need to." He pushed the glass along the counter in her direction. "You okay with orange juice? Or would you prefer water?"

"Orange juice is fine." She picked up the glass and took a sip. "Mmm, this is good. Is this hand-squeezed from your own orange tree?"

Another tease, he could tell by the gleam in her eyes. But he wasn't going there, merely giving a shrug as he opened his beer. "Are you hungry? I've got a casserole in the oven and some salad. Also a couple of special things for hors d'oeuvres and dessert."

Beth leaned against the counter and smiled. "Special things for hors d'oeuvres sounds fancy. And especially for dessert. What are they?"

"It's a surprise," Finn said.

"Oh, I love surprises." Beth's smile deepened. "Can I guess?"

He really wanted her to. And he wanted to drop hints, turn it into a game. Make her eyes sparkle, make her smile get even brighter, call the sunshine from her. Then he wanted to take her face between his hands and—

Shit. He had to get a handle on himself, stop letting his dick do all his thinking for him; otherwise, this was all going to get messy, and it was already far more messy than it needed to be.

But you're thinking of marrying her, so what are

you going to do if she agrees? Stay celibate all your life?

The thought stuck in his head, lit up in blazing neon.

Two months ago, before she'd appeared, he'd have said that yeah, staying celibate for the rest of his life seemed like a solid plan. Even a month ago, before they'd slept together, he would have been okay with it.

But now…all he could think about was how soft her skin had been beneath his hands and how sweet her mouth had tasted. How warm she'd been and how much pleasure she'd given him. And how celibacy seemed so cold and hard and bleak compared to her.

You can't do it, can you?

His breath caught. Dammit, he needed to think this through. He also was getting way ahead of himself, since she hadn't even agreed to move in with him, let alone marry him.

"No guessing." He shoved himself away from the counter. "Come on, let me give you a tour of the house."

She must have picked up on his tone because her smile dimmed, but she didn't make any protest, merely saying, "Sure, that would be great."

His place wasn't huge, so it didn't take very long, but he showed her the bathroom along the hallway and then the two bedrooms on either side of it.

One he used as a guest room and the other was an office. Up the stairs was his bedroom and a tiny en suite that Sheri had insisted on, and again he felt that discomfort of having Beth in a place his wife had occupied so intimately.

Especially when she lifted her head and looked up at the skylight in the ceiling he'd had put in so he and Sheri could look at the stars at night.

"That's so cool," Beth exclaimed with delight. "Do you stargaze in bed?"

Tension crawled through him, along with the intense urge to change the subject and walk away.

But if you're thinking about marriage, you're going to have to get used to her being in the same place Sheri was. You're going to have to get used to her liking the same things too.

That was true. Because what other option did he have? He'd built this house himself, along with help from Chase, Levi, and some of the Brightwater locals, and he couldn't see himself moving out of it permanently.

Plus it was also the place he'd lived with Sheri, and although the memories here were painful, they were also comforting.

He didn't want to leave. But if Beth agreed to be his wife, this was where she'd live too, and this was where she'd sleep. With him. Potentially in this bed. Watching the same stars he used to watch with Sheri...

Finn was conscious of Beth studying him, a slight crease between her fair brows.

"Are you okay?" she asked quietly.

"I'm fine." His tone was brusque but he couldn't seem to moderate it. "Let's go downstairs. There's something else I want to show you."

He didn't wait for her to respond, simply turning and heading back down the stairs and going back into the living room. Pausing beside one of the long glass sliding doors, he unlocked it and pushed it back, stepping outside onto the deck. Then he went down the steps that led to a small, white-shell path.

The path led not only to the bath that stood on the edge of the flat garden, but also to a tiny wooden cabin built into the side of the hill nearby. He could hear Beth's footsteps crunching on the shells behind him, so he didn't pause as he went up to the door of the cabin and opened it.

This was always going to be the real test, showing her Sheri's shed, where she used to paint and do the other arty things she'd loved. It had always surprised him how such a practical woman had such an artistic bent, but that had been one of the things he'd loved about her. There had been so much more to her than met the eye.

Initially he'd planned on setting aside some of his own workbench in the garage near the house for Beth and her jewelry making—because he had to give her a place she could work—but he'd known it wasn't going to compare to Clint's. The little art cabin, though, was perfect. It had a wide bench and lots of built-in cupboards, cubbyholes, and shelves. And it faced the view, with large windows for inspiration purposes.

Sheri had loved it out there, and instinctively he knew Beth would love it too. And he didn't want to show it to her—he really didn't. It was Sheri's place, not hers. But this reluctance wasn't going to help when it came to getting what he wanted. Which was her marrying him and creating a family for their child.

There wasn't much room in the cabin, since the storage and the big built-in desk took up all the space. So Beth remained in the doorway, gazing around at it. Then she looked at him and this time she didn't smile.

"This is gorgeous," she said. "But I get the sense you don't want me to be here, do you?"

"Of course I do." Again, he sounded far too brusque, which irritated him. He was supposed to be encouraging her to be here, not actively trying to scare her away. "This is where I thought you could set up your jewelry workshop."

She glanced around again, and he could tell she liked it, because her mouth softened. "This wasn't yours though, was it?"

Such a loaded question and asked so gently. Yet

he could feel all his barriers come up hard, the desire to keep his memories, to keep Sheri, all to himself. He didn't want to talk about her here, in this place she'd loved so much, a place that was hers and not for anyone else. Even he had to knock before he was allowed to come in.

Somehow, though, Beth knew, because she said quietly, "I don't have to be in here. I can set up my bench somewhere else."

Part of him was glad she hadn't explicitly mentioned Sheri, while another part was annoyed, hating how she pussyfooted around the topic, as if she didn't want to upset him.

Shit, he wasn't that fragile. Grief had done a number on him, sure, but it had been five years. The worst of it had passed. And bloody hell, he had to move on somehow. He was having a child, for God's sake.

"This was Sheri's art space," he said flatly, bringing up the topic so she didn't have to. "She used to paint and do other craft-type things in here, which is why there's so much storage. It's got a big desk though and lots of light. And it hasn't been used for years. You can put your jewelry stuff in here. It's a great space for it."

But Beth didn't look at the desk or the shelves around it. She only looked at him, and the sympathy in her eyes made something inside him throb.

She was so pretty, standing in the doorway

with the sun at her back shining in her pale hair and making her green eyes glow. The dress she wore clung to her figure, outlining every single curve. She was sunshine, every part of her, and he wanted to reach out and grab her, cover himself with her warmth.

He was so tired of being cold.

Yet his heart hurt, and he'd thought he'd be fine with her being here, but he wasn't. And he didn't know what to do about it except get out of here before he said something he regretted.

"Finn," she began.

But all he said was "Have a think about it."

And before she could say anything else, he pushed past her and headed back to the house.

Chapter 12

BETH STOOD FOR A MOMENT IN THE DOORWAY OF the gorgeous little cabin, watching Finn's tall figure stride back up the path to the house.

Her chest hurt, the warmth she'd felt the moment she'd stepped out of the truck and seen him standing on the deck waiting for her ebbing.

She'd loved his house, loved how it was full of light, how all the furniture was simple yet so comfortable looking, and that it was full of lots of different books and magazines and all sorts of other things a man with a curious mind might collect. She loved the kitchen with the beautiful, dark-golden cabinets Finn had made himself and obviously with a great deal of care and thought.

She loved this little cabin too, her heart instantly leaping at the sight of the wide desk and all the shelves and places to put things, and the magnificent view through the big windows.

But part of her also knew from the moment she'd stepped inside that this wasn't Finn's area. It was empty, for a start, and there were was something about it that made it feel like a more feminine space than masculine.

Then he'd said it was his wife's cabin, where she did her art.

That had felt like a punch to the gut, not so much it having been his wife's as the expression on his face when he'd said it. Hard. Fixed. A muscle in his jaw leaping, his mouth a carved line. His eyes had been so dark, no light in them whatsoever, just the raw edge of grief.

Of course. This was the house he'd lived in with Sheri, and here he was showing another woman around it. Another woman pregnant with his child.

Her heart ached. Because it was clear that though he hadn't wanted her to take the cabin and was deeply uncomfortable showing it to her, he'd brought her here anyway. Why? And why had he offered for her to move in? When it was still painful for him?

It's the baby he wants, not you.

The ache inside her deepened, though not for herself, because she already knew he didn't want her—not like that. They didn't have that kind of relationship anyway, which was something they'd agreed on. They weren't together and she wasn't disappointed about that, not when she didn't want anything more either.

What was clear was that they needed to talk about it. She didn't want her presence here to hurt him and if that really was the case, then obviously she couldn't move in. She wasn't his wife, and she didn't want him to feel as if she was taking Sheri's place.

Beth looked around the cabin, feeling the warmth and the welcome in it. The good energy that lingered in the air.

"Don't worry," she murmured. "I'll make sure he's okay."

Then she stepped back out again and walked back up the white-shell path to the deck.

Finn was standing in the middle of the living area, his back to the windows, his posture rigid. Karl had gotten up off his cushion and was nosing into Finn's hand, clearly picking up on the emotional tension in the air and wanting to offer his master some comfort.

Beth stepped through the doors and stood there a moment, wondering what to say that would help because she very much wanted to help.

Karl trotted over to her, gave her a sniff and licked her hand; then, as if deciding Finn was in good hands, he vanished out the door, onto the deck.

"Finn…I'm sorry," Beth began, hesitant. "I don't have to be here—"

"Yes, you do." He turned around sharply, dark eyes blazing. "You're pregnant with my child and that means you'll live here with me."

His deep voice was hoarse and his gaze so intense, so hot, she nearly went up in flames. But a thread of desperation ran through the words, the same desperation that burned in his eyes too.

A need gripped her to close the distance and touch him, run her hands across his tight shoulders and ease the tension in them, soothe him somehow with her presence the way he soothed her. But she got the distinct impression that wouldn't help.

"I made this," she said after a moment, her fingers brushing the pendant at her neck, "in the first couple of weeks I was in Brightwater. I found out what a koru was and that it stands for new life, peace, and strength. I loved the shape and the meaning, so I made myself a pendant I could wear." She swallowed, hoping she might be able to offer him something from her own experience. "I've never told anyone this before, so you're the first. I mean, I did try to tell Troy—he was my boyfriend before I came here—but he didn't want to hear it and certainly not after he left. I...I'd picked out a name for my baby when I was first pregnant. I named her Sunny. Because she was like a little ray of sunshine in my life." Beth closed her fingers around the pendant, her chest tight and sore. "She might not have been in my life for very long, but I was still her mother, and I didn't want grief to be her only legacy. I didn't want depression to be her monument either, not when her presence had made me so happy. So...that's what I chose. I chose the happiness she gave me. I pulled myself out of that depression and I came here to find a new future for myself, one that would be more worthy of Sunny's memory."

There were tears in her eyes, but she blinked them back because this wasn't about her and her own loss. This was about him and his. About how even in the depths of the black pit, there were still choices to be made and something to hold on to. Something to reach for.

She wasn't sure if giving him a small piece of herself would help, but she couldn't think of anything else to say.

Finn was silent, his expression taut, his dark eyes burning. Then he suddenly moved, closing the distance between them and taking her face between his hands.

She went still, her breath catching at the way he looked at her, at the desperation in his gaze. His palms were warm on her skin, his long, muscular body close, and she closed her eyes as his mouth came down, something inside her bursting into flames.

He kissed her hard, his lips hot and demanding on hers as if he'd been holding himself back too long and the leash had finally snapped and he was free. Devouring her as if he were starving and she were something delicious to eat.

It felt good to have him close, to have his mouth on hers and to taste him again. So *so* good. A relief, in fact. She put her palms flat to his chest and leaned into him, kissing him back as hungrily as he was kissing her, wanting his strength and his reassurance, wanting his hands on her giving her the pleasure she hadn't been able to stop thinking about for an entire month now.

He made a growling sound in his throat, propelling her over to the long, low leather couch that stood near the windows, then taking her down onto it.

His weight settled on her, and she wrapped her arms around his neck, her legs around his waist, arching up to press herself more firmly against his hot, iron-hard body.

He kissed her deeper, hotter, and she welcomed him, the rich taste of his mouth and the earthy, musky, masculine scent of him making her dizzy with desire.

She fumbled with the buttons of his shirt, desperate to feel the warmth of his skin. He helped, finally pulling it over the top of his head and off, and oh, he was glorious without his shirt. His torso was lean, every muscle cut, his skin smooth and tanned.

Beautiful. He was beautiful.

He didn't give her enough time to admire him though. His hands dropped to the hem of her sundress, pulling it up, and luckily it was stretchy so it didn't take much for her to wriggle out of it. He dealt with her underwear in seconds flat before getting rid of his clothes as well, and then she was being pressed back on the warm leather of the couch, both of them naked.

They were skin to skin, the heat being generated between them igniting into a bonfire of desire.

She couldn't think of anything but him, the feel of his body on hers, anchoring her, sheltering her, and the hot stroke of his tongue in her mouth. She kissed him back desperately, shivering with delight as he ran a hand down her body as if he couldn't wait to touch her, skimming over the curve of one breast, down her side, to her hip and thigh.

She spread her fingers out on his powerful shoulders, feeling the taut flex of his muscles, signs of his incredible strength. He made another of those delicious, demanding, masculine noises and shifted between her thighs, positioning himself.

"Tell me you want me, Beth," he growled in her ear. "I want to hear it."

"Yes, I want you," she gasped, ready to tell him whatever he needed to hear. "I want you so much, Finn."

"And where do you want me?"

"You know where."

"Tell me." Very gently he bit her earlobe. "Tell me specifically."

Oh God. Why was that so incredibly hot?

She swallowed. "I want you inside me. Now."

He didn't ask again, and he didn't hesitate,

pushing into her in a long, luxurious slide that had her moaning into his mouth. He felt so good inside her, so unbelievably good that she was shaking with the pleasure of it.

He went still then, his whole body tense, and she slid her hands down his back, stroking him, her hips lifting, encouraging him to move because she thought she might die if he didn't.

"Please," she whispered against his mouth. "Please..."

He began to move slowly, in a rhythm that left her panting and twisting, her nails digging into his back. His mouth moved too, trailing over her jaw and down her throat to the hollow where her pulse beat fast beneath the little silver koru nestled there. He kissed her, sucking gently, sending electric jolts of pleasure throughout her entire body.

She shuddered, his name a prayer on her lips, and she closed her eyes, sparks glittering and shimmering behind her closed lids. Everything had fallen away, all her fear of the future and what it might hold, all her worry she wouldn't be as strong as she thought she was, that she wouldn't be as brave— that she wouldn't be able to cope with what was coming and would fall into the pit again.

Yet now all of that was gone, crushed beneath the most glorious pleasure, a rush of delight and excitement and hope she hadn't felt in far too long. Not since the last time he'd held her in his arms.

Beth flung herself into it and surrendered, offering herself up to him, letting him take whatever he wanted and losing herself in pleasure.

He moved faster, harder, the sound of their combined breathing loud in her ears, and then he slipped a hand down between her thighs, stroking her so that suddenly everything broke apart in a shower of light and sparks, and she was trembling as ecstasy swamped her.

His movements became jerky, and he gasped her name in a hoarse, desperate voice before the pleasure came for him too and he buried his face in her neck, his breathing ragged and hot against her skin.

For long moments there was nothing but silence, not that Beth could speak even if she'd wanted to. She felt almost stunned by the speed and intensity of what had happened between them.

One minute she'd been talking to him about Sunny; the next she was on her back on the couch and he was inside her. Not that she was unhappy about it at all. Not when his body on hers felt good, a warm, heavy weight that wasn't crushing, only deeply reassuring.

She let her hands roam up and down the strong lines of his powerful back, stroking the oiled silk of his skin, admiring the tanned smoothness of it in the light coming through the windows. He didn't move and he didn't say anything, but his muscles relaxed under her touch, and it seemed to be something he enjoyed, so she kept doing it.

After what felt like a very long time, he finally lifted his head to look down at her, his gaze full of an expression she didn't understand.

"Are you okay?" he asked, his voice husky. "I'm sorry, I didn't—"

But she took one hand from his back and pressed a finger against the warm softness of his lips, silencing him. "Don't be sorry," she murmured. "I'm not."

The look in his eyes shifted and changed like the currents in a deep sea. "I wasn't supposed to do this again. It wasn't part of the plan for tonight. It wasn't part of the plan, full stop."

Beth met his gaze, letting him see that she wasn't disappointed about the way the evening was turning out, not at all. Some kind of tension had relaxed inside her, though she wasn't sure why, and maybe it was only the effect of a rather incredible orgasm, but whatever it was she felt good and not in a forced way.

This felt genuine. This felt real.

"Well," she said quietly, "maybe it should be."

He studied her face for a long moment and what he was thinking she couldn't tell. Sometimes she thought she knew what was going on in his head, and sometimes she had no idea. He could be hard to read.

"I wasn't thinking of only having you moving in, Beth," he said in a low voice.

"Oh?" She tried not to tense up, because she had a feeling she wasn't going to like this. "What else were you thinking about?"

Finn's dark eyes glittered. "I want you to marry me."

———————

He hadn't meant to come out with it like that. He'd meant to feed her some good food, let her relax, then bring the subject up as more of an idea to consider instead of an order she had to follow.

But he hadn't expected to be blindsided by his own feelings about her being here, in the same space he'd shared with Sheri. He'd genuinely thought it would be fine, because hell, it had been years since he'd lost Sheri, and everything else concerning Beth had felt so…easy and painless.

He hadn't expected to want her quite so intensely or feel the weight of the secret she'd given him, her baby's name. He'd been so short with her at the cabin, walking away without even an explanation, and yet she'd known what his problem had been anyway. Then had offered him a little piece of herself as a way to help. She was so generous with her caring that he'd been flooded with the most powerful desire for her.

He'd expected her to walk away or to change the subject, anything but notice his own grief and give him something to hold on to.

Then again, maybe he should have expected it. Beth seemed to be able to sense his emotions in a way that no one else was able to, not even his own brother.

He shouldn't have pushed her down onto the couch though, or taken her the way he had. It was exactly the opposite of what he'd told himself he was going to do. Sleeping with her had not been part of the plan, like he'd told her.

It was just…she was so beautiful, and he was so hungry. And looking down at her now, he knew that any thoughts of having a platonic marriage had just been a lovely fairy story he'd told himself to make himself feel better.

He wasn't going to be able to keep away from her. He didn't want to.

Beth's eyes went wide, the blush in her cheeks deepening. "Excuse me? You want to marry me?"

Finn held her gaze, unflinching. "I've been thinking about it a lot the past couple of days. Thinking about you and the baby and the future. I want our child to have my name and for both of you to have some legal protection. And…" He paused, letting her see how much this meant to him. "I want us to be a family."

She swallowed and he could see the pulse at the base of her throat start to race. Her body beneath his was tense, so he shifted to give her some space. But the movement and the heat of her skin and the sweet musky scent of sex and apricots was making him hard again.

He wanted to kiss her, run his hands over her skin, taste more of her, spend time on this couch exploring her lovely body, exploring all the brightness and sunshine that was part of her.

"Marriage," she repeated as if she didn't know the meaning of the word. "You want to marry me."

"Yes." He pushed back one of her pale curls, tucking it behind her ear, letting his fingers linger on the softness of her skin. "I should have said something earlier, but I was kind of hoping to build up to it."

"Finn, you barely know me. Also you could hardly stand for me to be in that little cabin out there just now. Your wife's cabin." There was no hesitation as she said the word *wife*, no flinching. As if she was confronting him with it. "Yet you want to marry me and presumably have me live here with you in this house? How is that even going to work?"

Good question. How?

Tension gripped him, though he tried to ignore it since he didn't want to ruin this moment by getting defensive.

But the problem was he didn't know how to answer her question. He didn't know how it was going to work. Because she wasn't wrong. They did barely know each other. And he had reacted badly to her being in Sheri's cabin. He wasn't even sure why.

She wasn't a threat to Sheri's memory. She

wasn't trying to replace her. She and Sheri weren't similar in any way. Hell, it had been five years. His wife's presence shouldn't *still* be weighing on him so heavily, right?

"I'll get you a cloth," he muttered, abruptly pushing himself away and off the couch, needing some time to think it through.

Or at least he tried to.

Until Beth's arms tightened around him, holding him where he was.

"Don't go," she said. "We need to talk about this."

"Beth..."

But she didn't let him go. "If you marry me, I'll be your wife, Finn. Have you thought about that? I'll be your wife, just like Sheri was—"

"No," he said sharply, before he could stop himself. "You won't be like Sheri. No one was like her, okay? You're different. You don't look like her, you don't act like her. You're pregnant. We're going to have a baby. It's not the same." His heart was beating very fast. "And I don't love you. That's why it works."

The flush of color had ebbed from her cheeks, leaving her pale, and he knew he'd hurt her, though why she should be hurt by any of this, when they didn't have feelings for each other, he had no idea. But she was.

With an effort, he got a grip on himself. "I'm sorry," he said with more gentleness this time. "I haven't had a woman in this house since she died and it's hitting me harder than I thought."

A tiny crease of concern appeared between her brows. "You haven't? Not at all?"

He hesitated a moment with the truth, because no one knew, and he wasn't in any hurry for people to find out. But Beth had given him a secret of her own and without being prompted. She'd simply offered it up, as if he was a man who deserved to know, a man she could trust. So how could he hold back now?

But it will make her important. It will make her mean something.

Yeah, well, she *was* important, and she did mean something. It wasn't love, but it was something all the same, and she deserved to know.

"No," he said. "In fact, I haven't been with a woman since she died." He couldn't stop himself from looking into her pretty green eyes, from holding her gaze so she could see the truth. "You're the first. You're the first in five years."

He could see the shock flicker over her face, and suddenly he didn't want to know what she thought. He couldn't bear any questions about it.

"Stay there." He needed to get some space, put some distance between them. "I'll get a cloth."

This time when he got up, she let him go.

He put on his jeans and stalked to the bathroom in the hallway, finding a soft cloth for her and turning on the hot tap for some warm water.

As the water ran, he muttered a curse under his breath. He shouldn't have said those things to her. Why had he? About Beth being different and how he didn't love her. About her being the first woman he'd been with in five years.

His emotions were all over the place and it wasn't fair to put them on her. She had nothing to do with Sheri, and all the issues he had were his to deal with, not hers. Especially when she had more than enough on her plate to handle as it was.

Then again, she did need to know where she stood, especially if she was going to be living with him and they were going to be married. A certain amount of honesty was required.

He'd learned that with Sheri in the first few months after they'd moved in together. He was a neat freak, and she was messy as hell, and things had been a bit fraught until they'd figured out a system that worked for both of them.

They'd had arguments after that, sure, but not very many of them. Sheri had been very forthright and honest, which had helped.

This is about more than her being untidy and you being neat. You don't even know if she is or not. You don't know anything about her.

Well, that was a lie. He knew she was bright and cheerful and pretty. He knew she'd lost a baby. He knew that she'd had postnatal depression and a partner called Troy who'd left her…

A heavy, powerful feeling shifted in his chest, but he shut it down hard before he could figure out what it was. Yeah, he knew bits and pieces about her. And he should probably be a little more forthcoming with her, but he could do that.

This thing between them would work. He'd make it work.

Turning the tap off and squeezing out the cloth, Finn brought it back to the living area. Beth had pulled one of the blankets that was hanging over the back of the couch around her, covering herself up, which was a pity. He loved looking at her naked.

She was looking at him, those big green eyes of hers full of emotion, sympathy, compassion, and all kinds of other things that made his soul ache and his spirit hungry. Suddenly he wanted everything he could see in her gaze, wanted it desperately, as if he'd been starved of it.

But that would involve him giving her things he wasn't ready to give, and he didn't know if he ever would, so he said nothing as he handed her the cloth.

She seemed to understand because she didn't say anything either, cleaning herself up wordlessly as he grabbed a shirt and put it on before going into the kitchen area to check on the casserole and start making the salad.

He was standing at the counter when Beth came over, still wrapped in the blanket. She watched him silently for a moment, then moved around behind him and put her arms around him.

Finn froze as the warmth of her body pressed against him. There was nothing demanding in it. It was simply her, giving him her warmth and comfort.

"I haven't been with anyone since Troy." Her voice was quiet. "So that's...probably about three or so years. You're my first since then too."

He didn't want to feel satisfied about that, but he did. Very, very satisfied.

"I didn't want it to be special," he said into the silence that followed. "I just wanted to...move on, I guess. But..." He hesitated but then said it, because she deserved to know. "It was special all the same. And so are you." He put his hands over hers where they rested on his stomach. "You're right—we don't know each other well, and yeah, I do have some issues about Sheri." He turned around, looking down at her, because this was important and he wanted to see her face. "I guess what I'm saying is that I'd like to get to know you. And I'll deal with those issues. I want this to work. I want you to live here and I want you in my bed. I want us to be together."

Her eyes were shadowed and full of that complicated mix of emotions he'd wanted so badly before, and her mouth was still full and red from his kisses.

And he felt desire rise again, hot and desperate,

bringing the knowledge with it that Beth deserved better than this—better than a man still living with the ghost of his first wife.

"I can't give you more than that," he went on, because he had to get it out now. "All I've got to offer is sex, financial support, and to be there for you when you need it. To be there for our kid too. But if that's enough for you…"

She didn't say anything, the emotions shifting in her eyes. Then she pulled the blanket from around her body, let it fall to the floor, went up on her toes, and kissed him. Hard.

And Finn forgot how difficult this was turning out to be and how complicated. Forgot about everything as desire gripped him by the throat, choking him. Nothing was more important than the woman in his arms and the feel of her mouth on his.

Nothing.

He lifted her into his arms and carried her upstairs to his bedroom, where he laid her down on top of the dark blue comforter, then pulled off his clothes.

She lifted her arms to him in wordless invitation, as if she'd been his lover for years, and it made his heart clench, made him hungry. And he realized it wasn't only because he wanted her body and the pleasure she gave him, but also because it was her.

She didn't ask him questions, didn't require him to explain himself. She didn't demand anything from him. She only offered—warmth, comfort, and pleasure. Little pieces of herself. A secret no one else knew that she gave only to him. Hers was a generous spirit, and there was nothing inside him that could refuse.

So he knelt astride her hips, took her raised hands in his, and kissed her knuckles. Then, holding her gaze, he pressed her hands down on the pillows on either side of her head and trapped them there.

"There're a few things I've been dreaming of doing to you, Bethany Grant," he murmured softly. "Will you let me?"

"Uh, stupid question," she said in a husky, throaty voice. "Of course."

"Then keep your hands there and don't move them."

He let her go, gratified when she obeyed, keeping her hands pressed to the pillows. Then he set his mouth to her throat and began to work his way down.

He made a meal of her, taking his time, tracing every curve of her body with his mouth, from the swell of her breasts to the tight little points of her nipples. He closed his lips around one, sucking hard, making her gasp and her body arch in delight, before transferring his attention to the other.

She murmured his name as he caressed her, stroking her like a cat, loving the feel of her soft skin beneath his fingers. She was so responsive to his touch and to the pleasure he was giving her, it made him feel like a god.

And when he pushed her thighs apart and bent his head, tasting her, and she cried out, it made him feel like even more of one.

He'd missed giving pleasure to a woman. Missed making her writhe and scream with ecstasy in his arms. Missed the feel of a woman's skin and the salty sweetness of her taste. Missed the soft heat and slickness between her thighs and her arms around his neck, his name being called in delight.

No, not just "a woman."

Beth.

He wasn't sure how you could miss something you didn't even know you were missing, but nevertheless, right here, right now, with Beth in his arms naked and gasping his name as he tasted her, he knew he'd missed her.

She was sunshine and sweetness, and he'd been in the dark, alone, for far too long.

He needed this and he needed her, and marriage was the only answer. He wouldn't accept anything less.

Finn slid his hands beneath her hips, lifting her so he could taste her deeper, driving her on toward the edge of the cliff and then straight over it.

And when she screamed his name, he felt nothing but satisfaction.

As she shuddered on the bed, panting and pink,

he lifted his head and moved over her, positioning himself between her thighs. Her hands were still beside her head on the pillow and that gave him a deep kind of thrill too.

"So?" he murmured as he eased into her, keeping it nice and gentle and slow. "Will you marry me, Beth?"

She gave a soft groan, arching back into the mattress. "You want an answer right now?"

"Yes." He lowered his head and brushed his mouth against hers, touching his tongue to her lower lip gently, tracing it as the slick heat of her body gripped him tight. "It could be good. We could have this every night."

She gave another little moan, as he eased deeper. "No fair. This is cheating."

"It's a simple question." He tilted his hips slightly, making her gasp. "Yes or no?"

Her pupils had dilated, making her eyes look huge and dark in her flushed face, and there were soft little curls of hair stuck to her forehead. She was so lovely. He couldn't think of anything he wanted more than to have her just like this, sleeping with him in this bed every night. Or rather not sleeping.

"You can't ask for an answer now...oh..." She gasped again as he shifted slightly, her hands still beside her head, now trembling. "Oh...F-Finn, that's...that's definitely not fair..."

"Yes or no?" He nuzzled against her skin, setting

his teeth against the cords of her neck and biting down gently. "Come on. It's not hard."

"You're such an ass. Oh..."

He heard her breath catch as he began to move, enjoying teasing her and making her gasp and writhe beneath him. Enjoying how flushed she was and how she could barely speak because of what he was doing to her.

"Oh?" He kept his movements deep and slow, drawing out the pleasure for both of them, feeling it roll over him with all the delicious heat of the summer sun. "You keep saying that."

Her mouth curved, her lashes fluttering, giving him flashes of the deep, shadowed emerald of her eyes. "You're...making it difficult for me to say anything else."

"I only need one word, honey." The endearment slipped out before he could stop it, but he could tell from the look on her face that she liked it. Just as she liked everything else he was doing—that was obvious too because she was moving with him now, giving him as much pleasure as he was giving her.

"Remind me what that word is again?" Her voice had gone husky and ragged, but the look she gave him was seductive as hell. "I keep forgetting it."

The emotional tension that had pulled taut between them down in the living room had dissipated now, and he was in no hurry to resurrect it. They were good like this, when they were flirting with each other, and he wanted more of it, so he relaxed and laughed, delighted at her giving back as good as she got.

"*Yes*," he breathed, bending to kiss her again. "*Yes* is the word you're looking for."

"Finn…" she breathed as he began to move faster. "Finn…"

"Wrong." He nipped at her bottom lip, angling his hips to go deeper.

She moaned, wrapping her legs around his waist, her hands coming up off the pillow.

"Nuh-huh," he murmured, grabbing them and putting them back down again. "What did I say about moving them?"

"Finn," she gasped, shifting and rocking against him. "Finn, please…"

"No." He bit her again. "The words you're looking for are *Finn, yes*…"

"But I—"

"Yes and then you can move your hands."

Beth gasped as he upped the pace, moving faster, harder. "You're a tyrant."

"I know." He slid one hand down to cup her breast, flicking his thumb over one hard nipple, then pinching it gently. "And you love it."

"Yes," Beth said breathlessly. "Okay, yes, Finn, I'll marry you."

Finn smiled, something expanding inside him that wasn't only physical pleasure. Something that felt like relief. "There. That wasn't so hard, was it?"

Beth muttered a curse, lifted her hands, and pulled his mouth down on hers.

And he finally let the pleasure consume them both.

Chapter 13

BETH SAT IN FINN'S TRUCK AS HE DROVE THEM both into Brightwater's town center and tried to ignore the nervousness roiling in her gut.

She didn't even know why she was nervous.

Actually, no, she knew why she was nervous. She and Finn were going into town to let everyone know that not only was she pregnant but also that she'd be moving in with him, and oh hey, they were getting married as well.

A surprise, sure, but no big deal.

They were going to visit the gallery first so she could tell Indigo and Izzy, then go on to HQ to inform Chase and Levi, then…whoever else was around, she guessed.

Izzy would be thrilled at the thought of her marrying Finn, and Indigo would be too, no matter how snarky she'd been earlier. Chase and Levi? Who knew? And the rest of the town…what would they think of her marrying one of their own? Sheri had grown up here, had been one of them, but Beth wasn't. She was an outsider, an interloper. Would they accept her? And more important, would they accept her and Finn's child?

"Don't be nervous." Finn gave her a quick glance before he looked back at the road. "Everyone will be okay with it."

"I'm not nervous," Beth lied, rubbing her hands on her thighs. "I'm fine."

One corner of his mouth curved. "Sure you are."

Damn, but he was gorgeous with that half smile of his.

He was gorgeous all the time, of course, but particularly when there was a tantalizing glimpse of that smile.

Not that it was his smile that had made her say yes to him the evening before, or even the way he'd teased her and given her the most intense pleasure. Sure, the sausage rolls he'd fed her after they'd come back downstairs had helped, and the eclairs he'd given her for dessert after she'd filled up on the delicious casserole he'd cooked had made her feel good about her decision, but she'd already said it by that stage.

She'd said yes because it was clear to her that he needed her to. He'd been so fierce when he'd asked her, his dark eyes full of intensity. It had been important to him—she could see that. Important that his child have his name, that they be a family.

Plus a small part of her had been thrilled when he'd told her she was the first woman he'd been with in five years—then been even more thrilled when he'd told her she was special.

She hadn't known she'd even wanted to be special to him until that moment.

You'd better not be hoping for more of that.

Oh, she wasn't. He'd been very clear about what he could give her, and she was fine with that. Sex and support, blankets and delicious food, and the odd endearment—what more could a girl want?

Of course she'd said yes. And if he'd said he didn't love her, then what of it? She didn't love him either, so it wasn't an issue. You could marry someone without loving them. You totally could. Just as you could love someone without marrying them.

After all, she'd thought she loved Troy and they'd talked off and on about getting married, but he'd never actually asked her. Not even after she'd gotten pregnant. In fact, she'd been debating bringing it up with him, since even though her parents' marriage had been dire, she'd still wanted it for herself.

She'd wanted to have the kind of family she'd dreamed of when she was younger, of parents who loved each other, no one criticizing or hurting each other. A family where a child could grow up without feeling suffocated by all the negative emotions that lingered in the air or feel as if they were being judged and picked at.

Finn wouldn't be a parent like that, she knew already. Even though they weren't in love, he wouldn't vanish suddenly like Troy had, without a word. Finn was up-front and honest, and he'd made it very clear that he took his responsibilities seriously.

She could do worse than marry him. It would make it easier with the town too. Marrying a local would ensure their child would be totally accepted.

I don't love you. That's why it works.

No. She wasn't thinking about that again.

"Okay, so I might be a little nervous," she admitted. "Indigo and Izzy will be fine. It's the rest of the town I'm worried about."

"You shouldn't be," Finn said. "They're all desperately concerned for my well-being, and me getting married and having a kid will be a weight off their minds."

Beth thought of the gossip she'd heard about Finn from various people around the town and the look in their eyes when they spoke of him. "I guess so."

"And I'll be relieved not to be asked ten times a day how I'm doing."

His voice was very dry and the sardonic humor in it made her smile. She knew how that went.

"That's kind of why I left Deep River," she said. "People kept looking at me like 'oh there's the poor depressed girl who lost her baby.'" She'd meant him to smile at that and she was gratified that he did, appreciating her black humor. "I got sick of it. I didn't want to be the poor depressed girl who lost her baby anymore. So when the opportunity to come out to Brightwater Valley presented itself, I took it."

Finn glanced at her. "You wanted a new life, huh?"

"Yeah. A new life and a new future." She rubbed her pendant between her fingers. "I wanted to leave the old me behind, the depressed me. I wanted to be a…different person here."

Finn didn't speak, but she knew he was listening.

"I wanted to be a positive and happy person," she went on. "A 'silver linings, count your blessings' kind of person. I thought it would be easy since no one knew me or my past. But…" She stopped because this wasn't exactly being positive or happy. This was depressing.

"Hate to tell you this," Finn said, "but I knew all of your cheerful crap was a total lie. It always felt kind of fake."

Beth stared at him. "What? Really?"

"Yeah." He gave her another of his dark, enigmatic glances. "I think that's why I found you difficult. Because it felt totally fake, and I didn't know what you were trying to do or trying to prove."

She blinked, feeling vulnerable, as if he'd ripped away a disguise she'd been wearing. "Oh," she said. "That's…embarrassing."

"It was only me, honey." His voice was quietly reassuring. "I don't think anyone else felt the same way. Actually, I *know* no one else felt the same way because I told Chase that once and he looked at me as if I was crazy and wouldn't hear a word said against you."

She studied his strong profile.

He wasn't looking at her, keeping his eyes on the road, but his large, capable hands on the steering wheel were loose and the tension she'd always seen in him seemed to be absent today.

Was it her agreeing to marry him? Or the sex? Or was it only that, now they had a direction and a decision had been made, he was more relaxed?

Perhaps it didn't matter. Perhaps all that mattered was that he was at peace with it.

"I'm glad someone was on my side," she said lightly, part of her annoyed that he'd seen through her, while another part was secretly relieved. Because now that he knew, she didn't have to pretend. "You might wish for me to start being fake again. Especially after the baby is born."

He gave her another fleeting glance, the glitter of something complicated and fierce in his eyes. "No, I won't. You don't have to fake anything with me, Beth. You never have to fake anything with me. Got it?"

She swallowed, a small lump forming in her throat. "Yes."

"Your previous boyfriend, Troy, right? He out of the picture?"

"Yes and pretty much completely. He didn't do

grief or depression or any of that tough stuff, and after I lost the baby, he just…up and left."

Anger flickered briefly across Finn's face. "Good. Sounds like an asshole to me. And just so we're clear, I'm not going to be like him. I don't run away when things get hard. I'll be around for the duration."

The lump in her throat got bigger. "Okay."

"I think we probably need to talk more about how this is going to work." Finn was clearly on a roll now. "But I want to get our announcement out of the way first."

Last night it had been late after they'd finished dinner and dessert, and she'd been tired. So he'd tucked her up in his bed, telling her he'd call the farmhouse to let Indigo know she'd be staying over.

She expected him to sleep with her, but if he had, she hadn't noticed, since she'd been alone when she'd fallen asleep and alone when she'd woken up that morning.

They'd talked a lot over dinner about how they were going to tell people and when she'd move in—all the practical stuff and nothing at all personal. Which was fine and she'd gone along with it. But…was that how their marriage was going to be? Discussions on practical matters and nothing else?

He'd said he wanted to get to know her though, so maybe not. Maybe there would be more. Eventually.

"Yes, fine," she said.

"That reminds me…" He hesitated slightly, which was uncharacteristic of him, then went on, "I should have told you earlier, but…Chase already knows."

Beth frowned. "Chase already knows what?"

"He knows that we slept together. And he knows you're pregnant."

An unexpected stab of anger caught her. She'd been very clear she hadn't wanted people to know and Finn had agreed.

"How?" she demanded. "Did you tell him?"

"Yes." Finn was unflinching. "I did."

"Why?"

"Because he made a comment about my good mood after we slept together and wondered if it was because I'd gotten laid."

Oh great. Men.

"So, what? You just decided to tell him? After we agreed to keep it secret?"

They'd come into town by this stage, Finn pulling into the gravel parking area in front of HQ and stopping the truck.

Then he turned his full attention on her. "Chase isn't a gossip. I told him not to say a word, and he wouldn't—didn't. I thought it wasn't going to go anywhere then, and he already knew I was attracted to you because he's my brother and he knows me too well."

Beth bit her lip. "And the pregnancy?"

"Again, he's my brother. And he has a kid himself. I needed his advice."

As quickly as it had come, her anger dissipated.

She couldn't be mad at him. Chase would certainly pick up on Finn's moods, because while Chase might be a bit of an ass, he was also a perceptive ass unfortunately. And she couldn't fault Finn for wanting his brother's advice either, especially after finding out he was going to be a father.

Hell, it was a moot point now; everyone was going to find out anyway.

She sighed. "Well, okay then. I guess that's all allowed."

Finn stared at her a moment longer, the fierce light in his eyes burning. Then he reached out, and before she could move, his fingers were in her hair and he was bringing her in close and his mouth was on hers.

She gave another little sigh, this one of pleasure as his lips moved on hers, warm and very, very welcome.

It was a deep, slow kiss, and she didn't even realize that there had been a purpose to it until he let her go and she realized that Bill was sitting outside his shop, Mystery the mystery dog sitting near but not too near him, and had seen them.

"Uh, as announcements go," she murmured, "that's quite something."

Finn smiled, making her breath catch, because

truly, when he smiled, the whole world really did light up.

"Come on," he said. "Let's go turn this town upside down."

———

Finn got out of the truck and went around to Beth's side, opening the door for her and handing her out. Then he curled his fingers around hers, settling her hand in his.

It was a declaration—just as he'd seen Bill sitting there and decided that the kiss should be a declaration. He wanted everyone to know that she was his, and what better way to do so than to kiss her in front of the town's biggest gossip?

She was blushing adorably now, which made her look even prettier, even though she was still in yesterday's sundress—not that he was complaining *at all* since that sundress looked bloody great on her.

He definitely wasn't complaining about the kiss mark on the side of her neck either, the one that he'd put there yesterday.

His mark, which satisfied him a great deal. Turned out he *was* kind of a caveman about certain things.

"Bill?" Beth murmured as they walked toward the general store and the gallery. "Really? He's the first one to know?"

"Technically Chase was the first person to know. But Bill's great. Once he knows, the rest of the town will before the end of the day."

"True." Her fingers squeezed his. "You're a sneaky bugger, Finn Kelly."

Warmth glowed in his chest at the teasing note in her voice. God, but he loved it when she said stuff like that to him. He wasn't sure why.

Sure you do.

He shoved that thought away, hard.

"Nice use of Kiwi slang," he said instead. "I think you're getting the hang of it."

She gave him a sassy grin that made him want to kiss her again. "I try."

"Enjoy those sausage rolls, did you?" Bill said as they passed by the general store, his gaze dropping to their linked hands and then back up again.

"You could say that." Finn paused by the wooden bench Bill was sitting on. Mystery thumped his tail but made no move to beg for treats. The dog knew that Finn was already taken. "Thanks, Bill. The eclairs were excellent too."

Bill glanced at Beth, then back at him again. "You don't say."

Finn had another reason he'd wanted Bill Preston to be the first to know, not only that he and Beth were together but about the baby too; the townspeople were quite protective of their own, and Beth was an outsider. Bill had also been one of the people who hadn't been happy with the influx from Deep River and had been vocal about it, and Finn didn't want him being unpleasant to Beth out of some misguided protective impulse.

So he looked the old man in the eye and said, "Beth agreed last night to be my wife." He paused a moment and then added, "And we're expecting our first baby."

Bill's blue eyes went wide, and his mouth dropped open.

Beth's fingers in his tightened, and he gave her a little reassuring squeeze in return. If anyone was awful to her, he would punch them in the face, so help him.

"Is this true?" Bill just about leapt off his seat, staring at Beth, who'd gone three different shades of pink. "You're expecting?"

"Yes. It's true."

Much to Finn's shock, Bill suddenly turned to him and gave him a sharp, fierce hug. "Oh, my boy," he said thickly. "I hoped you'd find happiness again and you have. That's such wonderful news." Then the old man released him and stepped back, looking up at Finn and grinning hugely, his blue eyes a touch misty. "Wonderful...just wonderful."

Mystery gave a bark in agreement.

Finn was still struggling to process that when Bill went on, "And to such a lovely girl too." He gave Beth the same misty-eyed glance but mercifully spared her a hug. "That's special…just very, very special."

Beth abruptly dropped Finn's hand, stepped forward, and gave the old man a hug herself. "Thanks, Bill. I appreciate it."

Bill smiled and patted Beth on the shoulder. "You take care of this one for me, won't you?" Obviously meaning Finn.

"Of course I will," Beth said. "Don't you worry." She reached out and took Finn's hand again. "Come on, Mr. Kelly. We have some other people to tell."

Then she pulled him away in the direction of the gallery.

"That was…unexpected," he muttered, still unable to get over Bill's reaction. "I thought he'd be less…"

"Like he was going to cry?" Beth was smiling. "He must care a lot about you."

Finn could hear the question in her tone, and since there wasn't any reason not to tell her, he said, "Bill used to look out for Chase and me when we were kids. Dad got into the drink after Mum died, and he often forgot to buy food, so Bill would give us stuff from the store. Make sure we got fed."

They came to the door of the gallery and paused outside it.

Beth was looking at him concernedly. "Really? How awful for you. I didn't know that."

Finn shrugged. "Ancient history. It's fine." He

decided not to tell her about how Bill had tried to push food and other things on him after Sheri had died.

What? Did you think people didn't care?

No, he knew they did. He just…hadn't wanted to have to deal with their worry for him on top of his own grief, and clearly Bill had been worried for him.

I hoped you'd find happiness again…

Yeah, and that made him a touch uncomfortable because Bill clearly thought he and Beth were in love, which wasn't the case at all. This was a marriage of necessity rather than feeling, and he wasn't happy with lying about it.

Are you really lying? Doesn't she make you happy?

Yeah, no, he wasn't going there. Just as he wasn't going to go around explaining the exact nature of his and Beth's relationship.

Easier to give people the facts and let them draw their own conclusions, even if they were the wrong ones.

Beth's gaze became sharp, clearly not believing his "it's fine" take on it, but he didn't want to get into a deep and meaningful discussion with her right here on the street, so he pushed the door of the gallery open and, still holding her hand, strode in.

Izzy was at the counter, with Chase on the opposite side, while Indigo sat on top of it with her project bag held protectively on her lap, a disapproving look on her face. Levi had leaned a provocative elbow on the counter right next to Indigo and was obviously in the middle of pissing her off.

The four of them all looked up at as the door opened.

"Beth!" Izzy exclaimed. "We were wondering where…" She trailed off, her gaze dropping to where Beth's hand was safely enclosed in Finn's.

Chase noticed too and Finn didn't miss the grin that spread across his face.

Indigo's eyebrows shot up, her mouth opening.

"Hey," Levi said. "You two are holding hands. Don't know whether you've noticed that or not. Just thought I'd point it out."

"Yeah." Finn met four pairs of eyes squarely in turn. "I'd noticed. And before anyone says anything, Beth and I have an announcement." He glanced at her. "Do you want to go first?"

She was obviously nervous, so he squeezed her hand again, letting her know she wasn't doing this alone, that he was with her.

She smiled gratefully, making a warm feeling unfurl inside his chest, then she turned to the others. "Okay, so, I'm pregnant. And, uh…Finn asked me to marry him."

"Oh my God!" Indigo squealed, her project bag slipping from her fingers and onto the floor. "Seriously?"

Levi, who was clearly far too close to the squeal, put a finger in his ear and wiggled it. Then his handsome face broke into a smile and he shoved himself away from the counter, striding over to where Finn stood and clapping him on the back. "Mate, that's great news! And so totally unexpected."

Finn realized that he'd been subconsciously bracing himself, ready to square up to anyone who might criticize his decision, and in fact he hadn't expected anyone to simply be pleased for him. A tension he hadn't known was there, prickling through his muscles, eased and he found himself grinning back at his friend. "Thanks. And don't tell me you knew already."

"You really thought I wouldn't see the way you looked at Beth?" Levi's hazel eyes took on a wicked glint. "Good catch there, mate. Stole her away before I could get to her."

Beth laughed. "Like you could."

The look on Levi's face became suddenly smoldering. "That's because you haven't seen me bring out the big guns yet."

Indigo had jumped off the counter and was now sidling past Levi to get to Beth. "Shut *up* about your big gun," she muttered. "I bet it's not even that big."

"Baby, don't tempt me," Levi purred.

Luckily Indigo didn't seem to have heard, too busy throwing her arms around Beth's neck and giving her a hug.

Meanwhile Chase had approached, doing a good job of pretending to be totally surprised by the news when of course he wasn't. "Good to hear, little brother." He gave Finn a clap on the back too. "Always hoped I'd be an uncle."

Izzy had rushed to join Indigo in hugging Beth to death, the pair of them obviously thrilled, which pleased Finn to no end. Not that he'd thought they wouldn't be supportive; it was just nice to know they were actively pleased for her too, since he didn't like the thought of Beth having no one at all.

"So that was morning sickness?" Indigo was asking her. "That day when you were ill on the couch and Levi was being a dick?"

"Hey," Levi said, sounding injured. "I was *not* being a dick. I was being a gentleman and giving a lady a ride home."

"So," Chase said expansively, squeezing Finn's shoulder, "I think this calls for a celebration at the Rose tonight. What do you think?"

"Amen," Levi muttered fervently. "A—the hell—men."

Izzy fluttered her hands. "Oh yes, let's do that. But I want to organize it."

"Sweetheart," Chase said patiently, "it's not an event, there's nothing to organize."

"And I just told Bill," Finn added. "Drop a word to him and the whole town will be there."

He wanted the town to be there, he realized. He

wanted his brother and Levi there. He wanted Izzy and Indigo and Gus and all the people who were important to him to be there.

He wanted everyone to be there. Because this was a goddamn celebration and it had been too long since he'd had anything to celebrate. He had a baby coming, and soon they'd be a family together, and the thought made him...

Yeah, okay. It made him happy. And he couldn't remember the last time he'd been simply...happy. Without any complications or expectations. There had been moments out in the bush or with the horses when he'd been content. Peaceful. But he hadn't felt like this, where thinking about the future made him feel hopeful instead of...well, nothing.

Beth laughed, warm and free, and he thought if sunshine could be turned into a sound, it would be the sound of Beth's laugh. It lit up those dark places in his soul.

He looked at her, unable to drag his gaze away. She was glowing, her hair in that messy bun he found so sexy and the green of her eyes enhanced by her dress. Her lush mouth had curved into the most gorgeous smile as Izzy excitedly gave her yet another hug, and there was nothing fake about this smile, nothing forced. As if she was as genuinely happy about the future as he was, and that made him happy too—that being with him was something that pleased her.

It's her. She makes you happy. Go on, admit it.

Well, and what if she did? He could allow that, couldn't he? It wasn't love and it never would be, because he'd given his heart to one woman already and she'd taken it with her when she'd died. He couldn't give away what he didn't have.

So yeah, Beth did make him happy.

And he was fine with it. Absolutely fine.

"She said yes, I take it?" Chase asked from beside him.

"What do you think?" Finn watched his lovely fiancée, unable to look away as she stood there glowing while the other two women asked her excited questions.

"And you're okay with it?"

Finn knew what his brother was really asking him. *Are you okay with getting married again? After Sheri?*

"Obviously I'm okay with it." He kept his voice very neutral. "I wouldn't have asked her if I wasn't."

"But you thought it all through, right?"

Yeah, they were not going to have that conversation here. They were not going to have that conversation at all.

Finn turned and looked at his brother. "It's okay, Chase. I'm fine."

But Chase's gray gaze was far too perceptive, far too knowing. "Are you though? Have you talked about it with her?"

"No," Finn said far more sharply than he'd meant to, his patience thinning.

Chase opened his mouth, obviously wanting to say more, hesitating then shutting it again.

Good choice.

Finn took a breath. "Let me have this moment, Chase, okay? I just…want to be happy without all that other shit getting in the way."

His brother nodded slowly, then glanced over to where Beth stood. "Sure. But make sure she knows where you stand." He looked back at Finn again and he was not smiling this time. "Because she looks really happy, and I'd hate to see her get hurt."

"She knows," he said flatly. "Don't worry, I told her."

Yet this didn't seem to make Chase any happier. He only gave Finn an oddly assessing glance before nodding and moving over to give his congrats to Beth.

She reached up to give his brother a hug, then glanced over at him and smiled, green eyes dancing, and Finn felt an echo of that strong, powerful emotion he'd experienced the night before twist hard in his chest.

Does she really know?

She should. He'd been clear about what he was prepared to give her. She hadn't protested. She hadn't said a word.

Which was great. Because he didn't want her to fall in love with him, just like he didn't want to fall in love with her. And they wouldn't. They would be...married friends. Who slept together.

It was good.

Everything was going to work out just fine.

Chapter 14

BETH MOVED INTO FINN'S PLACE OVER THE course of the next couple of days, the process a surprisingly simple one. Not that it was ever going to be too difficult, considering she didn't have a lot of stuff.

She felt compelled to check with Indigo more than once to make sure her friend didn't mind living on her own at Clint's, but Indigo was very cheerful about it.

"Are you kidding me?" she'd said, blue eyes wide. "Of course I don't mind being alone. I *like* it."

Considering Indigo had lived with only her grandmother since she was a child and then completely alone after her grandmother had died, Beth could see her point. But still, Beth worried for her.

Indigo was unfazed, muttering happily about having more room in the big shed for dye pots and how great it was going to be, and there was no question she was genuine about it.

The issue of transport she shrugged off.

Levi offered to be her taxi service, and when this was refused, he offered to teach her to drive. This was refused also in favor of getting rides from

Shirley, who lived just up the road from Clint's place and who'd also offered to drive her.

Anyway, it wasn't going to be for too long, since Finn had made no secret of the fact that he needed to get someone to manage the horses permanently for him at some stage, which meant they'd be taking over the farmhouse. It would also mean Indigo would need to find yet another place to live, but she insisted on crossing that particular bridge when she came to it.

Beth had been slightly afraid of it being weird moving into Finn's house, but it turned out to be not as much of a drama as she'd thought. He made no comment about her taking over Sheri's little art cabin, and if he didn't visit her there after she'd set up her jewelry-making stuff, she decided not to make an issue of it.

The first night she'd moved in, after Finn had cooked dinner they'd sat at his big dining table and he'd asked her easy questions about growing up in Deep River. She didn't talk in-depth about her childhood, but she'd let him know that it hadn't exactly been a happy one. He'd then offered her bits and pieces about his own childhood in Brightwater. His hadn't been happy either from the sounds of it, what with his dad's drinking and his mother's death, but when he talked about hiking in the bush and fishing on the lake, and building huts and playing at being stranded on a desert island in the wilderness, she could see how growing up here could be idyllic.

It made her even more certain that she'd done the right thing by moving in with Finn and living here.

Then after the talking was done and they'd both cleaned up, Finn had held out his hand and without a word had led her up to his bedroom, that was now their bedroom since he'd cleared space in his drawers for her and in the tiny en suite bathroom too.

That set the pattern. They'd do their own thing during the day, then they'd have dinner together at the dining table, talking about all kinds of things but definitely sticking to subjects that were impersonal. And after that, they'd go upstairs to bed and have sex, and every night it was phenomenal.

In the aftermath, Finn would wrap his arms around her and pull her in close, holding her, and if sometimes she looked up at the skylight and at the brilliant stars shining through it long after he'd fallen asleep, feeling like something was missing and not knowing what it was, that was a minor thing.

On the whole, she had no complaints.

A couple of weeks after she'd moved in, they were sitting out on the deck in the early evening twilight. A couple of bellbirds in a nearby manuka tree were chirping away, along with a tūī providing a counterpoint, filling the air with a peaceful, liquid song.

Finn had thrown a ball for Karl—a futile endeavor since Karl never brought it back—and was talking about one of the horse treks he was doing the next day. It was a day trip, and the weather was supposed to be really good, and he liked taking newbies out as a lot of them got starry-eyed about the horses and he enjoyed being their introduction to riding.

Beth enjoyed hearing him talk about it too. He'd become very animated, discussing each of the horses and their personalities as if they were people, before going into long, detailed explanations about all the treks Pure Adventure NZ had on offer and his plans for new trails over previously unexplored parts of the valley.

He was so sexy when he was talking about something he loved. He got all lit up inside and she could completely understand why some of the female tourists got starry-eyed about more than just the horses.

She'd never gone on a trek he'd led. In fact, what with the gallery opening and then all the pregnancy and moving-in drama, the only outdoor activity she'd done was a trip to Glitter Falls over a month ago.

It was clearly something she needed to rectify and soon, since they were moving into fall, and as everything was weather/season dependent, she'd miss her chance to do any of it before the baby was born.

To get out into the wildness of the New Zealand bush and take in all that magnificent scenery. Get some inspiration for a series of necklaces she'd been thinking about, a botanical theme yet again, with emphasis on native flowers maybe.

Nothing to do with wanting to spend time with the beautiful man sitting next to her, watching him in his element doing what he loved.

No, nothing at all.

"I'd love to come with you," she said impulsively. "I mean, I've been wanting to do some of this outdoor stuff for ages. Do you have room?"

Finn was sitting in an old armchair that had been dragged out onto the deck, the stuffing coming out of several holes in the arms and back. He held a beer between his long fingers; the rustic wooden coffee table sitting between them was loaded up with a glass of orange juice for her and plates containing a mixture of pregnancy-friendly cheeses, crackers, and olives.

The food, naturally, had been Finn's idea. Her morning sickness came and went, and on good days he took his role of providing for her very seriously, cooking meals or putting together little grazing plates for her. Often, he'd bring her back a sausage roll from town whenever he'd finished leading a tour, or he'd slip into the gallery and leave one on the counter.

"That man is wooing you with food," Izzy had commented.

Beth had told her that she didn't need wooing. She'd already been wooed.

But Izzy had only shrugged. "The Kelly men are like that. Chase cooked me breakfast and brought me constant coffees. Just saying…"

The thought had made Beth uncomfortable, though she couldn't have said for certain why, so she tried not to pay too much attention to it. However, since Izzy had brought up the subject, she couldn't help noticing that Finn was definitely on a mission to make sure she ate well.

Now, he gave her his trademark enigmatic look, dark eyes impenetrable. She'd thought he'd become easier to read, since they were living together and getting to know each other, and while that hadn't entirely been the case, she had learned that when he looked at her like that he actually had quite a few thoughts on the subject and was trying to figure out which particular one he was going to go with.

"You don't want me to come," she said before he could reply, trying not to feel hurt about it. "Do you?"

"I didn't say that."

"Yeah, but you're giving me that look."

"What look?"

"The Finn Kelly 'I am mysterious and I am trying to hide my true feelings' look."

He glanced down at the beer bottle in his hand, but she saw the way his sexy mouth curved. She'd amused him.

The hurt feeling lessened. Getting a smile out of the man was like getting blood out of a stone, so when she succeeded…it felt like winning the lottery.

"I'm hiding my true feelings, huh?" He glanced up again, not bothering to hide his smile this time, the sight sending a wash of heat through her the way it always did. "As it happens, my true feelings are that I'd love you to come if you want to. But I'm concerned about you riding. Have you ever been on a horse before?"

A small, hot glow of joy unfurled inside her. He'd "love" her to come…

Don't be stupid. It's only a horse trek. That "love" doesn't mean anything and you know it.

Of course it didn't. She was being stupid and needed to calm the hell down.

Beth shook her head. "Nope, not once."

"Okay, well, I'm not sure—"

"It's a beginners' trek, you said," she interrupted before he could get going and forbid her entirely. "So presumably there will be others who also haven't been on a horse before."

"Yes, but—"

"And the horses are all quiet, steady, good beginners' horses?"

"Again, yes, but—"

"And it's a gentle ride through farmland and a bit of bush, no difficult terrain?"

Finn just looked at her, dark eyes glittering with amusement.

"I'm going to take that as a yes." Beth smiled in what she hoped was a winning manner, because now she'd decided she really wanted to go. "So what's the issue? If you want me to come, why don't I?"

"You have an answer for everything, don't you?" He raised his beer to his lips and took a swallow.

"When it comes to getting something I want, yes, I do." She picked up a cracker with some cheese on it and took a bite. "Come on, let me come. What's the big deal?"

"The big deal is you being pregnant."

"So? I've heard this wild rumor that pregnant women are actually not made of glass. And in fact can withstand some fairly strenuous treatment." She gave him a sultry look from beneath her lashes that she knew turned him on. "Which you proved thoroughly last night."

As she'd hoped, heat flared in his gaze. "I can prove it again if you like."

"I do like. But only if I can come with you tomorrow."

Finn leaned forward and put his bottle down on the coffee table. Then he beckoned to her in a preemptory fashion. "Come here, woman."

"'Woman'? Really? You're going to order me around now?"

"You love it when I order you around." The look in his eyes intensified. "Come here, honey."

Desire gathered inside her, and although she loved teasing him, she loved being in his arms even more, so Beth put down her orange juice, got out of her chair, and went over to him.

Finn pulled her down, nestling her in the crook of his arm, and she relaxed against the hard planes of his body, relishing his heat.

"Why do you want to come?" he asked.

"Well, because apart from going to Glitter Falls once and Queenstown a couple of times, I haven't done much looking around the area. And I'd like to." She met his gaze. "I'd kind of like to see you at work too. Plus the environment here is important to you, and since I'll be sticking around here for the fore-seeable future, I'd like to get to know it. Especially for our child's sake."

His gaze flickered. "You didn't consider moving back to the States? Bringing our kid up there?"

Beth frowned, puzzled by the question. "Why would I do that? I agreed to move in and marry you, Finn. And I assume that means staying here."

"Yeah, it does. It just struck me that I hadn't asked you how you felt about staying in New Zealand. I thought I'd better ask."

She was touched he'd thought about it, but she'd already more or less decided when she left Deep River that she wouldn't be going back anytime soon. She'd left that life behind and the decision she'd made still held.

"No," she said. "I haven't considered moving back. I wanted to leave Alaska behind and I have. Brightwater Valley is where I want to stay."

He nodded slowly. "Okay. Then if you want to bring up a real Kiwi kid, you really do need to get to know the country. Tomorrow, you can come. But you'll ride next to me."

The little glow of joy expanded at the thought of spending a whole day with him, doing something he loved and doing it together.

You are such a goner.

But she ignored that thought, smiling and reaching up to twine her arms around his neck. "I can do that. Now…" Slowly she drew his head down. "How about I do some ordering around for a change?"

———

The weather the next day was pretty much perfect: blue skies all the way and warm, with a fresh breeze that prevented it from getting too hot.

Finn's little group of tourists gathered in the gravel area in front of the stables at Clint's farmhouse, all of them excitedly clustering around him as he explained where they were going and what it was going to involve.

Levi was there to help everyone mount up and

get them settled, soothing any nerves and answering any questions while Finn got the group organized.

It wasn't a hard trek. Just a ride along the ridge-line on Clint's land before heading down a gentle hill, through some bush, and out onto a little pla-teau above the lake that gave some magnificent views.

Lunch—which had already been dropped at the site by quad bike—would be served and everyone could relax for a half hour before riding back to the farmhouse.

Soon everyone was on their mounts and ready to go, so Finn swung into the saddle on Jeff's back. Karl used to follow the treks when Clint had lived there, loping along beside them with his tongue hanging out, and Finn saw no reason why he shouldn't continue to enjoy a run with them, so he'd been brought along too. The horses were used to him and didn't even flick an ear as he barked excitedly now, wanting everyone to hurry up so he could get going.

Beth was on Carol, the most bombproof horse he had, a steady old mare who spooked at nothing and knew the trail so well she could probably go there and back with her eyes closed.

She was as safe as houses, yet Finn was still vaguely uneasy about Beth being on a horse. When she'd asked him the night before whether she could come, his instant response had been *hell no*.

Because what if she fell? What if she was thrown? What if something terrible happened and she was hurt and lost the baby?

It was ridiculous thinking, and he knew it, and his response to it had annoyed him so much he'd decided that yes, she would come. Especially after she'd explained why she'd wanted to: to see him at work and to connect with the environment for their child's sake.

Yeah, he'd liked that a lot. Brightwater Valley and the lake and the mountains were his home, his place. He was connected to them on a level that went deeper than merely the physical, and Sheri had been too. They'd shared that connection.

But Beth hadn't grown up here and she didn't have that same connection, and the fact that she'd picked up how important it was to him and wanted to find it for herself felt like a gift.

The whole of the past two weeks felt like a gift, if he was honest with himself. Having her living in his house, sleeping in his bed, sitting out on the deck with her in the evenings and hearing about her life in Deep River...

It was good to have her around. To talk with and to hold. To sit with and spend time with. She was bright and funny, and his house felt as if the summer sun had come inside to stay.

She made him smile, even when he didn't want to, even when his mood turned dark, and he'd found himself looking forward to getting home at night so he could see her.

She made him feel…lighter than he'd felt since Sheri died, and he didn't want to analyze why that was; he was just pleased to feel it.

So of course he wouldn't deny taking her for a trek. It was a beginners' trip, which made it the perfect introduction.

She hadn't been nervous of the horses, only excited as he'd introduced her to Carol and given her a carrot to feed to the mare. Beth had stroked the horse's soft muzzle and neck, smiling hugely, then had given a little gasp of excitement as he'd boosted her up into the saddle.

She was sitting there now as he helped the others, looking like a total newbie, it was true, but also like a kid taking their first ride on a Ferris wheel, wide-eyed with excitement, nervousness, and delighted anticipation.

She wore an old pair of jeans, a worn white T-shirt with a dark-green fleece thrown on over the top, her white-blond hair in a long braid down her back, and a riding helmet, and quite honestly she'd never looked lovelier.

She made his chest ache and he had to turn away from her just so he could concentrate on what he was doing.

Eventually all his charges were mounted and ready, and he turned Jeff in the direction of the start of the trail, leading the way with Beth beside him.

"Relax," he murmured as the horses walked at a leisurely pace. "Your shoulders are up around your ears."

"Oh, what? Like this?" She put her shoulders down and glanced at him, copying his loose hold on the reins.

"Yeah, that's good. Also, you can look around at the view. Carol knows where she's going."

"I know. But I want to feel like I'm actually riding and not just sitting on top of the four-legged equivalent of a quad bike."

Finn grinned. "After the baby's born, how about I teach you to ride?"

She glanced at him, her eyes sparkling. "Oh, you would? I'd love that."

The ache in his chest deepened, warmth flickering through him at the look on her face and the way her eyes lit up. There was nothing fake about her now and there hadn't been for the whole past two weeks she'd been living with him.

But make sure she knows where you stand… because she looks really happy and I'd hate to see her get hurt.

Chase's voice from that day a couple of weeks ago when they'd made their announcement drifted through his head, though he tried to ignore it.

She *did* know where he stood. He'd told her.

And seriously, what more could he do? Remind her every five seconds that he couldn't give her anything emotionally?

She hadn't asked him to anyway, and if she was happy, what was he worrying about?

He dismissed the nagging doubt in the back of his mind, concentrating instead on the trek.

It was an easy ride along the trail and then up a short slope to the ridgeline, which they then followed, the dense green of the beech forest below them, the rolling green fields and the sparkling, deep-turquoise blue of the lake beyond.

The air was warm and full of the scents of dry grass and late-blooming gorse flowers, along with the earthier, distinctive spice of the bush.

"What made you want to buy Clint's farm?" Beth asked as they rode. "Was it always something you wanted to do?"

The sun was warm on his back, and he was feeling relaxed, and even though it was a subject that ventured into painful territory, he didn't mind answering her.

"I spent a lot of time with the horses here after Sheri died," he said. "Clint let me manage them, and then I got the idea of adding horse trekking to Pure Adventure's list of activities. It turned out to be pretty popular, so when Clint said he wanted to leave, it seemed like a good idea to buy the ranch for the business."

"I can see why it's popular." She waved at the view. "This is gorgeous." Her hand dropped to Carol's neck, and she gave it a little stroke. "And who doesn't like a horse?"

"Oh, there are a few people."

"They're idiots then." She tipped her head back and closed her eyes. "Mmmm, that sun is wonderful."

Not just the sun. She is too.

Finn found himself staring at her, unable to tear his gaze from her face. She looked so peaceful, wholly in this moment, enjoying the sun and the view and the animal beneath her.

But that was Beth, wasn't it? She'd told him she was here to leave behind the Beth she'd been in Deep River. To be someone different, happy, and positive. Which implied that back in Deep River she hadn't been that person. And it was true that when she'd arrived here, he'd thought her relentless cheerfulness a put-on. Perhaps sometimes it had been.

It wasn't now though.

Beth Grant didn't need to force herself to be happy and positive in order to be a different person. She already was that person.

She didn't have to try. She was made of sunshine, and she radiated it simply by existing.

A deep, heavy feeling shifted in his chest, and suddenly he couldn't breathe.

"I need to go check up on the tourists," he muttered.

And he turned Jeff around and rode back along the trail.

Chapter 15

BETH WATCHED FINN RIDE AWAY WITH SOME puzzlement. What on earth had prompted him to be so abrupt? Had it been the mention of his wife? When she'd asked him about why he'd bought Clint's horse ranch, she'd just been interested to know. She hadn't realized it had been linked to Sheri's death; if she had, she wouldn't have asked.

So is this what your marriage is going to be like? Everything's good until you say the wrong thing?

She swallowed and glanced away from Finn, who was checking in with each of his charges. Carol clopped peacefully along the trail, obviously knowing where she was going and requiring no input from Beth.

The ridgeline was clear and open, providing the most magnificent views of the jagged, snow-capped mountains and the glitter of the lake. A warm breeze ruffled the ends of her braid, bringing with it the by-now-familiar scents of the bush and the fields—spicy dry grass and sun-warmed earth.

Much farther along, the trail finally dipped down into the bush—mainly silver and black beech, with a couple of red beeches thrown in—before coming out again into the sunlight.

A weird thought caught at her. That would be their marriage, wouldn't it? Sunlit spaces and moments of happiness. The scent of his skin when she kissed him. The warmth of his arms around her. Then the darkness of the bush as she said something that hurt him without meaning to, that would cause him to close up and pull away from her.

She'd never know which thing it would be. She'd be walking in darkness, surrounded by quicksand and thorns, trying desperately to stay on the path and not blunder into disaster.

Growing up in her parents' house had felt like that, with her father constantly seething about things she didn't understand and exploding at the most innocuous things. Then there were her mother's emotional outbursts that would come out of nowhere and end up with her mother lying in bed for days on end.

Was that what she and Finn were destined for? Was that what their child would grow up with?

Despite the sun, an icy shiver went down her back. She didn't want that for their baby. She couldn't bear for them to grow up in the glass house she'd grown up in, where the slightest wrong move could cause something to break and then the whole thing would shatter.

But isn't that what you've been doing for the past

two weeks? Tiptoeing around Finn? Letting him direct all the conversations? Not pushing him, not demanding anything of him? Feeling lonely...

Beth blinked at the trail ahead, unseeing, a cold sensation prickling all over her.

Yeah, that's exactly what she'd been doing. She'd been keeping the peace, not wanting to rock the boat. Happy to take the moments as they came and exist in them while they were there, thinking that this could be the happy life she'd wanted, the bright, positive future she'd hoped for.

But was it really? Avoiding the past, avoiding all those thorns and briars and quicksand worked for a while, but she was always surrounded by it— always having to watch her footing in case she fell in.

That wasn't the path to happiness, and it wasn't the path she wanted their child to take either.

She swallowed because she knew what the alternative was, and that was uprooting the thorns, razing the briars, and filling in the quicksand. That was confronting those painful subjects and talking about them.

If you want happiness, you have to choose it. And then you have to work for it.

"Damn," she whispered under her breath.

It felt unfair. She'd worked hard for the happiness she did have, pulling herself out of the pit back in Deep River and putting it behind her by choosing to come here. Yes, it had been hard to put on that brave face all the time, to be cheerful and positive, yet now it didn't feel like quite so much of a struggle.

Now, she was in a good place. She felt almost happy in a way she hadn't for a long time, and she didn't want to have to go back to the struggle.

She wanted to live with Finn the way they were, taking whatever he had to give and being content with that.

But that isn't enough for you, and it never will be. You don't want to just take. You want to give as well.

She drew in a shaky breath, momentarily forgetting she was riding a horse along the most incredibly beautiful ridge on a warm late-summer day.

All she could think about was Finn's dark eyes and the intensity that burned in them at night when he held her in his arms. When he was demanding and fierce, as if there were a furnace burning inside him and he had to let all that heat out somehow. Because he was trapped in that heat, burning himself alive…

Tears abruptly prickled in her eyes and she had to blink them back, shocked by the upwelling of grief inside her. She hated the thought of him being in so much pain. She *hated* it. Because he was in pain—she could sense it. He was trapped by his grief, and she knew how that felt. She *knew*.

He was riding next to a woman who seemed nervous on her horse, leaning in to say a few words to her, utterly in command of himself and the

animal he rode. He radiated assurance and quiet
confidence in what he was doing, and there was
something so soothing and reassuring about that
confidence. As if the world could go to hell, but if
you were with Finn Kelly, you'd be okay because
he'd know exactly what to do.

But…did he have anyone he looked to for reassurance? Did he have anyone he shared his fears
with? His hopes and his dreams? Had they all died
with his wife, or did he keep them to himself now?

*You know he keeps them to himself. He shares noth-
ing of himself with anyone.*

Beth looked away, raising a hand to scrub away
her tears. Stupid man. She got why he'd want to
cut himself off from people. It was hard to reach
out after you'd lost someone. It had been hard for
her to pick up the phone and call her doctor that
first time she'd realized she needed help, but she'd
done it.

You couldn't isolate yourself. That wasn't the
answer.

*Aren't you a fine one to talk? Wanting to handle
everything yourself?*

She had, it was true…until he'd come along and
shown her it was okay to let someone else help to
carry the weight. Then there was Chase and Izzy,
leaning on each other, helping each other out.

The town as a whole was like that too: Evan
McCahon bringing his paintings down to the

gallery—if reluctantly. Shirley helping Bill in the general store. Everyone helped each other here.

But who helped Finn? She remembered the hug Bill had given him and Bill's misty-eyed look. Remembered Evan striding in with a painting because Finn had asked him to. Remembered the other things people had said about Finn over the past couple of months she'd been here.

They all cared about him. He had his brother and Levi, so it wasn't as if he didn't have the support. But it was true that Finn distanced himself, kind of a part of things but not really. Why was that? Because of his wife? Because he was still grieving?

Beth gripped the reins tighter, a deep certainty shifting and settling inside her.

She didn't want him to be alone. She wanted him to have someone, and she wanted to be that someone. In which case she was going to have to let him know that, to tell him that he didn't have to close himself away, that he could share things with her—it was okay. Because she'd been through the fire like he had.

He wasn't as alone as he thought he was.

She sat up a bit straighter on Carol, determination stiffening her spine, and when he came up beside her again, she turned and gave him a radiant smile. "You're very good with the tourists. It's sexy."

That got her one of his half smiles in return. "Don't flirt with the tour guide. It's one of the rules."

"Oh really? And what if I break it?"

"Then you won't get the surprise I brought along for lunch just for you."

Beth's heart gave a little leap, because of course he'd brought her a surprise. "What surprise?"

"If I told you, then it wouldn't be a surprise." He gave her a measuring glance. "Ever tried trotting?"

"Um…how different is it to walking?"

"The same except bouncier." With effortless grace, he urged Jeff into a trot, and she found Carol doing the same, following Jeff down the gentle slope as they headed into the bush.

Then all thoughts of Finn vanished; Beth was too busy trying to keep her seat. Finn was grinning as he rode back and forth along the line of tourists, making sure everyone was okay. There were laughs of delight and a few curses but no one fell off, and soon they were riding through the cool of the beech forest, sunlight dappling the ferns and the thick leaf litter that covered the trail.

"Just so you know, Finn Kelly," Beth said breathlessly as Finn came up beside her once again, slowing his horse and thus everyone else's horses, "trotting is *not* the same as walking."

He smiled. "We'll do a canter on the way back. That's easier."

"Oh, I'm sure going faster makes all the difference."

He laughed, and her heart turned over in her

chest at the way it lit the darkness of his eyes. He was gorgeous when he wasn't smiling, but when he was laughing…oh, man…

You are so in trouble.

No, she wasn't. She was only…appreciating him.

"You'll love it," Finn said, still grinning. "You'll see."

They rode through the bush for another half an hour or so, Finn urging Jeff back and forth along the line of tourists, giving a spiel about the different species of trees and shrubs in New Zealand's South Island bush. He assigned each person a specific bird or animal to spot, and soon everyone was calling out and pointing as the bush around them came alive with wildlife and the sound of birdsong.

There were bellbirds and saddlebacks, tiny pīwakawaka flitting in the air. A fat kereru eyed them from the safety of a black beech, while a kaka made loud screeching sounds. New Zealand didn't have any large native mammals, but it sure had a lot of birds.

Beth loved it. Finn had assigned her a kea, the kaka's cheekier cousin, and she spent a lot of time craning around trying to spot one and failing. Until one swooped down to land on one of the other tourists' riding helmet, tilting its head this way and that, studying them all curiously. Delighted, Beth grabbed for her phone along with everyone else, wanting to take a picture. But the kea knew exactly what was going on and apparently wasn't here for a performance, since it flew off exposing the bright orange and yellow feathers beneath its wings, before anyone could snap a photo.

Soon they were heading out of the bush and to the little picnic area situated on a small, grassy plateau with towering cliffs above and below. Finn helped people dismount, then gave everyone instructions on how to deal with their horses. They were such a placid lot, it mostly involved letting the reins dangle and allowing them to graze.

Beth helped him with the picnic lunch that had been dropped off earlier along with blankets, flasks of hot coffee and tea, and bottles of water. Lunch was sandwiches and cookies, though Beth was surprised to see that he'd set out something a bit different for her.

Laid out on a checked blanket, apart from the rest of the group, were some neatly cut sausage rolls, crackers, her favorite hard cheeses, and a jar of Teddy Grange's special olive marmalade.

"Oh my God," she breathed as she sat down and reached for the jar. "How did you know?"

Finn sat down on the blanket next to her, looking extremely smug. "I asked Izzy what you might like on a picnic, and she mentioned you'd gone a little crazy for Teddy's olive marmalade."

"But she said there were no more jars left."

His eyes glinted. "Oh, she found one for me."

A lump rose in Beth's throat for absolutely no good reason.

Finn Kelly was a special man. He'd done nothing but look after her since he'd found out she was pregnant, making sure she was well and comfortable, that she had whatever she needed for her work and the food she liked to eat. He made things easier. He made things better.

He makes you happy.

He did. He really did.

She leaned forward and brushed a kiss over his mouth.

"Thank you," she said quietly. "If that's your surprise, then I love it."

He smiled back and cupped her cheek, his thumb brushing over her cheekbone, and she shivered, the warmth of his touch settling down inside her. "It's only a jar of olive marmalade."

"I know. But it's a jar of olive marmalade you went out of your way to get, and I really appreciate that."

"You can show me your appreciation tonight then, hmmm?" He kissed her gently. "Now, I'd better go check—"

"Finn." Beth gripped his wrist. "What do you like?"

He frowned. "What do you mean?"

"You've been doing so many things for me. Nice food and blankets and all kinds of things. But what about you? What can I do for you?"

Wickedness glinted in his eyes. "You already do it. At night. In bed."

Naturally he'd make it about sex. He was a man, after all. But she didn't want this to be just about sex. She wanted it to be about him not cutting himself off all the time, but opening up and trusting her with more than just his body.

"I'm not talking about sex, Finn," she said. "I'd like to do things for you the way you do things for me. I'd like to...you know, take care of you. Be there for you."

"You don't need to be there for me. I'm fine." Gently he pulled his wrist out of her grip. "And I'm not the one who's pregnant, you know."

She could sense his withdrawal, could see the glint in his eyes vanish, the door to the furnace closing. He was uncomfortable and distancing himself.

"So it's okay for you to take care of me, but it's not okay for me to take care of you?"

The lines of his gorgeous face hardened slightly. "I don't need taking care of, Beth. I mean, don't get me wrong, I appreciate you thinking of me like that, but it's not necessary, okay? Now." He shifted and stood up. "I'd better go check on the rest of the group."

Beth watched him stride away, an ache in her heart.

He said he didn't need taking care of.

But he was wrong.

Finn took them all for a brief canter on the way back to the farmhouse, and everyone, predictably, loved it far more than the trotting. There were lots of smiles and laughter as he led them back to the stables, where Levi had returned to dole out apples and carrots for everyone to give to their mounts as a thank-you.

He'd thought the brisk ride back would rid Finn of the tension that had settled between his shoulder blades after the conversation he'd had with Beth at lunch, but it hadn't. And he wasn't sure exactly why it had made him so tense.

He didn't want her to look after him. He didn't need it. That was *his* job, not hers, and it wasn't something he was going to ask of her.

"You look happy," Levi commented, leaning on the stall gate as Finn got Jeff settled. Toby and one of his sons would be coming soon to deal with the other horses, but Finn liked dealing with Jeff himself. "Happy as in you don't look happy at all, but really pissed off about something," Levi went on. "What's up? Trek not so good? Someone do something dumb?"

"No," Finn said, not wanting to talk about it. "Trek was good. People had fun. And I'm not pissed off."

"Yeah, and I'm the Queen of England. Bow before Her Majesty, please."

"Levi…"

His friend's hazel eyes flicked over him in that disturbingly perceptive way Levi sometimes had. People always thought he was fun and charming, easygoing and relaxed, until they hit the steel that lurked beneath his exterior. He was ex-SAS, like Chase, and there was a certain…similarity between them, such as the sharp focus Levi turned on him now.

"This is about Sheri, isn't it?" All the good humor had vanished from Levi's voice.

Finn set his jaw. "I'm not talking about—"

"Sheri and Beth," Levi went on, as if he hadn't heard. "This dad stuff is getting to you, I think."

Finn picked up some straw and began to rub down Jeff's sides with it, annoyed now. Because Levi was standing at the gate, blocking his exit, and leaving would be a drama. Shit, doing anything but standing there rubbing down the horse would end up being a drama.

"It's not." He tried to keep his voice very level. "I'm fine with it. And you're wrong. It's got nothing to do with Beth."

"If it's got nothing to do with Beth, then why is she currently staring at you like a kicked puppy?"

Finn cursed under his breath, a sudden pain gripping him. He hadn't meant to hurt her, he really hadn't. He'd just…

Wanted to put some distance between you and her? Keep her at arm's length? How is that fair to her?

He remembered the expression in her eyes as he'd told her that he was okay, that he didn't need looking after, and how for a moment she'd appeared stricken. As if looking after him was something she'd wanted to do.

Which would have been great if that had been something he'd wanted too, but he didn't.

Bullshit. You want it. You're desperate for it.

No, he damn well wasn't. He was happy giving to people; he didn't want to take. Taking involved opening himself up, sharing himself with someone, and he didn't want to do that either. Not again.

Hell, even if he actually wanted to, he suspected he couldn't. Sheri had been the only person he'd ever given himself over to wholly. He'd fallen in love with her with all of his soul, and he suspected she'd taken a good portion of that soul with her when she died.

He had nothing left to give anyone else, not even Beth.

Yet despite that, his chest felt tight, an ache inside him.

"I don't know why she's staring at me like that," he said shortly, shoving the pain away. "I didn't say a bloody word to her."

There was a silence behind him, but he could feel the pressure of Levi's skepticism like a weight pressing down on his back.

"Sure you didn't." Another pause. "Right, better get this lot back down to HQ."

Finn didn't turn.

Levi's footsteps moved away, crunching on the gravel, and then came the sound of his voice calling all the tourists together and getting them organized in his truck, Karl yipping excitedly. Some of them rode in the deck behind the cab, which wasn't technically allowed, but the tourists loved it. They were all ordered to keep their riding helmets on, and Levi drove very slowly too, so no one was in any danger of being tipped out.

Finn stayed in the stall until he heard the truck pull away down the driveway and silence fell.

"Finn?" Beth's voice came from behind him.

He tensed, feeling the heat that inevitably rose whenever she was around rise again, bringing with it yet more of that subtle ache and fierce hunger.

Hunger for the sunshine inside her, because it didn't seem to matter how much he had, he always wanted more.

But he couldn't have it, just like he couldn't have her taking care of him.

It would be selfish to take when he couldn't give anything back.

She'd been through so much. She'd lost her baby, survived postnatal depression, then come halfway around the world to find a new life for herself, and the last thing she needed was some brooding widower who couldn't give her what she truly deserved.

He took a breath, dropped the straw in his hand, and turned.

She was standing at the stall gate, holding her helmet in one hand, strands of pale hair blowing loosely in the breeze.

He remembered the hair brush he kept in a drawer in his nightstand, with golden strands of hair still caught in the bristles.

"I'm sorry," he said, because she deserved an apology from him. It wasn't her fault he was a moody asshole. "About back at lunch. I was short with you, and I didn't mean to be."

"That's okay." She lifted a hand and pushed some hair out of her face. "But I...I think we need to talk."

Talking was the last thing he wanted to do, but she wasn't wrong. And if he wanted this to work—and he really did—he was going to have to suck up some unpleasant things.

Marriage was about compromise after all, and he'd found it with Sheri. He didn't see why he couldn't find it with Beth too.

"About anything in particular?" A stupid question, since he knew full well what she wanted to talk about, but it would be good to hear it from her directly. So he could prepare himself.

"I think you know," she said quietly. "You said you want this marriage to work, but it feels like there's a whole lot of stuff that's off-limits with you, subjects you don't want to talk about, and I don't like having to feel my way around it. I don't want to end up inadvertently hurting you or making things difficult. So...I'd like to work out a road map. I think we both need one."

She's not wrong.

She wasn't. And even though he didn't want to talk or think about any kind of "road map," he knew he was going to have to. It wasn't fair to her otherwise.

"Yeah, okay." He let no hint of his reluctance show in his voice. "I guess we do need to talk about that. So when do you want to discuss it? I've got to finish up here and get back to HQ, then help Cait with getting the projector set up for tonight."

The projector was for town movie night, which happened in late summer or whenever someone was bored and wanted to do something social. It involved a projector and screen being set up beside the lake, chairs from the Rose being hauled out, drinks and snacks being handed around, and about a mile of extension cords to sort out.

Everyone loved movie night though. Sitting by the lake in the evening, watching a movie on DVD, sipping a beer and eating chips, and sometimes talking more than actually watching the movie. Sometimes there would be a few tourists lingering by the lake and they often joined in too.

It was a great social occasion.

"Okay," Beth said. "Then maybe after the movie. I presume you're going?"

He nodded because he always went. He, Chase, and Levi were at all the town occasions since they were all believers in supporting the town however they could.

Movie night had, in fact, been Levi's idea, and surprisingly, for a suggestion from someone who hadn't grown up here, everyone had taken to it wholeheartedly.

But Finn felt bad that she'd had to ask him if he'd be there. It would be her first movie night here, since they hadn't had one for a couple of months, and he knew she'd love it. Yet he hadn't talked to her about it, hadn't mentioned even going together.

Sheri liked movie night too.

"Are you going to come with me?" he asked far, far too late. "I'm sorry, I should have mentioned it to you earlier."

She lifted a shoulder. "It's fine. Izzy told me about it. I'm meeting her and Indigo down there."

So she'd assumed she wouldn't be going with him and maybe not even sitting with him.

You didn't even talk to her about it so are you really surprised?

He shouldn't be, yet irritation caught at him that she'd be with her friends instead of with him, even though he knew he had no right to be annoyed. Not when he'd put her at arm's length and kept her there.

Beth's gaze met his briefly before she glanced away. She pushed back some more hair that was blowing over her face. "Well, Indigo has made me some tea so I might go and—"

"Beth, wait," Finn said before he could stop himself, not liking the guarded expression on her face.

She looked back at him. "Yes?"

He came over to the stall gate, opened it, and stepped outside. "I'm sorry about movie night. I should have said something to you. It's a fun evening and I think you'll enjoy it."

Beth smiled, though it wasn't the radiant one she'd give him when he'd revealed the treat he'd brought along for her, which made regret sit like a stone inside him. And she didn't come over, put a hand on his chest, and rise up on her toes to kiss him the way she sometimes did.

"Yeah, it does sound fun," she said. "I'm looking forward to it."

She stayed where she was, not far from him, yet suddenly it felt as if there was a giant gulf between them, a chasm miles deep.

A chasm you put there.

Oh, he knew. He'd done it deliberately. And not just with her, with everyone, and he'd never felt the need to bridge it.

Yet he did now. He wanted to close that distance,

grab her and haul her into his arms because the ache in his soul, the hunger for her that wouldn't leave him alone, felt too much to bear.

Except that would be a bad move. He couldn't put that on her. The distance had to remain.

"Okay." He thrust his hands in his pockets to keep them to himself. "I'll see you down there then."

She nodded. "Then we'll talk after."

"Yeah, we will." He extended a hand for her helmet. "I'll deal with that for you if you like."

Beth held it out to him, and he didn't miss that she carefully avoided brushing his fingers. And when she murmured a thank-you and turned back to the farmhouse, she didn't look behind her.

He didn't want that to feel as if someone had wrapped their fingers around his heart and was squeezing it hard, but for some reason it did.

And they kept on squeezing as she walked into the farmhouse and closed the door behind her.

Chapter 16

MOVIE NIGHT WAS JUST AS ADORABLE AS BETH thought it would be.

Deck chairs, old armchairs, stools, pub chairs, dining chairs—just about any chair you could think of—had been hauled onto the grassy bank by the lake, all of them facing a giant projector screen on a stand. Long extension cords powered the projector and DVD player that had also been brought out, the cords running directly across the main street and into HQ, which was the closest building with a power outlet.

People sat chatting as the long, late-summer twilight lay over the town, the air still warm, the sky still a deep blue but now tinged with the pinks and oranges of what looked to be a truly beautiful sunset.

A cooler of drinks had been brought out, Jim managing the distribution, while Cait was doing a roaring trade in cooked sausages wrapped in slices of bread and topped with tomato sauce—the kiwi version of a hotdog.

There was lots of laughter and much discussion about how to get the DVD player working with the projector, something that was clearly Levi's territory since he was crouched in front of it, steadfastly ignoring all the suggestions called to him from various townsfolk.

Izzy, Indigo, and Beth were sitting on an old couch that Chase and Levi had carried out of HQ just for them, which had resulted in cries of "no fair," to which Chase had merely responded that it was for Gus. No one minded Gus having a special seat, but it was noted that there seemed to be more than enough room for Gus *and* Izzy *and* her friends as well.

It was all in good fun. Kiwis, Beth noted, enjoyed teasing people they liked; the more they liked you, the more they teased. In fact, judging from the way they teased her, Izzy, and Indigo, it must mean they were held in *very* high esteem.

"So how are you feeling?" Izzy asked her companionably as the three of them sat together on the sofa. Gus had gone off to beg yet another sausage from Cait, while Indigo and Izzy were cradling cold shandies—half lemonade, half beer.

Beth stuck with the ginger beer that was apparently a Shirley special—good for morning sickness, Shirley had informed her sagely—and was finding it to be very, very good indeed.

"I'm okay," she said. "Not feeling too bad. And… "—she raised her glass—"this helps."

"Yeah, ginger's great for nausea," Indigo said.

"But you know, what Izzy and I really want to know is how are you and Finn."

Izzy frowned at Indigo. "Hey, I was going to work up to that."

Indigo only shrugged. She had her knitting in her lap in a pile of blue wool and whatever it was didn't appear to have grown appreciably given all the time she spent knitting it.

Beth wasn't quite sure what to say to that. How were she and Finn? Good. On the surface. If you didn't mention things like feelings. If you were fine with sex at night with an unbelievably sexy man who did sweet, caring things for you during the day. And if you didn't care about what the future would hold or worry about how your heart was going to resist falling for said sexy man.

A man who insisted on shutting himself away and you out.

Izzy frowned. "I get the feeling things aren't great?"

Beth had talked with Izzy and Indigo after the pregnancy/marriage announcement and had explained to them the nature of her relationship with Finn. She hadn't thought pretending it was something it wasn't was a good idea, so she'd been up front. No, they weren't in love. Yes, they were sleeping together. Yes, they were still getting married. Yes, it was kind of weird.

The other two had seemed to sense it was a

complicated situation and so hadn't pressed her for answers or other explanations. She'd been grateful for that, since she hadn't wanted to talk about it herself. But now...

Beth sighed and took a swallow of her ginger beer. She felt achy from the ride that morning, but the place that ached the most was her heart. She'd been up front with Finn about wanting to talk. About needing a road map for this marriage of theirs, and she had seen the reluctance in his dark eyes.

He didn't want to talk about it, that was clear, and quite frankly it was starting to hurt. No, scratch that. It was already hurting. She'd been honest with him about her various issues, yet he didn't talk about his. They'd chatted about his childhood, but he didn't mention Sheri. He never visited the little cabin either, and every time she dropped a hint about having an outdoor bath, he changed the subject.

She didn't want to demand things of him he wasn't ready to give, but she didn't want this to be the whole of their relationship either.

She...wanted more than that.

"No," she said. "Not great."

"Oh no," Indigo murmured feelingly. "I'm sorry, Beth."

"Why?" Izzy asked. "What's going on? You don't have to tell us if you don't want to, of course. I'm not going to push."

"Oh, it's okay. I could probably use some advice,

to be honest." She looked over the heads of the people sitting in front of them, over to where the tall figure that was Finn stood with Jim, helping hand out drinks. Gus was standing next to him eating her sausage and bread, and he was smiling down at her, his face lit up.

He was so handsome when he smiled like that, and it was clear he loved being with his niece. He'd love their child too, of that she had no doubt.

But he'll never smile that way at you.

Pain hit her, a great throbbing ache. He did smile at her, but it was never like that. Never as if she was someone he loved being with.

Never as if she was someone he loved.

Oh, you idiot.

Yes. Yes, she was an idiot. She wanted to be someone Finn Kelly loved. And she knew why. She'd known for a week or so now yet hadn't wanted to acknowledge it.

She was in love with him, that's why.

"So what's up?" Izzy asked.

Beth took a gulp of her ginger beer. Well, she certainly wasn't going to tell the others that, not yet. Maybe not ever. Hey, maybe if she ignored it, it would go away.

"Finn's great, don't get me wrong," she said. "He's very supportive and caring. Does a lot of stuff for me. But…there's this distance between us. He's shutting me out."

Indigo wrinkled her nose, obviously not impressed with this. She put her shandy down and picked up her knitting. "So, uh, you never really went into detail about the…um…exact nature of your relationship with Finn. Emotionally, I mean."

Beth sighed. "It's complicated."

"Of course it is," Izzy said comfortingly. "Kelly men do tend to make things unnecessarily complicated."

"He did lose his wife." Beth rubbed at the condensation on the side of her glass, feeling defensive of him. "And there's no magical 'moving on' date. You never stop grieving. You just learn where to put the grief so you can keep living."

Izzy's gaze was full of a compassion that made Beth's throat close up.

"That sounds like the voice of experience," her friend said quietly.

It wasn't the right time, and it wasn't the right place, just before a movie was supposed to start and with the town gathered around, all talking and laughing. But the words slipped out of Beth before she could stop them.

"I've been pregnant before. But I…lost my baby. She was a late-stage miscarriage. And then I had some terrible postpartum depression." She swallowed. "People knew. That's the reason I left Deep River. I wanted to get away from all those pitying stares, find myself a new life. Somewhere more positive and happy."

"Oh, Beth." Izzy reached out and grabbed her hand. "I'm so sorry."

Then Indigo took the ginger beer bottle out of Beth's other hand and laced Beth's fingers through hers, the two women holding on to her tightly. They didn't speak, but then they didn't have to. Beth could feel their support and their sympathy, their compassion flooding into her—a wordless offer of comfort and caring that brought tears to her eyes.

She had been afraid to tell them. Afraid to lay bare her experiences because no one else had wanted to know. And no one else had stayed to support her or care for her. She'd had to do it all on her own, and she had.

But it had led to an immense distrust of the people around her—people who didn't deserve that distrust. Like Indigo and Izzy. They were here for her, she realized. They would never abandon her.

She swallowed again, blinking back the tears fiercely. "Thanks," she said in a husky voice. "Thanks, you two. I know I haven't said anything about it before, but...I didn't get a lot of support from my family, and I find it a bit difficult to trust people."

"You can trust us," Izzy said firmly. "You can trust us with anything."

"Amen," Indigo murmured. "You can."

She took a breath. "I'm in love with Finn Kelly."

"Oh," Izzy said, smiling. "Not surprising."

"At all," Indigo added.

Beth was a little miffed. She thought it was surprising. "Well, I only just figured it out." She sniffed. "It wasn't supposed to happen. We were supposed to have one night together and that was it, go our separate ways."

"Uh-oh." Indigo squeezed her hand tighter. "Getting pregnant must have been a shock then. No wonder you looked like a ghost."

"Yeah," Beth said, feeling inexplicably lighter now that all her secrets were out. "That's kind of an understatement. Finn wants a family and he wants to be around to see his kid grow up, be a father, and he wants some legal protection for the child and for me. And when he suggested marriage, I thought, why not? I mean…we're virtually already married. Living in the same house, sharing the same bed. We're just…not in love. Or rather, he's not in love with me."

Izzy gave her hand a last squeeze, then let go, taking a sip of her shandy. "Are you sure about that?"

"It looks like he is to me," Indigo said, picking up her knitting again.

Beth's heart thumped painfully. "He's not. He was very clear that he wasn't. It looks that way because he's a good guy. He helps everyone; it's not just about me. And he was very clear about what he could give me and what he couldn't."

Izzy's brow furrowed, but all she said was "So what are you going to do? Or rather, what do you want to do?"

Beth rubbed at the slick surface of her glass. "I don't know. I thought I'd be fine with what we have, which is pretty good. But...sometimes I say things or ask about things that clearly hurt him. I grew up in a house constantly full of anger and emotional distress, and I don't want that for our kid."

"You shouldn't want that for you either," Izzy pointed out, her dark eyes full of kindness and warmth. "You deserve better than that, Beth."

Tears filled her eyes yet again, and she had to put her hand up to scrub them away. "Stupid pregnancy hormones," she muttered.

Izzy glanced away to give her some time to pull herself together, which Beth was grateful for.

"He deserves better too," she said in a firmer voice. "I want to look after him the way he looks after me."

"Yes," Izzy said. "He really does deserve that."

"You need to talk to him," Indigo muttered. "Just lay it all out."

Izzy nodded. "Agreed. If you're going to be married, you have to be honest with each other. You can't let this stuff fester, especially when a kid is involved."

As one, they all looked to where Gus stood, wiping her hands on her jeans, obviously pleading for something from Finn, who was shaking his head.

Chase's first wife had left Brightwater Valley when Gus was five and she hadn't been back since. Beth could never understand how a mother could leave her child like that, with not even one visit.

"No," she said. "You're right. I can't. I already told him we need to talk, but I'm not sure how he's going to take it."

"And if he doesn't take it well?" Izzy glanced back at her. "What will you do then?"

Beth's heart squeezed tight.

"I don't know," she said bleakly. "I really don't know."

———

Gus, in true Gus fashion, was pleading for a shandy, and since she'd already had one, Finn wasn't inclined to allow her another, even if the ones Jim made for her were mostly lemonade.

"Please, Finn." Gus danced around in front of him. "Just one more."

"That's a no, Gussie. And I think you heard me the first time."

Gus scowled. "I'm going to ask Dad."

"You do that. I'm sure he'll be much more understanding."

Gus rolled her eyes, sniffed, then stalked off, the epitome of a young teen in high dudgeon.

"Don't tell me," Levi said, wandering over to

him, having finished fiddling with the projector. "She wanted another shandy?"

"Of course she wanted another shandy." Finn put his hands in his pockets and scanned the crowd, his gaze coming to rest, as it always seemed to do, on Beth, who was sitting on the couch from HQ with Izzy and Indigo.

The other two were holding Beth's hands, obviously in solidarity about something, while Beth looked down at her lap. Her loose ponytail had fallen over one shoulder, a lock of white-blond hair hiding her expression. She was in a loose, white shirt this evening and a pair of worn jeans, simple clothes that nevertheless seemed to highlight how pretty she was, how she glowed like the sun.

"She looks about as happy as she did up at the farmhouse," Levi observed, picking up on the direction of Finn's gaze.

"Don't you have something better to do, Levi?" Chase's voice came from behind them, and Finn swung around to find his brother standing there.

"No," Levi said. "I don't."

"Are you sure?" Chase did not sound happy.

Levi glanced at him and then at Finn, then clearly deciding discretion was the better part of valor, he said, "Perhaps I'd better start the movie."

"What is it tonight?" Chase asked, coming to stand next to Finn.

Levi's wicked grin came out to play. "*Die Hard.*"

Finn shook his head. "Again?"

"Hey, everyone loves it."

It was true, everyone did, though Chase got rather prudish about the language when Gus was around.

Predictably, Chase sighed. "Isn't there anything more…family friendly?"

Levi shrugged. "Hey, the town voted, and they all voted for *Die Hard*. What can you do?"

The "vote" consisted of a box on the bar of the Rose, where everyone noted down their preferred movie on a slip of paper. Only one vote was allowed, but Levi had been known to cheat shamelessly.

"Come on, Levi," said Teddy Grange, who'd placed her deck chair right in front of the screen, as close as she could get. "Let's get this movie going."

"Yes, come on." Shirley, who was sitting next to her, agreed. "Hurry up."

"Coming, ladies." Levi grinned and moved away to deal with the DVD player and the projector.

"He's not wrong," Chase said after he'd gone. "What are you doing to that poor girl?"

It took Finn a moment to realize what Chase was talking about. "Who? Beth?"

"Of course Beth, you bloody idiot," Chase growled, grumpy and not bothering to hide it. "Look at her. She's upset."

It was true. He could tell she was upset by the way her head was still bowed and the way the other two were gripping her hands. The sight made him ache, though he tried hard to ignore it.

"I didn't do anything to her," he said flatly, as if he could make himself believe it. "And why do you assume it's got anything to do with me anyway?"

"Because she's been happy right up until the time she got together with you and fell pregnant. Ever since then, every time I see her she looks bloody miserable."

"She wasn't happy right up until then," Finn couldn't help pointing out. "She was just pretending."

"Right," Chase said. "Like you're pretending."

Finn tensed. "I'm not pretending."

"Don't be a dick. Of course you are. You're pretending you don't give a shit about her, and quite frankly you're not doing a very good job of it."

Finn turned sharply to stare at his brother, defensive anger twisting in his gut. Chase stared back, gunmetal-gray eyes glinting silver in the twilight dusk.

"I don't know what's going on between you and her," Chase went on, obviously in the mood to deliver a lecture, "but it's clear she's unhappy, and I don't like it when my brother is making a perfectly lovely woman unhappy."

Finn wished he could deny it, tell Chase that it was nothing to do with him, but he knew that it was. He knew that he was being unfair to Beth, because she sure as hell didn't deserve it. The issue was, he didn't know what to do about it.

"I'm trying not to," he said after a long moment. "Believe me, I'm trying. But…"

"But what?"

Finn let out a breath and glanced back at the women sitting on the couch, trying to figure out what to tell his brother. "I have to keep some distance, Chase. I can't…let her get close."

Chase scowled at him. "Why the hell not? You're going to marry her. How are you going to keep some distance when she's your wife?"

"You know we don't have that kind of relationship. It's not the same as you and Izzy. You love Izzy and—"

"And what? You don't love Beth?"

"No."

"What about if she loves you?"

A muscle leapt in Finn's jaw. "She doesn't."

"Yeah, we've had this conversation before, and you said the same thing, but I'm not so sure about that now. Look at her, Finn. That is not the picture of a happy woman."

The ache in his heart deepened, became a raw pain. He'd never wanted to hurt her, not after what she'd already gone through with losing her baby and having her boyfriend just up and leave her.

But he was hurting her—he could see that. Yet what else could he do?

He couldn't let her in, couldn't bridge the gap between them. He had nothing to give her. Nothing at all.

She deserves better than that, you selfish asshole.

Yeah, well, what else was new? The only alternative was to let her go and he couldn't do that. Not when she was expecting their child and definitely not when everyone else in her life had left her.

"I can't let her go," he said. "She's been through a lot, and I can't just abandon her."

"Did I say anything about abandoning her?"

Finn let out a breath, not wanting to talk about it. "Drop it, Chase."

"Hell no, I'm not going to drop it. You're being an asshole, Finn Kelly, and I want to know why. Is it because of Sheri? Is that what this is about?"

A cheer went up as Levi finally got the projector going and the DVD started playing. Someone yelled "yippee ki-yay," thankfully leaving off the swear word out of deference to those with more sensitive faculties.

Finn glanced over to where Beth was sitting. She was leaning back on the couch now, chatting with the other two. If she'd been upset before, she didn't seem to be now, but that light he'd always seen in her, that bright glow…it felt dim. As if someone had turned down the brightness on her.

Your fault. You're making her miserable.

"I don't have anything left, Chase," he heard

himself say flatly. "I gave everything to Sheri. Every last piece of me. And when she died…that was it. She took it all with her. There's nothing left now, nothing at all." He gritted his teeth. "And certainly nothing left to give Beth."

There was a long silence.

The opening credits were playing, everyone settling down to watch.

"That's the biggest heap of bullshit I've ever heard in my life," Chase growled. "Sheri was your first love, and she was your first loss, and you don't get over that. I get it. But she didn't take your heart with her, and quite frankly she'd be more than a little pissed with you thinking she had."

Finn bit down on the thing he really wanted to say, which was to tell his brother to butt out of his goddamn business. But sadly, Chase wasn't wrong. Sheri hadn't been the least bit sentimental, and she *would* be pissed with him and the candle he was continually holding for her.

"I'm not loving anyone like that again," he said instead, a hint of a growl in his voice too. "I can't."

"Won't, you mean," Chase snapped.

Finn barely resisted the urge to take his brother's strong neck in his hands and strangle him. "Screw you. You don't know a thing about it."

"Maybe not. But what I do know is that you'd better sort your shit out because what you're doing now isn't working."

"You think I don't realize that?"

Chase's gray gaze was very direct. "Sheri's gone, Finn. But Beth isn't. Beth is right here. Which means you need to figure out what you want. And if that's a big happy family without having to make any sacrifices or take any risks, then you're going to have to think again. Life doesn't work that way and you know it."

Then Chase stalked past him, going over to the couch where the three Deep River women were sitting. Izzy's face brightened as soon as his brother appeared and she held out a hand to him, glowing with happiness.

At the other end of the couch, Indigo knitted and smiled as Chase said something to her.

Sitting in the middle was Beth. She glanced at him, but there was no bright smile for him on her face. She looked pale and drawn instead.

Then all of a sudden, she got up and began threading her way through the arranged chairs in the direction of the gallery.

He shouldn't follow, not when anything he had to say she probably wouldn't want to hear. But he couldn't help himself.

He headed off after her.

Chapter 17

BETH SHUT THE DOOR OF THE GALLERY BEHIND her, the sound of the movie abruptly muting. Then she began to do a slow inventory of the displays, noting what was on show and what wasn't and thinking about what gaps there were.

Anything to distract herself from meeting Finn's dark gaze across the heads of the people watching the movie and feeling her heart tumble like an acrobat over and over in her chest.

Seeing the walls behind his eyes. Walls he was never going to lower for her, and she knew that. She could sense it. He was protecting himself fiercely, locked up tight like an oyster.

She understood. Letting people in was hard. But she could still feel the pressure of Izzy's and Indigo's grips on her hands, steadying her, letting her know they were there, and she knew while it was hard, it was also worth it to lower those walls and let people in.

People you trusted. But maybe that was the problem.

She loved him, she could admit that now, and while she'd never demand his love in return, she did need his trust. And it seemed obvious that he wasn't going to give it to her, or the most secret, essential part of himself.

In which case how was it ever going to work between them? How would their marriage survive without trust? How would they ever be a family together?

If he doesn't let you in, then you're never going to be a family.

Beth's throat closed, the thought much more painful than it had any right to be.

Oh lord, but she was tired of feeling like crying every five seconds. It was getting old.

She moved over to the counter to have a look in the stock book, then heard the gallery door open behind her. She turned to find Finn coming in, closing the door behind him.

Her heartbeat sped up, her palms feeling sweaty. Ridiculous to feel like this every time he was near, especially given she'd been living with him for the past two weeks. But then that seemed to be her stock response to him. He made her feel like an over-wrought teenage girl in the grip of her first crush.

He took a couple of steps toward her, then stopped, his hands where they customarily were, which was in the pockets of his worn jeans.

God, he was gorgeous. Dark and brooding and powerful. No wonder she felt like a teenager when he was around.

No wonder you're in love with him.

Yeah, well, she could do with being in love with him a little less, because quite frankly it sucked every bit as much as she'd thought it would.

"Hi," she said, the word coming out breathless. "Did you…want something?"

"You wanted to talk, Beth. So here I am."

"Oh, I thought we were going to do that after the movie."

"I saw you leave, and I've seen the movie before." He lifted a shoulder. "If you want to talk, here I am."

Crap. She did want to talk, but now that he was standing there with his dark, enigmatic gaze on hers, she felt nervous.

She swallowed, reaching for her pendant and feeling the reassurance of the cool silver against her palm. Sunny, her daughter, a reminder of what Beth had promised her—to find happiness and strength, a new life worthy of her daughter.

She could do this. She *had* to. For their child's sake.

"Okay, fine." She lifted her chin. "So…what are we doing, Finn? How exactly do you see our marriage working? Because right now it feels like it's not going to, and we're not even married yet."

He didn't move, not saying anything for a moment. But that was the way with him. He took his time before he spoke.

"So, what do you need?" His voice was low,

husky. "What do you need from me? You said something about a road map."

She had. She'd wanted some way of navigating around the topics he didn't want to talk about, some way of knowing what his boundaries were so at least she wouldn't end up inadvertently hurting him.

But that wasn't going to work now. Because actually she didn't want to avoid those topics. She wanted him to trust her enough to talk about them, and if he couldn't fill in the parts that were quicksand and briars, at least she could help make them less boggy and sharp.

That was what a partnership was, wasn't it? It was supposed to be about mutual support, about sharing the load.

She'd never had that with Troy. When she'd needed him, he'd left. But she could see herself having that with Finn. And what was more, she wanted it.

"I did say that," she said. "But I don't think a road map is going to be enough for me anymore."

He was very still, watching her in that steady way he had, no hint of his emotions on his face. "Then what else do you want?"

"You," she said, just coming right out with it because why the hell not? "All of you. Not only you looking after me or cooking me dinner. Or you holding me at night. I want you to feel like you can confide in me. Share things with me. Lean on me. I want you to trust me."

A muscle leapt in his jaw. "I do trust you."

"No, you don't," she said sadly. "Because if you did, you wouldn't change the subject whenever I try and talk about that bath. You'd come into my workspace in the cabin. You wouldn't tell me you are fine every time I ask if you're okay. You'd let me take care of you. You'd let me give you what you give me."

The muscle leapt again and he looked away, those wide shoulders stiff with tension. "I can't, Beth. I'm sorry, but I can't."

Her stomach hollowed, though really she should have expected this response. He'd been clear with her from the beginning that a relationship, a real relationship, wasn't what he wanted.

"Can't what?" she asked anyway.

He glanced back and it was as if that door to his soul had been opened and she could see through it. She'd always known he was intense, but the ferocity of the emotion that burned in his eyes now stole the breath from her body.

"If you're expecting love," he said in a low voice, "I can't give it to you. Sheri was the love of my life, and I will never love anyone the way I loved her. Not ever."

It was nothing she didn't know already, even though he'd never said it so explicitly before. And it wasn't surprising. Finn was a man of deep, fierce emotions, and when he committed to something, he committed with his entire being.

Yet Beth's heart squeezed tight all the same. "I'm not asking you to love me like that. I would never ask you to love me like that. All I'm asking for is some trust."

"Trust? That's all you want?" His dark gaze blazed. "Shit, Beth, you should ask for more than that. You deserve more than that."

Did she? Did she really? No one else had ever said anything about what she deserved before. Her father hadn't wanted anything to do with her depression and her mother made it all about her and her own fragility. And Troy had just left.

No one had said *you deserve more*.

"I don't know," she said thickly. "Do I?"

"Of course you do." Finn took an involuntary step forward, an anger she didn't understand leaping high in his gaze. "You're beautiful and funny and smart. And so damn talented. You light up the room. You bring sunshine everywhere and you just…you just bloody dazzle."

She blinked, her eyes prickling for about the millionth time that day. "Well, if I dazzle and I'm so damn talented and funny and brilliant, why can't I get more from you?"

The words hung in the air, heavy and weighted.

She probably shouldn't have said them, but she didn't take them back.

Finn didn't look away this time. "Why? Why do you want more from me? What the hell can I possibly give you that you can't get from anyone else?"

There didn't seem to be much point hiding what she felt for him, not now. And why shouldn't he know anyway? It was the truth.

"Because I'm in love with you, you idiot," she said huskily. "And look, I don't much care if you love me back or not. I just want you to let me love you."

The expression on his face shifted, shock giving way to something else, something bright and fierce and raw. The he shut it down.

"No," he said in a guttural voice. "Don't do that. Don't say you love me. Love wasn't part of the deal, remember?"

"Actually, I don't remember any kind of deal. You talked about what *you* could give *me*. But there weren't any rules about what I could give you."

"No," he repeated, and this time she could hear the desperate note in his tone. "That's not happening. I won't let you. I don't want you giving me one goddamn thing."

It should have hurt, that rejection, because it *was* a rejection. And maybe if he'd been gentle and firm about it, it would have. Maybe it would even have broken her a little.

But he wasn't gentle and firm. He wasn't even hard and uncompromising, the way he could sometimes be when his will was tested.

No, she'd seen that expression on his face, the fierce, bright one. It was longing—she was sure of it. And it came to her suddenly that he wasn't arguing because he didn't want what she had to give. He was arguing because he did. He wanted it desperately.

He stood there rigidly, his jaw tight, everything about him radiating tension. And part of her wanted to end this conversation and stop pushing him, tell him it was okay, they could discuss this at a later date, never if that's what he wanted.

But she knew she couldn't do that. Because deep down, she suspected he *didn't* want that. He was hungry for connection. She'd felt it every time he took her in his arms, in the care he lavished on her and on the animals he looked after. In the town he protected with his quiet, steadying presence.

He wanted it, yet for some reason he was denying himself.

"Why not?" she asked quietly.

———

Beth stood in front of him, curvy and perfect, her white-blond hair glowing in the last rays of the sunshine streaming through the windows of the gallery. Her green gaze was direct and he could see the strength inside her. Not a brittle strength but supple, flexible. Willing to bend but not break.

She loved him, she'd said. The one thing they'd

promised each other wouldn't happen. The one reason why all this worked.

He didn't love her, but she loved him.

It wasn't supposed to be this way. It wasn't supposed to happen.

This wasn't supposed to be complicated. It was supposed to be easy. And that was the problem, because nothing was easy when feelings got involved; everything became that much harder, that much more painful.

He didn't want pain for her, not after everything she'd been through.

He'd told her the truth when he'd said that she deserved more, because she did. She deserved happiness and stability. She deserved love. She deserved the life she'd come here to claim and a man who could love her the way she should be loved, which was with every part of him.

But he wasn't that man. He'd never be that man. He didn't have the ability anymore, not after Sheri. And he couldn't allow her to give him her heart while he kept his locked away. It wasn't fair to her.

Liar. Don't make this all about her when it's your own damn cowardice you're protecting.

The thought wound through his brain, but he shoved it away.

He wasn't protecting himself. This was for her sake and cowardice would be letting her love him while he gave nothing back. He could tell himself all he liked that bringing her the food she liked and looking after her when she was sick and moving her into his house was enough, but it wasn't, and he knew it.

Beth Grant was a woman who needed to be loved.

"Why not?" he echoed, trying to ignore the way his chest ached and his hands longed to reach for her, to pull her close. "Because it's not fair, Beth. It's not fair to you. Not after all you've gone through."

Her gaze flickered. "Don't give me that. Don't make this about me. Anyway, aren't I the one who gets to decide what's fair to me?"

A strange agitation gripped him. He pulled a hand from his pocket and shoved it through his hair. "So what are you saying? You'd be happy to marry a man who doesn't love you? You came here for a new life, Beth. To find happiness. And I can't give you that happiness. I can't."

She watched him, and he didn't understand the look in her eyes because by rights she should be angry with him, yet there was no anger at all there. Only what looked like compassion, which made the restless, antsy feeling inside him even worse.

"But you want to," she said quietly. "Don't you?"

He stilled, his heart beating way too fast.

You do. You want her. You want to be with her, have her in your house, in your bed, in your arms. You want to talk to her, confide in her, share everything with her, and you have since the day you first met her.

No, shit, he didn't want that, and he didn't know where this weird, restless, agitated feeling was coming from. He couldn't give her that even if he'd wanted to because he'd given all of that to Sheri and he had nothing left in his heart for Beth.

Nothing.

"It doesn't matter if I want to or not," he said flatly, trying to calm the hell down. "The fact is, I can't. Sheri died and everything I had to give died with her. I've got nothing left for anyone, not even you."

"And our child?" Beth asked in the same quiet voice. "Does that include them too?"

His heart twisted. "That's different."

"Is it? So I suppose Gus is different too. And Chase. And Levi. And everyone in this whole damn town. You love them because it's different."

It's not different. You love all those people, so why can't you love her?

No. Bullshit. Of course it was different. Those people were family, and you had to love family. You didn't get a choice with family.

But he had a choice with Beth.

Beth was someone he could love and love intensely. She was so bright, so beautiful, and she was having his child. She was compassionate and strong. She was the light to leaven his dark and she wanted his intensity. She reveled in it in a way Sheri never did.

She suited the man he was now far better than Sheri.

Which meant he couldn't have her. Ever.

He couldn't give himself to another person again, not like that. Losing Sheri had nearly killed him. He'd been a shell of a man afterward, his heart dead inside his chest, and it had taken him a long time to come back to himself again. A long time to heal.

Beth was wrong. He didn't want to be the one to give her happiness. Yes, he wanted her in his bed and in his arms, but that's it. He didn't want her in his heart. He didn't want to let himself love anyone the way he'd loved Sheri ever again.

Keeping his heart to himself ensured he could be there for the people that needed him, and that was the most important thing.

Even if it meant shutting out the one person who didn't deserve it.

"Yes." The word sounded flat in his ears. "It's different."

"How?"

"I don't have a choice with them. They're my family."

Beth was standing so close, her scent surrounding him, and he could see the silver pendant at her throat and the frantic race of her pulse beneath it.

Could see the compassion and sympathy in her eyes, as if he was the one who deserved it, not her.

"And I'm not?" she asked gently. "Is that what you're saying?"

"I'm saying you're a choice." He couldn't be anything but hard now because that would at least keep her at a distance. "And I can't choose you."

It was a shitty thing to say, and he wanted her to turn from him and walk away. To take her bright, shining presence away, along with the temptation to throw himself into her light and burn there.

But she only nodded, as if this was something she expected him to say. "I get it, Finn," she said. "Maybe if I'd lost someone like you lost Sheri, then I might make the same choice. And I'm not going to demand you make a different one. It's hard to love again when you've had a loss, and it's hard to trust when you've been let down. It's hard to reach out, to make yourself vulnerable." She took a little breath. "But if there's anything I've learned while being here it's that suffering alone doesn't help. You need people around you, and you need to let them in." She took a step toward him, coming close, but didn't touch him, though he could tell she wanted to. "You taught me to trust again, Finn Kelly. You taught me I was strong enough to ask for help and that *is* a strength, no matter what some people might say. And I want you to feel that strength too. So...if and when you decide to make a different choice, I'll be here."

He stared at her, not understanding at first. "What do you mean you'll be here?"

She smiled, even though her eyes were full of tears. A genuine, beautiful Beth smile. "Well, I'm hardly going to walk away from you, am I? You were always there for me. Why shouldn't I be there for you?"

"Beth, I—"

"No, don't say anything. You don't have to now. We'll sort things out later." She hesitated a moment. "I'm going to give you some space though. So I hope you don't mind if sleep at Clint's tonight."

He felt as if the ground was abruptly sloping away from him, his balance shot, unsteady on his feet. He wasn't sure what he'd expected, her to walk away, get angry, shout at him, anything but this compassion and sympathy.

Even Sheri would have shouted at him, since she'd had no patience with his "fussing" around her, as she termed it.

Yet Beth wasn't doing any of that. She was only smiling at him as if he'd given her a gift, not flung her love back in her face.

"I can't marry you, Beth," he said bluntly, ignoring the growl of his more possessive self, because it seemed she didn't understand. "You know that, right? Not now."

A tear slid down her cheek, which didn't make any sense to him because she was still smiling. "That's your decision. If you don't want to, you don't want to. Just know that whatever you decide, I'm not going to go back to the States. I'm staying in New Zealand. And I'll stay in Brightwater Valley."

Relief gripped him, so intense he could hardly breathe. All he could do was nod.

Then without a word, she walked up to him and touched his cheek gently, as if she was saying goodbye. Then her hand dropped away, and she went past him, out into the night.

Chapter 18

FINN SAT ON THE DECK IN THE DARKNESS NURSING a beer.

He liked the night. Liked the blackness broken by the scattering of stars, liked how they glittered like jewels against the sky, undimmed by any city lights. And he liked how quiet it was here. How he could hear nothing but the crickets, a distant morepork calling, and the sound of Karl's claws on the wood as the dog came over and put his head in Finn's lap, as if Finn needed comforting.

Which was ridiculous, because he didn't.

He'd come straight from seeing Beth at the gallery to his house, needing to be in solitude and quiet to escape the damn noise in his head.

She was probably going to move out, and he was okay with that. He'd come to some equilibrium of having her in the house, of balancing her and Sheri, and it had worked for the past couple of weeks. But he couldn't ask her to stay, not after their talk.

He wasn't sure where that left them with the child, but he'd figure it out.

A heavy, dark feeling coiled in his gut, telling him he was a liar, that he needed her and she needed him, and was he really going to let her walk away?

He ignored it. He'd made his choice. Being alone was easier, less complicated, and it required nothing at all of him emotionally, which was what he'd preferred all along.

No, you don't, you damn idiot.

The thought irritated him, so he ignored it, scratching Karl behind the ears. The dog's head whipped up all of a sudden and he turned, looking into the blackness. There was no barking, but abruptly he took off down the driveway.

Finn stared after him, puzzled. Until Chase's tall figure appeared, striding up the slope, Karl trotting along behind him.

Tension crawled along Finn's back. Shit. Looked like his brother was in full-blown protector mode.

He got to his feet as Chase stormed up the steps to the house, coming to a stop in front of him, glaring furiously.

"What the bloody hell do you think you're doing?" Chase demanded straight out. "I have one upset fiancée, one upset daughter, and Beth, who should be upset, trying to make sure my fiancée and daughter are okay."

That was very Beth, wanting to make sure other people were okay, even when she was the one who should be upset.

And what are you doing? Sitting on your deck

having a beer after you flung her love back in her face.

Guilt shifted inside him. He ignored it and the pulsing ache in his chest.

"What do you mean, what am I doing? This is about Beth, I take it?"

"Of course it's about Beth," Chase growled. "She came out of the gallery, watched the rest of the movie, and then when Izzy asked her why she looked so pale afterward, she dissolved into tears."

Finn gripped his beer bottle so tight it was a wonder it didn't snap in two. "She told me that she was in love with me," he gritted out. "And I told her that I couldn't return the feeling. That's it."

Chase's gaze narrowed into thin, sharp slivers of iron. "What goddamn bullshit. Of course you can return the feeling, you dick. You were in love with her the moment she appeared."

He's right. That's why you could never be friends with her. That's why you had to push her away.

Finn ignored the thought and the raw ache in his chest. "No, I'm not. I wanted her, Chase. That's it. It was entirely physical, nothing more."

"Again, I call bullshit. You've been running around after her, doing things for her, wanting to support her and marry her, fluffing your fucking nest in preparation for her to sit in it."

This time anger came to the rescue. "It's about

the kid, Chase," he growled back. "That's it. There's nothing more to it than that, okay?"

"If it were just about the kid, you wouldn't be sleeping with her every night, which is apparently what you've been doing."

"Yeah, and?" Finn took a step, getting in his brother's face. "What business is it of yours anyway?"

"It's my business because I can't stand seeing my brother finally getting something good happening in his life and then throwing it away for no apparent reason," Chase shot back. "Beth is an amazing woman. She's good for you and I think you know that. She's perfect for you—"

"I don't care what she is," Finn interrupted sharply. "Don't you get it? I loved Sheri. I had the best marriage with Sheri. She was all I ever wanted and now there's someone else and I..." He stopped, breathing fast and hard, his whole body vibrating with the force of an emotion he didn't understand. He'd told Beth loving her was a choice and he'd made that choice. He didn't want to love her. He didn't.

But all the words were sounding weirdly hollow, like justifications, like excuses.

He took a breath, trying to get some air into his lungs. "You don't understand. What happens if I'm happier with her than I was with Sheri? Does my marriage to Sheri then matter at all? Was it a mistake? If I fall in love with Beth, is she the love of my life instead of Sheri?" He took another step, his heart pounding, struggling to articulate all the doubts suddenly crowding in. "Will I forget her, Chase? If I fall in love with Beth, does that mean Sheri doesn't matter anymore?"

Chase didn't move. "No, and I think you know that, Finn," he said gruffly. "That's all bullshit, just excuses. Loving someone else doesn't mean Sheri didn't matter and it doesn't cancel out your marriage. You were a different person then. Sheri was perfect for you when you married her, and Beth is perfect for you now, you bloody idiot. Can't you see that?"

"It's not about me," he shot back, though something inside him whispered that that was a lie. "This is about not wanting to tie Beth to a relationship where she doesn't get what she needs. And it's about protecting her—"

"No it isn't," Chase said sharply. "You think I don't know what you're doing? I did the same goddamn thing when the shit hit the fan with Izzy. I thought I was protecting her, but I wasn't. I was protecting myself."

He's right. Because it's easier to do that than it is to risk your heart again.

Well, wasn't he right to protect himself? Hadn't he been through enough? Didn't he deserve something easy for once? Something that didn't hurt?

"You're shit-scared," Chase went on, his silver

gaze roaming over Finn. "Don't think I can't see that. And I get it. You lost Sheri and I know you're grieving. I know it hurts. But she'd have no patience for this crap. She'd tell you to pull your head out of your ass, stop building a shrine for her, stop standing vigil, and go and be happy."

The barb struck home, because of course Sheri would say that. She'd tell him he was being ridiculous. Tell him he was being too sentimental.

She did always want you to be happy, remember?

He did remember, especially those last moments. He'd held her hand and she'd given him the most lovely smile. "Stop looking so sad," she'd said. "I'll be okay. But I want you to be happy, okay? Promise me?"

He had. He'd promised her, all the while knowing he'd never be happy again.

So what good is that promise when you never meant to keep it?

He couldn't stand the look in his brother's eyes, couldn't stand the way his thoughts kept circling, so he turned away, walking blindly down the steps and heading to the edge of the flat lawn, where the ground sloped down into the bush, where the bath was.

He stopped, staring unseeing into the darkness.

"How can I do that?" he said, sensing his brother nearby. "Losing her nearly killed me and I can't...I don't want to do it again."

"I don't know." Chase's voice was flat. "I got no advice for you about that. All I know is that loving someone else doesn't mean you stop loving Sheri. Love doesn't work that way."

"I don't know if I can go through that again."

"Then figure it out, dumbass," Chase said impatiently. "Because you know what? You were right, it *is* about her. And Beth deserves better."

It took Finn a long while to realize that Chase had gone and that he was standing alone in the dark with the outdoor bath in front of him.

That stupid bath.

Sheri had wanted it put in, then had taken one bath in it and decided she didn't like it and hadn't gone in it again.

Beth wanted to use it. She'd love it.

She would. He could see her loving sitting in the warm water and looking out over the bush, washing that beautiful hair of hers.

He looked down at the bath, his heart twisting around in his chest. Hell, he'd made that damn bath a holy relic to a woman who hadn't even liked it. Just as he'd turned the cabin into a big deal by never visiting, so he couldn't see Beth in Sheri's place. Never talking about Sheri, guarding her memory jealously.

But no, it wasn't her memory he was guarding, was it?

It was himself. It was his heart.

Chase was right, Sheri would be appalled at him. She'd never had any patience with his intensity, and she'd be horrified at him not wanting Beth to use the bath because of her. A waste, she would have said. She would have been happy to see it being used, just like she'd love to see Beth using her cabin.

She would have been happy to see him using his heart too.

Be happy, she'd told him.

So why aren't you honoring the promise you made to her?

Finn went very still, his breathing fast. *You're shit-scared*, Chase had told him. And yeah, he was. He could admit that now.

He was scared of loss, scared of pain. Scared of risking his heart again.

Well, and who wasn't? Who'd choose to throw themselves into that fire again willingly?

Beth did.

The breath left his body in a sudden rush because it was true. Beth had. Even after losing her baby and her partner, even after experiencing depression, she hadn't chosen to lock herself away as he had; she'd chosen to come to New Zealand. To find happiness for herself.

She'd chosen to love him. And even when he'd flung it back in her face, she hadn't walked away. She'd told him she'd be here for him if he ever changed his mind.

Her courage and quiet strength made a mockery of everything he'd thrown at her, all those stupid excuses. Everything he'd believed about keeping his heart to himself and remaining strong.

It's hard to reach out, to make yourself vulnerable...

That's what she'd said, and she was right—it was hard. But she'd done it. She'd made herself vulnerable; she'd let him in.

Only for you to fling it back in her face.

Pain splintered in his chest. Goddamn, what an asshole he was. What a selfish, self-absorbed asshole. He'd given her nothing but excuses, while she'd given him honesty. She'd given him love.

Finn took a ragged, painful breath and stared at the stars glittering overhead.

Could he give her that back? Could he make the choice to love her?

It's too late to choose, you dumb idiot. You already love her. You loved her the moment you first met her.

He felt something moving through him then, something wild and passionate and hot. Familiar but different, because love wasn't the same this time around. It wasn't new, and he was older, with more life experience. Yet it was just as powerful, just as intense.

Yes. He loved her. He loved Beth. She was the light in his life, and he'd craved it. But it was a different craving to the one he'd had for Sheri. That had been new and wondrous. First-time love.

That love was still there. He'd always have it, he could see that now. He wouldn't lose it. She would always be with him. He felt it in his heart, in his bones. She wasn't in that bath or in the cabin, and she wasn't in that hairbrush he still kept in his drawer. She was in his heart, and while he loved her, he'd never lose her. Because love…love was immortal like that.

Yet he had a future ahead of him, a future that she wouldn't be part of, and he suspected she wouldn't want to be part of it anyway. Because this was *his* future. His and Beth's.

Finn stood there for a long moment. Then he shook himself and went into the house and up the stairs to his bedroom. And he pulled open the drawer and took out the hairbrush.

Sheri's hairbrush with strands of blond hair still caught in the bristles.

He'd kept it for some reason he now couldn't fathom, because she wasn't there in that brush either. But he picked it up and took it downstairs, out into the night.

He stood on the deck and carefully pulled loose a strand of gold hair and held it up between his fingers. Then he opened his fingers and let it go.

"I've fallen in love again, Sheri," he said quietly to the night and the spirit of the woman he'd loved and still did. "And she's not like you." He pulled another strand loose and set it free to drift in the night air. "But I think you'd really like her." He pulled the last strand free. "I know I could be happy with her. So what do you say? Shall I do it?"

The night didn't say a word, but he didn't need it to.

He knew the answer in his heart already.

Be happy, Sheri had told him.

Perhaps it was time to do what she said for a change.

Finn let loose the final strand of hair and watched it drift away. Then he put down the hairbrush, walked down the steps, and set about making some preparations.

———

"You know men are really terrible," Izzy said. "And I include Chase in this sometimes too."

Beth was sitting on the couch on Izzy and Chase's deck, trying not to think about how it reminded her of sitting out on Finn's deck with him.

She felt bruised and sore, like her heart had been ripped out of her chest, but fundamentally, she knew she'd be okay.

She hadn't wanted to cry in front of Izzy and Indigo, but she hadn't been able to help it when they'd asked her what was wrong. And instantly she'd been surrounded by warm, feminine comfort. She hadn't had that before, and it felt good, so she'd let herself have it.

What Finn would do now was anyone's guess, and she wasn't sure what would happen if he was serious about not marrying her. She would go on, though. Because this was only heartbreak. It wasn't grief or the black pit of depression. And this time she wasn't alone. She had her friends—hell, she had the whole town—to help her through it.

"They are," she replied, wishing the chamomile tea Indigo had thrust into her hands was whisky instead, because she could sure use it now. "I hate them."

"Me too," Indigo said in solidarity. "They're the worst."

"And Finn Kelly is the worst of them," Beth added.

"He is," Izzy agreed.

"Stupid Levi comes a close second," Indigo muttered.

"Beth?" The voice was deep, male, and utterly unwelcome.

The three women turned to see Finn standing at the bottom of the steps in front of Chase's house, staring at them.

Izzy stood up, frowning furiously at him. "You're not allowed here, Finn Kelly. Why don't you go back home?"

Beth's throat had closed, because he was looking at her intensely and for the first time there was nothing guarded in his expression. Every emotion was laid bare for her to see.

He didn't look at Izzy. "Beth, I want to talk to you. Please."

"Why?" She didn't move. "Have you come to a decision? Because if you have—"

"I was wrong," he interrupted quietly but very firmly. "I gave you a whole bunch of excuses about what I could and couldn't give you, but in the end, it was all bullshit."

A shiver whispered over her skin, her eyes filling with tears. "What do you mean?"

"I was protecting myself because I was afraid. Afraid of loving you and what it would mean, and how it would affect my memories of Sheri... God, it was so much crap." He took a breath. "Losing her hurt...it hurt a lot, and I didn't want to open myself up to that kind of pain again, but..." His black eyes burned. "You did. You opened yourself up to me and to the town, even after everything you went through. You showed me what true bravery is, Bethany Grant, and I can't...shit, I can't let that go." He took a step toward her. "Because the truth is, honey, love was never a choice when it came to you. I've been in love with you from the moment I met you."

The breath caught in Beth's throat, her vision flooding with tears.

"Well," Indigo said. "That's quite the speech."

Finn didn't even blink. "Beth, you're my sunshine. You light up the dark places inside me. You're strong and understanding and generous and caring. You're brave and beautiful. Sheri wanted me to be happy, and I know I can be. But I can only be happy with you."

Beth took a ragged breath and got to her feet and found herself almost running down the steps to him. Because how could she hold back after that?

She couldn't. She didn't want to.

She'd told him she'd be here for him, and she was. She always would be.

Finn held out his hand to her, oddly formal. "Please, come with me. I want to show you something."

Perhaps it was a mistake. Perhaps she shouldn't have believed him. But he was here and she couldn't refuse.

Izzy made shooing motions, looking a bit misty-eyed, while Indigo gave her a big thumbs-up. So Beth took his hand and he led her back up the driveway to his house. Then, strangely, over to the outdoor bath that was full of hot water and was steaming gently. There were rose petals floating in it.

"Sheri wanted an outdoor bath," Finn said. "So I made her one. She had one bath in it, then decided she hated it and never used it again." He glanced at her, his gaze full of intensity, the door to his heart wide-open now, letting her see everything. "She'd be horrified if it was never used though. She'd want it to be enjoyed, and so would I." He lifted Beth's hand, grazing a kiss over her knuckles. "I'll always love Sheri. She'll always be part of me. But my future is with you, if you want to share it with me."

Tears were falling down Beth's cheeks, but she didn't stop them. Instead, she reached up and cupped Finn's cheek with her hand. "Of course she's part of you. Sunny is part of me. We don't lose them. We loved them, and because we did, we get to keep them forever. Love is the best way to remember, don't you think?"

Finn smiled and not just a half smile this time, but a full-on, blinding, joyous one that dazzled her completely.

Turned out that when Finn Kelly smiled, the entire planet lit up.

"Did you just read my mind?" he asked. "Because I was just thinking that very thing."

"I can, you know," she said, teasing just a bit. "You should watch those thoughts of yours."

He laughed and pulled her in close. "Take your clothes off, honey, and let's have a bath. I have a couple of other thoughts to share with you."

And he did, and much to her delight, they were suitably filthy ones.

But afterward, as she leaned back in his arms in the warm water of the bath, and they both stared up at the stars glittering in the sky, they shared other thoughts, deeper thoughts. Secrets and truths and futures. And the hidden depths of their souls.

It was going to be a good life, she knew.
It was going to be the life she'd always dreamed of.
And it was going to start right here, right now.
With him.

Epilogue

INDIGO JAMESON STOOD IN THE HALLWAY, facing the entrance to the living area, the broom clutched in both hands raised high, staring at the horror that sat in the middle of the living room rug.

It was huge.

She'd never seen an insect that big in all her life.

It was all long, segmented legs, quivering antennae, and sharp, pointy bits of chitin.

It was like something out of a prehistoric nightmare.

She'd just gotten off the phone with Beth after discussing the latest development in her housing woes. Finn had finally found a manager for the horse ranch, which meant she was going to have to find a place to live. The farmhouse was part of the employment package, and even though she wasn't going to be forced out, she'd decided she didn't want to live with some stranger.

What she'd wanted was to sit on the couch with a nice cup of chamomile tea and think about her options. Except she'd been foiled by the horror sitting on the rug.

She hated insects. She hated them. And the last

thing on earth she wanted to do was deal with this one, but since she was alone in the farmhouse and the only person to help her was herself, she had no choice.

Ah, well. What else was new? She'd been taking care of herself since she was fifteen, and quite frankly she'd done a damn good job of it, thank you very much.

One spiny, horrible insect was *not* going to get the better of her.

"Okay, Mr. Insect," she said aloud, because of course the insect was male, and men were the worst. Especially ones who menaced innocent females with their sharp, pointy bits. "We can do this the easy way, or we can do this the hard way."

"I'm all for the easy way myself," a deep, melted-honey voice said from the direction of the front door. "What's up, Indy? You look like you've seen a ghost."

Instantly Indigo's heartbeat sped up.

Great. Naturally it would be him. The bane of her life.

Levi King.

Where had he sprung from? She hadn't heard a car come up the farmhouse's long gravel driveway. Then again, she'd been involved with Mr. Insect over there and not listening out for visitors.

But she had no time to be annoyed by Levi's sudden appearance, not when that thing on the rug might dart at her. Hell, perhaps it could even fly. Now there was a horrifying thought.

"It's okay," she said determinedly, because she certainly didn't need him to help out. "I have it under control."

"You've got what under control?" Levi strolled up beside her and glanced into the living room. "Oh, you mean that wētā?"

Indigo blinked. "Wētā?"

"Yeah. That big insect sitting on the rug over there." Levi stepped into the living room and walked casually toward the horror. "Don't worry, I'll get rid of him for you."

"Don't touch it!" Indigo shrieked, not caring about her dignity as he bent down toward the insect. "It'll probably kill you!"

The bastard only laughed. "If you shriek like that, he might." Levi reached out and much to her shock scooped the wētā into his palm. "Come on, Wally. Let's take you outside. What did I say about scaring the ladies?"

"Wally? Don't tell me that thing has a name."

"All wētās are Wally." Levi straightened and gave the insect a little stroke. "It's the law."

She didn't care what it was. She wanted it out of her house.

Indigo pressed against the wall of the hallway, trying to put as much distance between her and the insect yet also trying not to look like she was.

Levi strode unconcernedly past carrying the wētā and disappeared outside.

Five seconds later he was back, grinning that ridiculously attractive grin that made her go hot and shivery and breathless at the same time it made her want to punch him in his stupid, handsome face.

"There," he said, hazel eyes dancing with an amusement she felt sure was at her expense. "Don't worry, I didn't hurt him. I gave him a good talking-to, then let him go."

Indigo realized she was still holding her broom aloft. She lowered it, tried to grab hold of the remaining shreds of her dignity, and sniffed. "I had it under control."

Levi glanced at the broom. "Sure you did."

Indigo sniffed again. "Why are you here, Levi? You didn't even knock."

"No, I didn't." The amusement in his eyes gleamed brighter, taking on a hint of wickedness that made her skin prickle with heat.

Damn man. He was up to something; she'd bet her life on it.

She'd also bet her life that it would annoy the hell out of her.

"Indy," he said, using the nickname she pretended to hate but was secretly delighted by, "I think I might have a solution for your housing difficulties."

Acknowledgments

Many thanks goes to Deb Werksman, my editor, and to Helen Breitwieser, my agent. Also to the entirety of central Otago for being such a special setting. The usual suspects, too, deserve a mention. You know who you are. 🩶

About the Author

Jackie Ashenden has been writing fiction since she was eleven years old. Mild-mannered fantasy/SF/pseudo-literary writer by day, obsessive romance writer by night, she used to balance her writing with the more serious job of librarianship until a chance meeting with another romance writer prompted her to throw off the shackles of her day job and devote herself to the true love of her heart—writing romance. She particularly likes to write dark, emotional stories with alpha heroes who've just gotten the world to their liking only to have it blown wide apart by their kick-ass heroines.

She lives in Auckland, New Zealand, with her husband, the inimitable Dr. Jax; two kids; one dog; and one cat. When she's not torturing alpha males and their obstreperous heroines, she can be found drinking chocolate martinis, reading anything she can lay her hands on, or being forced to go mountain biking with her husband.

Find Jackie online at jackieashenden.com, Instagram @jackie_ashenden, or facebook.com/jackie.ashenden.

Also by Jackie Ashenden

ALASKA HOMECOMING
Come Home to Deep River
Deep River Promise
That Deep River Feeling

SMALL TOWN DREAMS
Find Your Way Home

FIND YOUR WAY HOME

Small-town romance heads to the mountains of New Zealand
in a brand-new contemporary series by Jackie Ashenden

Brightwater Valley, New Zealand, is beautiful, rugged, and home to
those who love adventure. But it's also isolated and on the verge of
becoming a ghost town. When the town puts out a call to its sister
city of Deep River, Alaska, hoping to entice people to build homes
and businesses in Brightwater, ex paratrooper Chase Kelly is all for
it. But former oil executive Isabella Montgomery and her plan to
open an art gallery don't seem up to the test. Now Chase is determined to help her learn the ways of his formidable hometown.

"The heroes are as rugged and wild as the landscape."
—Maisey Yates, *New York Times* bestselling author,
for *Come Home to Deep River*

For more info about Sourcebooks's books and authors, visit:
sourcebooks.com

THE NEXT BEST DAY

Bestselling author Sharon Sala brings a new contemporary romance filled with second chances, new beginnings, and a small Southern town you won't want to leave

After two back-to-back life-changing events, first grade teacher Katie McGrath left Albuquerque for a fresh start in Borden's Gap, Tennessee. She's finally back in the classroom where she belongs, but it will take a little while for her to heal and feel truly like herself. She'll need to dig deep to find the courage it takes to try again—in life and in love—but with some help from her neighbor Sam Youngblood and his adorable daughters who bring her out of her shell, her future is looking brighter than she dared to imagine.

"Sharon Sala is a consummate storyteller... If you can stop reading, then you're a better woman than me."
—Debbie Macomber, #1 *New York Times* bestselling author

For more info about Sourcebooks's books and authors, visit:
sourcebooks.com

THE WEDDING GIFT

Heartwarming Southern fiction from bestselling author
Carolyn Brown—available for the first time in print!

Darla McAdams is on the verge of breaking up with her fiancé, Will
Jackson—only a week before the wedding. Darla's sure that her
Granny Roxie will understand when Darla tells her that her first
love, Andy, has come back to town, making her doubt everything.

Granny has been married fifty-five years—she can certainly
sympathize with Darla, and she's perfectly willing to share her
wisdom. A long conversation in the bridal room about marriage,
anniversaries, and what saved her own half-century marriage might
just help Darla settle those pre-wedding jitters...

"[You] will flip for this charming small-town tale."
—*Woman's World* for *The Sisters Café*

For more info about Sourcebooks's books and authors, visit:
sourcebooks.com